ELEMENTALISTS
INCOMPLETE

SI FOOTE

LEAVES FROM THE VINE PUBLISHING

Copyright © 2023 by SI Foote

Published 2024

ISBN: 9781962793001

Published by Leaves From the Vine Publishing, LLC

Cover Design by Kristin Murray

Editing by Glysia Gretz

Additional Images Created by Samantha Foote

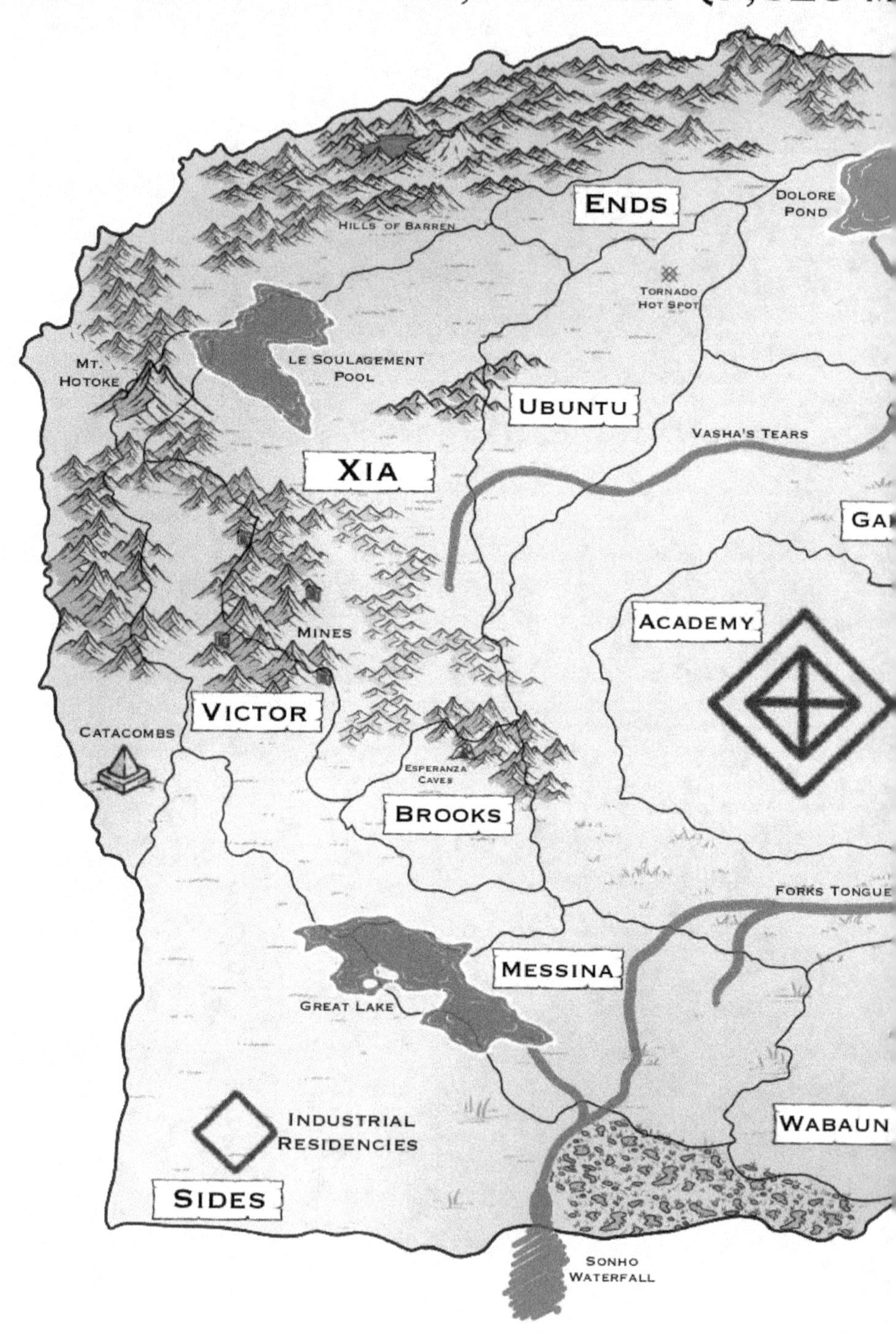

ELEMENTŌRUM P
BASE ELEVATION: 25,000 FEET (7,620 M
ENDS
DOLORE POND
HILLS OF BARREN
TORNADO HOT SPOT
MT. HOTOKE
LE SOULAGEMENT POOL
UBUNTU
VASHA'S TEARS
XIA
GA
ACADEMY
MINES
VICTOR
CATACOMBS
ESPERANZA CAVES
BROOKS
FORKS TONGUE
MESSINA
GREAT LAKE
WABAUN
INDUSTRIAL RESIDENCIES
SIDES
SONHO WATERFALL

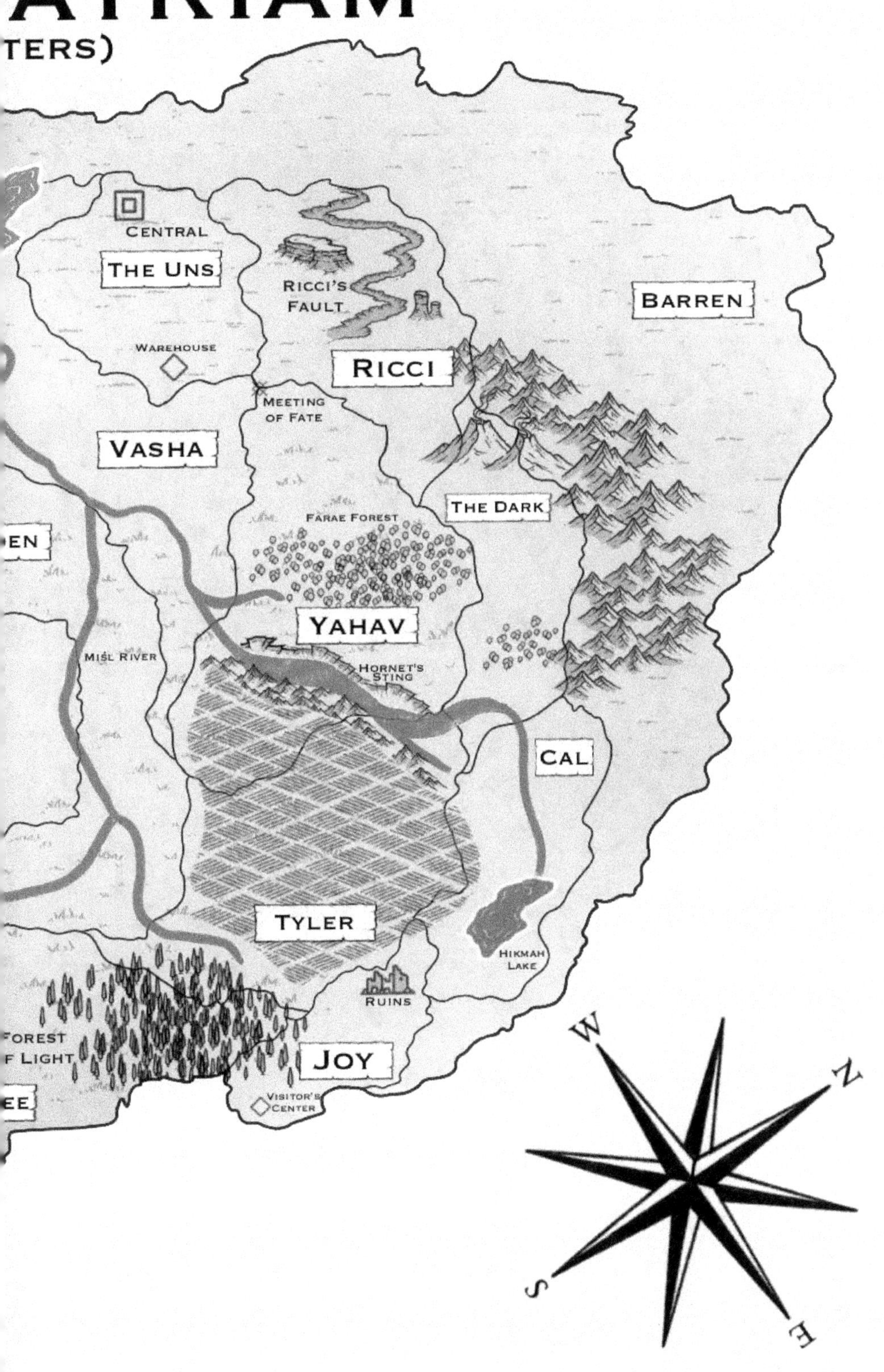
CENTRAL
THE UNS
RICCI'S FAULT
BARREN
WAREHOUSE
RICCI
MEETING OF FATE
VASHA
THE DARK
EN
FARAE FOREST
YAHAV
MISL RIVER
HORNET'S STING
CAL
TYLER
HIKMAH LAKE
RUINS
FOREST OF LIGHT
JOY
EE
VISITOR'S CENTER
W
N
S
E

Content includes mentions of suicide and rape.
Content includes descriptions of abuse, torture, beheading, and war crimes.

So, I'm pretty sure that the first book you write is supposed to have an obligatory dedication to your family.

My parents are awesome, so this book is dedicated to them.

However, I feel like this whole series should be dedicated to my friend, Jeff Orren. He is my sounding board. Half the time, he just has long strings of texts to read where I worked out the problem just by texting him. The other half he was helping me work out issues.

I seem to have a lot of those.

TABLE OF CONTENTS

CHAPTER ONE
Expiration

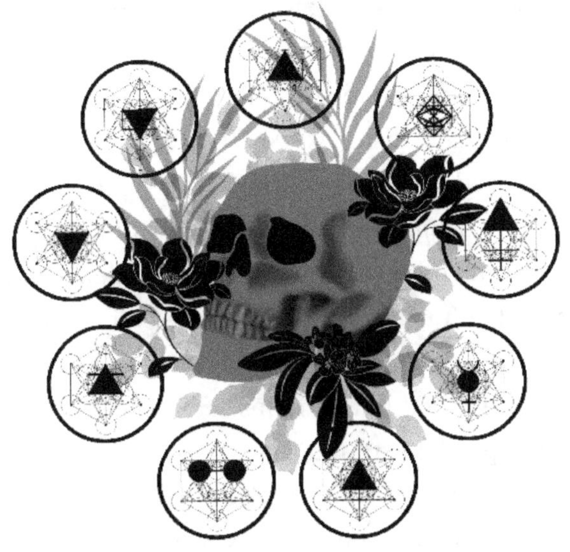

June 30, 2316

Mongolia Sector, City of Xia, Elementōrum Patriam

Ethan's legs gave out. He groaned in pain when his knees hit the dry-packed earth of the open field. A small fire burned a few feet away from him. Despite its size, it blazed with suppressive heat. The proctor for his test, Taylor, stood over the fire and controlled it with an outstretched arm. His cool blue eyes pierced through Ethan like knives. Ethan returned the look with venom. He knew the Council planned to kill him if he didn't pass the test.

He didn't care.

It didn't matter how much Professor Taylor pushed him; he wouldn't be able to control Water like they wanted. The last-ditch effort to save his life.

With a low groan, Ethan hoisted himself on shaky legs and took several aggravating steps toward the fire. He stretched out his left arm. *No use,* he thought bitterly. No fiber of his genetic make-up allowed him to gather the available water in his body, or in the air, to extinguish the flames.

Ethan's body pitched forward, and he caught himself on the ground with his hands. The dirt and gravel dug into his palms and knees. He dropped his head to the ground, and his sweaty red hair dragged through the dirt. His eyes settled on the upside-down world framed by his legs. None of the houses faced each other—a design to help cut down on traffic in neighborhoods—tightly packed with barely any landscaping. Each garage accommodated two slim, circle shaped hover cars which took up half the space of a tired vehicle. Each roof had its own solar panel dish.

He dragged his head up. Taylor watched Ethan with little interest, annoyed at the teenager's lack of ability. Ethan didn't blame him. Professor Taylor had a reputation as one of the harshest graders at the Academy, but even the nicest teachers couldn't help him pass his element tests. When his eyes met Taylor's, his pounding heart and the hum of air-conditioners intensified. Ethan drew in a deep breath and the sound rattled in his ears. A bead of sweat ran down his cheek and fell to the parched ground.

"Put it out, Silverspoon," Taylor growled. Even in the heat, he dressed in a professional black suit with a white-collared shirt. A red tie, pushed up to his throat, rested over the buttoned seam. He didn't break a sweat. With a flash of Taylor's blue eyes, the fire grew larger, and Ethan choked on rising bile.

"I can't." He shook his head.

Ethan leaned back on the balls of his feet and pulled his sweat-soaked shirt from his body. He threw it to the side and fell onto his butt. Ethan tugged up the hem of his jeans and pushed his high socks down, bunching them at his ankles. He stared at the fire and kicked his legs forward. Taylor tapped his foot. Ethan shuddered. He didn't want to cross a powerful, fully trained elementalist, and he didn't have the resolve to try. Ethan had no plans to do what Taylor wanted. Rather, he couldn't physically do it. He took a steady breath and propped his torso up with his hands extended behind him.

"Do it," Taylor commanded.

Ethan remained ready to fail.

He couldn't control water. The Academy gave him every chance to prove his worth in all seven elements, and he failed every time. He dropped his weight from his arms, and his back hit the solid ground. Ethan winced as pain ripped through his body. The injured nerves calmed, and he took in the blue sky.

Clouds scattered. No birds. The sky *too* blue. The kind of dark blue that settles at sunset, sprinkled with the beginnings of the constellations. If the sky had the pale, translucent look it did on the surface, it would look like Nevada. For a moment, the fateful afternoon of the Black Rider's descent clouded his vision. Hoof beats echoed across his memory. The slap of a boot against the tile floor of the kitchen. A body hitting the wall.

Ethan pushed his fingers through the dirt and tried to seek the switch Taylor wanted to trigger. It didn't exist. Genetics gifted him the body of an elementalist from birth, but he would never be one of them. When the Council called for him, they'd give him what he desired. Long-awaited death.

"If you don't pass this test, it'll be reported as another fail on your record," Taylor said.

"Awesome." Ethan kinked his neck up, so he could look farther behind him.

A wood fence leaned nearby. No longer a popular choice, wood often remained a forgotten material. People preferred the invisi-fences. Ethan's gaze shifted back to the sky. A black dot formed at the corner of his eye, and he focused on it. When he blinked, it vanished.

Heatstroke.

"Are you not going to try?"

"I *have* tried." Ethan threw his arms into the air. He clenched his fists and momentarily tried to focus on gathering water from his body. Nothing clicked. Sweat dripped from his fist and onto his cheek. Ethan pulled a face and used his sweaty shoulder to wipe it away. He dropped his hands back to the ground. He didn't have the strength to move his body.

The heat ebbed away, and Ethan could breathe again. Taylor kicked dirt onto the fire, and Ethan wondered momentarily if he could pass the test with the secondary method.

Professor Taylor would forcefully keep the fire going, he mused. *He's a Fire elementalist. But then again, Earth is stronger than Fire...*

It took him a while to find the will to sit up. With a slow breath, he reached for his shirt and straightened out the muddy material. Ethan located the tag and tugged the Henley on. It felt disgusting. His toes curled when the seams stuck to his skin in the wrong places. After a few moments, he yanked it off. He'd return to the Academy shirtless.

Ethan turned to Taylor. He held a thin glass phone in his hand and tapped the screen with his free hand.

Ethan shook his head. A few strands of hair clung to his forehead, and he pushed them back. He forced himself to stand. His head swam, and he staggered to the left. A new black dot formed on the horizon, but it didn't vanish when he blinked. It grew. A smile taunted his lips.

The transportation pod came to a halt in front of them. It didn't touch the ground, nor did it disturb the ground with its slipstream. Its gleaming glass exterior reflected distracting and blinding flashes as it met the sun. Unlike the hover cars, the pods didn't need steering mechanisms. They floated flat and cylindrical with room to recline on the inside. Groups often traveled in pods over the smaller cars. The circular doors opened automatically to the side and revealed the plush, blue velvet cushioned interior. Taylor gestured for Ethan to enter the pod before him, and he gladly took the opportunity.

No matter how much he hated the Academy, he'd rather be there with a known fate than in City of the Uns or on the Earth's lower surface.

He settled into the soft seat of the pod and leaned his head against the glass. His hair left behind streaks of sweat. When Professor Taylor boarded the pod after him, neither of them made a move to start a conversation. Ethan failed the examination with full knowledge of the consequences. The Council would rule him as Rogue, and they wouldn't hesitate to kill him because of it. He watched them do it before. Rogues presented a danger to elementalist society.

Nobody in Elementōrum Patriam knew the members of the Council by name, but they ran the country like any other government. They made laws and allowed the people to vote on important matters. However, Elementōrum had few elections as they flaunted a near perfect society above the humans. The seven-member Council carried out their duties to the country without hesitation. Ethan thought of their role as mostly symbolic. They represented the seven natural elements: Earth, Water, Fire, Air, Storm, Fortune, and Life. Supposedly, the strongest elementalists made up the Council. The original nine Council members created their country and continent. No one knew why they doubled representation for two of the elements. To honor each creator after splitting Pangea, they named nine of the cities after them.

Ethan loathed the original nine. They separated the elementalists from the humans and created a divided world. They named the Uns as a separate entity who deserved despotism in lawless ground; he knew the Uns was a fancy name for humans born to elementalists. The nine created the law which killed people like Ethan—Rogues. Those with superior elementalist bodies who couldn't control one of the seven elements.

Ethan failed the last of his tests. He didn't need Taylor to input an official grade to know. He collected bits and pieces from each, but he couldn't control a single element in full. He remained a danger to elementalist society. He knew he deserved the Rogue label.

While Rogues had the same genetically mutated body as the elementalists, the mutation chose a form which refused to allow them to control one singular element of the seven. Instead, it created a "glitch" where they could control bits and pieces of the seven elements without control. To spare their people the pain of dealing with a Rogue, the Council killed them. Ethan met his first Rogue at age five. The Council decapitated him in the middle of the street.

The silver transportation pod lifted smoothly into the air once Taylor sat in his seat and the door latched shut. Ethan cracked one eye open to watch his teacher. Taylor occupied himself by inputting Ethan's marks on the examination. Occasionally, Taylor's fingers hesitated over the keystrokes, and a frown pulled at the corners of his mouth. Ethan wondered how quickly the letter from the Council would arrive. He assumed they used an automated system for the most part. He doubted they really kept track of all the students approaching Rogue status. Taylor's thumb hesitated over a lower portion of his screen, again. He caught Ethan's eye, opened his mouth, closed it, and tapped the screen before quickly tucking it into the inner pocket of his suit jacket. Ethan's clear, glass phone alerted him when the completed scores hit his report. He pulled it from his left pocket and stared at the notifications.

Grade change.

Examination input.

A letter from the Council.

Expected.

Ethan took a deep breath, cleared his throat, and unlocked the phone with his fingerprint. He opened the email from the Council first. His phone glowed blood red when he did. Pity settled on Taylor's face. Ethan knew none of the teachers wanted to fail a student into Rogue status, but after too many examinations, he stopped caring about the result. Nineteen-years-old, four years of testing. His eyes scanned the message.

>*Ethan Silverspoon,*
>
>> *We on the Council regret to hear of your failure in the Water element examination. We hope you will join us for breakfast tomorrow morning. We will discuss your future promptly at ten o'clock.*
>>
>> *Please report to the locked door on the third floor by the tall windows. We are sure you know the one.*
>
>*Enjoy the rest of your day,*
>
>*The Council*

"Breakfast," he snorted. It wouldn't make a difference if they told him, *We plan to kill you at ten o'clock tomorrow, please make sure you're there.* Perhaps they used "breakfast" as a code for poison. He didn't know how they would do it, but if he had to choose, he'd pick something quick and clean.

The pod broke through the upper field of sky outside the City of Xia, one of the nine. As they climbed, the closer cities came into full view. Behind them, the wasteland of the City of Barren. To the south, the mines crossed the mountain range between the City of Victor and Xia. Directly ahead, the large cave structures in the northern corner of the City of Brooks shrouded the cities below in its shadow. Ethan thought he could faintly make out the edges of the Great Lake where it crossed between three cities: Victor, Sides, and Messina.

The pod turned northeast to straighten its course to the Academy at the heart of the nation; its buildings and towers rose higher than anything else in the country. They followed the mountain range on the south side of the City of Garden until they swung toward the parking structure. Ethan only caught the barest glimpse of the Forks Tongue River in Garden on their descent. The City of Garden hosted all the Mediterranean architecture and cultures. A beautiful fade between each style of housing. Ethan loved the Morocco sector the most.

Houses surrounded the Academy and glimmered with flashes of gold in the night; in the day, they shone like pure silver. They followed similar architecture patterns from the City of Garden. If Ethan could be a Wind elementalist, he'd spend his nights gazing at the city from above. The elevation of the land allowed the citizens to see the stars shimmer throughout the day. They winked at those occupying the large outdoor study areas and cobblestone paths. The Storm elementalists maintained the weather. It rarely snowed, but it rained once a week. The sunny weather helped the students at the Academy remain positive about their education.

The Academy acted as the training grounds for elementalists, a city not unlike the mythical Mount Olympus. Historians theorized the ancient religious site originated from the elementalists' country, Elementōrum Patriam. Large castle-like spires rose into the sky above floors no longer distinctly Greek in style. The buildings had bits and pieces taken from cultures around the world. The Bullet—a train system without rails, and their main transportation around the country—shot between buildings near light speed. Aqueducts, turned into walking paths, wove between and over smaller buildings. Several transportation pods lifted into the air and shot off across the landscape. A handful of towers floated in the air without support. A large pond structure toward the south side of the Academy housed underwater classrooms. Ethan envied those who studied in their natural element.

The transportation pod circled the Academy until it reached the entrance for the parking area. Several pods rested near the walls where elementalists worked on the mechanical components. The other vehicles waited in neat rows and glistened in the low light of the workspace. At the end of the long row of pods stood a single set of doors. The pod stopped in front of them and opened the door for its occupants. Taylor exited first, and Ethan followed close behind him. The program in the vehicle directed the pod away to the wash station, and the elementalists headed for the doors into the Academy.

Light filtered across the open hall from magnificent floor to ceiling windows between columns. At the end of the hall, a healer from the Academy infirmary waited for Ethan. He tapped his foot impatiently, and the gold buttons from his azure uniform sent sparks of light dazzling across the walls. The outfit had a slight glow from the reflection against the silver lining on the seams. The stunning uniform helped set them apart from other employees in the building. Only the best Life elementalists could work in the Academy. When the healer spotted Ethan, his annoyed frown deepened, and a flicker of horror shot through his eyes.

"I didn't almost kill anyone this time." Ethan gave the man an uneasy smile and a thumbs up. The Healer sighed and gestured for the teenager to follow him.

During one of his two Life element exams, he mixed some chemicals together and created a deadly poisonous gas. He caused an emergency evacuation of the infirmary. Healers tended to run in the other direction when Ethan approached in anticipation of what havoc he left in his wake.

"I'll see you later, Mr. Silverspoon," Taylor called after him.

He wouldn't.

The Healer led him through the brightly lit hallways of the elementalist indoor classrooms. At the end of a long corridor, they walked into the open Infirmary. The infirmary reeked of iodoform. Ethan crinkled his nose.

Like the hallway from the garage, the infirmary hosted floor to ceiling windows. The large columns of light moved from east to west, and the afternoon light gave Ethan's red waves of hair a soft, fiery glow. The white cotton sheets were itchy but overall, more comfortable than the dorms. Soft downy feather pillows and mattresses made from finest polyester with soft cotton stuffing made the stay enjoyable. The few beds near the end of the ward hidden behind blue curtains were saved for highly injured elementalists, an uncommon occurrence.

They restricted him to one of the open beds by activating the invisi-walls saved for troublesome patients. He figured it must be a security precaution in case of a nearby cart of chemicals (not like he'd play with them for fun); they didn't want a repeat. He adjusted the glass reader on a stand next to his bed. It contained all records information on file. Curious, he opened the folder with his ELE ID attached.

Name: Ethan Aaron Silverspoon

Age: 19

DOB: June 1, 2297

Eye Color: Brown

Hair Color: Red

Height: 177.8 cm (5 ft 10 in)

Time Spent at the Academy: 5 years

Non-Element GPA: 3.692

Element GPA: 0.0

Element: Rogue

He nodded along with the information. All correct. Ethan let out a huff and fell against the bed. He pulled out his phone to clear the grade change notification. In the application, he scrolled through his past results.

December 31, 2312- End of Eighteen-Month Initiation to the Academy

> **GRADE**: Pass
>
> Elementalist shows positive signs for being able to control one of the elements. He is not affiliated with any of the currently inhabited elements. Individual elementalist testing will prove successful.

Every three months after the initiation months, Ethan took a test for each of the seven elements, and each element got two opportunities.

Storm

> He changed the path of a tornado in Ubuntu that nearly killed the entire Lesotho sector. The proctor barely managed to get it under control, and one of his classmates, who got sucked into the tornado, miraculously made it out alive. They thought he might be a rather clumsy Storm elementalist until he, and several other students nearly drowned in a tsunami during his second test.

Fortune

> Ethan had to influence the luck of those around him, but he had no golden glow. Several other students did worse on their test in his presence than they did in class and bullied him over bringing them bad luck instead. When he tested alone the second time, the proctor

stabbed themselves with their pen, but ruled it as an accident and gave him the fail.

Life

The notorious incident with the chemicals. Almost everyone in the Academy knew about him from that point forward.

Air

Ethan couldn't lift himself off the ground any higher than he could jump. He almost took down another student when the Air instructor threw him off the top of the Academy like a baby bird, and he gripped his fellow student for dear life as they plummeted.

Fire

Ethan used a spark starter (he vehemently refused to admit to cheating) and set fire to the City of Garden. Luckily, the Fire test occurred far enough from homes to not affect the public, and the elementalists got it under control quickly enough. However, he did destroy a large section of endangered foliage which the Life elementalists spent weeks recovering. The gardens section had a poster of him hanging in the front office banning him from the grounds.

Earth

Somehow, during his Earth test, a large pit opened in the ground and trapped several Academy professors and students. If they weren't Earth elementalists, they would've suffocated under the weight of the collapse. Every student except Ethan passed.

Water

His most recent test with Taylor in addition to nearly drowning a student three months prior. He didn't have a good track record for doing much other than nearly killing others around him. The exact qualities they looked for in Rogues.

If normal grades counted for anything, I'd be brilliant, Ethan thought. He coughed and looked across the room for the Healer who would tend to him before sending him back to the dormitories. With the ongoing examinations, the infirmary was busier than usual.

"How are you doing today?" The sweet voice of a Healer behind him nearly made him fall off the bed. He slowly rolled over until he saw the woman assigned to care for him. She had pretty blue eyes and black hair. "I'm Rose Sylvester."

"Ethan Silverspoon." He put out his hand. Rose took it politely, and she gestured for him to sit up.

"I'll be examining you today to make sure all your vitals are in the right place."

"Alright," Ethan sat up on the bed and allowed her to examine him.

Rose waved her hand over his body, and a soft green glow emanated between them. She stored information from the scan in the glass screen by his bed. He could see his heartbeat on the monitor next to several other health related items. One highlighted with red.

"You're only a little dehydrated, no need for an IV," she said. "I'll bring you some water while the rest of these stats update."

Rose walked away and left Ethan with the quiet space again. *If water is my only issue, I can drink water back at the dorms*, he huffed. Several minutes passed before Rose returned with a gallon of water. The screen showed his temperature as only one hundred and four, so Rose ordered a prescription to help return his temperature to the normal one hundred and six minimum for elementalists. Once she ensured his other vitals normalized, she discussed his release with a supervisor. Ethan drank a quarter of the gallon while he waited to distract his thoughts from the irony of visiting the infirmary with his death less than twenty-four hours away. A few minutes later, she returned with instructions on what to do when he returned to the dorms. On his way, his mind drifted to a conversation with his Water element Professor the day before.

Professor Emma VonBerg approached him after class. His things scattered across the room, held him back. The more proficient elementalists in the class bullied him relentlessly and sent his belongings to the farthest corners of the classroom. He found one of his erasers under a nearby desk when Professor VonBerg addressed him. He whipped up and cracked his head on the metal support beams. She quickly apologized and handed him an ice cube from her hand, which he took to be polite.

"Ethan, you realize if you fail this Water element test you are going to be classified as a Rogue elementalist." Professor VonBerg took a seat at the next desk over. Ethan walked calmly to where his things were and rummaged longer than necessary in the pockets.

"I am quite aware of the situation, yes." His tone echoed a lifetime of fear hidden behind his brown eyes.

"I suggest you do a bit of study and practice. It might help you with your exam tomorrow," Professor Vonberg said.

"No amount of study and practice is going to help me tomorrow if it hasn't helped me thus far. I don't think any of the teachers at this school would really be disappointed if I failed."

"I've been instructed to give you this." She held out a blood red envelope with gold writing curling fancily into Ethan's name on the front. She held it like it burned her fingers, barely touching the corner. He snatched it from her hand. He half expected it to shout at him.

"Thanks," Ethan mumbled, tossed his bag over his shoulder, and made to leave.

"And Ethan?" Professor VonBerg called. "Good luck."

He glanced over his shoulder for only a moment before exiting the room without a 'thank you'. He blindly followed the colored lines on the wall indicating each element's dorms and classrooms. Near the end of a hall where the colors ended and hosted the undefined dorms, he climbed the flights of stairs. He didn't feel the marble under his feet or the railing in his hand. Ethan watched in envy as Air elementalists pushed themselves effortlessly through the spiraling staircase. If they chose, they would never walk anywhere again. Water elementalists teasingly jetted the flying students; a few of the kind Fire elementalists stopped the water from hitting them. Ethan ducked, avoiding lightning bolts and bricks. Passing students glanced at the red envelope in his hand, but none of them said a word. He stumbled into the boys' dormitory. The other nineteen-year-olds glanced up as he entered and hastily looked away.

His bag hit the post of his bed with a loud clunk. Ethan collapsed on his firm mattress a moment later and groaned into the pillow. The stiff landing did nothing to comfort him. The corners of the letter, clenched in his hands, poked painfully into his side. After a moment, he slit it open. Most of the other boys who hung around in the dorm had left, and the ones who stayed ignored him.

Good luck,

The Council

Ethan groaned and rolled over. He pressed his face into the cotton pillows. Ethan had two options: study or sleep. But sleep wouldn't come anytime soon. He went into the bathroom and filled his water cup to the brim. Ethan brought it back into the main bedroom and concentrated hard for the next few hours. By the time the others returned to bed, he still couldn't manipulate the water in the cup. He was better off attaching the water cup to a string and spinning it with centrifugal force or rolling water in fumed silica than attempting to summon water to his will.

July 1, 2316

The Academy, Elementōrum Patriam

Ethan walked through the dormitory halls, shoulders drooping. He took the longest route through the building but still had plenty of time until the Council expected him. He spent the quiet moments of solitude contemplating what his existence meant. Fate gave him too many chances to keep living. He approached the end of the line. He took care to focus on each breath in and out. In and out. In and out. One of them would be the last.

People would praise the day Ethan left their world alone—he wouldn't be a danger anymore. They would hear stories of all his misdeeds but never of the man resigned to death. The smile at the corners of his lips would be the last his body formed. His last title: Rogue.

He brought his thumb to the pulse in his wrist and focused on his heartbeat. He counted. Twenty pulses uniquely his. Twenty more at a steadier pace. Twenty telling him to stay alive. Sixty counts that wouldn't prove his existence when his body stilled.

Ethan didn't remember the rest of his walk through the cream halls and admiral tiles. He didn't remember losing sight of the colored wall stripes telling him which classrooms and dorms he neared. A door in the middle of the hallway, alone, read THE COUNCIL in black on gold. Ethan scratched the space between his eyebrows and stared at the ornate bronze handle. Once he touched the knob, he committed to entering the Council's domain.

Taking a deep breath, Ethan stretched out his hand and clenched it into a fist. He counted to ten, uncurled his fingers, and twisted the knob. It gave way, and he pushed the door open. He couldn't see anything short of a few feet inside. The only illumination came from the hallway. He stepped into the dark, and the door swung closed behind him. Ethan thought he heard footsteps then a hand pushed him forward. He tried to spin around, but the person vanished. The darkness pulled him back. Terror filled his veins—he could barely move.

Something forced him into a chair, and he flew down the hall on the mobile furniture. Ethan's hair pulled back from his forehead. He had no time to think before the chair hit an inhibitor, and he launched forward. Ethan tried to brace himself with his non-dominant arm, but his shoulder connected with the ground first. He rolled until he hit a wall.

"Welcome, Ethan Silverspoon. We're so glad you could join us." A female voice reverberated, and the lights clicked on. Momentarily blinded, Ethan shook his head to return his lost sense.

Floodlights exposed the basketball stadium sized room. Stained white walls reflected the light, and upon closer inspection, he noticed dry and cracked blood. Above him hung a silver box lined with windows, tinted dark on one side. It resembled a fancy box for spectators at a sporting event.

"I'm not ready to die," he said. The sudden realization shocked Ethan to his core—he accepted his fate, but he wanted hope. His last wish faded. His fight and adrenaline drained from his body.

"Good-bye, Ethan."

Hidden panels on the walls slid aside and six Lūminis Sclopētum, a weapon that resembled a rifle, mechanically clicked into place. Another *click* loaded the ammunition. Ethan pressed himself against the wall. He closed his eyes and clenched his jaw.

Crack.

CHAPTER TWO
Epitaph

June 2, 2302

Harlowton, Wheatland County, Montana, United States of America

Five-year-old Ethan peered around the corner at his mother. With music playing in the background, she fixed dinner. She hummed along and flipped the vegetables in the pan as they sautéed. Ethan's father passed him on his way into the house and ruffled his son's red hair.

"Hi," Amber greeted.

Aaron smiled and pressed a light kiss to her lips. The washing machine in the corner made a sound to alert them to its finished task. Aaron took over dinner, so his wife could tend to the laundry. When she spotted Ethan around the corner, Amber gestured for him to join her. Ethan ran over to his mother, and she set him on top of the washing machine. She opened the front load door and moved the clothes to the dryer. Amber pressed a warm kiss to her son's cheek.

"How is my baby boy doing?"

"I found a new bug today."

Amber smiled and lifted a hand to separate the strands of his hair. They heard the click of a television. Ethan's favorite television show played first. He tried to wiggle off the washing machine, but Amber stopped him. "Let daddy watch the news for a bit."

"Okay." Ethan placed his hands in his lap and watched his mother fold the towels. She handed him a small stack of washcloths, and he folded them into messy fourths. "Can I help with the big towels?"

"I'm almost done." She took the messy pile from him and set the folded pieces in the basket. Amber lifted him off the machine. "You can put these clothes into the washing machine."

Amber pulled down the box of detergent. A loud beeping sound from the TV startled them.

"We have breaking news for the occupants of Harlowton. A Rogue slated for death in Elementōrum Patriam escaped earlier today. According to the GPS in the transportation pod, he is on his way here. The Council informed us they are in pursuit of the Rogue. They've asked all civilians to remain where they are to reduce fodder for the Rogue to use. Please do not go outside."

Elementalist—the school mentioned them recently after a child was collected from their class. Since Ethan first learned about them, he wanted to see one, but everyone he talked to feared them. Curiosity overtook him, and he darted away from his mother into the living room. He propped himself on the back of the couch and moved the curtains aside to stare out the window. Ethan hoped the elementalists would pass close to his house where he could see them in person. Police officers stood in the street and directed people quickly into their homes for safety.

At the end of the street, a man barreled through the line of officers. Seven people in blood red robes followed hot on his heels. Amber grabbed her son and pulled him away from the window, but not before Ethan saw the glimpse of fire escaping behind the Rogue. It leapt onto the dry grass lawns and crawled toward the houses. The trees crackled and screamed as the fire broke past their protective bark. One of the seven broke away from the main group and sent jets of water across the burning area. A second dropped back and placed their hand on the destroyed ground. The area restored healthier than before. The other five continued down the street after the Rogue.

The Silverspoons couldn't tear their eyes away from the window. The elementalists' cloaks fluttered around them as they moved, and the Rogue tripped. He crawled across the ground on all fours, like a crab, with his stomach toward the sky. The heat outside rose, and the front windows of the house shattered. Aaron threw himself over his wife and son to protect them from the glass.

"Don't kill me!" the Rogue wailed. Sirens rose above the din of whispers as the Council converged. "I didn't do anything wrong!"

The seven cloaked figures rejoined and created a ring around the man. One of them stepped forward, the smallest. The Council member held out their black-gloved hands, and a thin rope of fire connected them. The Rogue, surrounded, hung his head and kneeled. He clenched his fists, and the rope lowered in front of his neck.

Amber pulled Ethan firmly into her body, a poor attempt to shield him, but the child refused to let her face him away. The Fire elementalist took a step away from the Rogue, and in one swift movement, pulled the fire directly through their neck, cauterizing the wound. The head teetered. Tears spilled to the pavement. A moment later, the head rolled. The body collapsed behind it, and the head came to a stop at the feet of one of the Council members. The Council immediately transferred it to a body bag.

"We're extremely sorry for interrupting your daily lives." They bowed. "We will make sure this doesn't happen again."

They disappeared as swiftly as they came.

August 16, 2306

Goldfield, Esmeralda County, Nevada, United States of America

Nine-year-old Ethan stared out the bright window of his grandmother's office building. He lived with his mother's parents since his parents' deaths. Harlowton was wiped off the map after the Rogue elementalist incident. A deadly toxin left behind after the Rogue's death made Ethan the only survivor.

None of the doctors could figure out why he lived with extreme exposure while all the other children died.

Ethan squinted at the streets a few floors below. The sun made the green patches of grass glow. His head rested on his arms. He wanted to play outside with the other boys in his neighborhood, but both his grandparents had to work. They held him hostage in a boring office instead of paying for childcare. An equally annoyed huff came from behind him as his grandmother worked on the computer; the system she worked on had crashed. She muttered a few unintelligible words under her breath and hissed in frustration as one of her co-workers asked her if she knew why the heavily used program in every office stopped working. Ethan snorted in derision; only an idiot would keep the program past 2304 because it needed significant upgrades.

"Alright Ethan, you've got your wish. We're heading home. The tech advisors have to come in again to work on the system."

Ethan perked up and followed his grandma to the elevators where he enjoyed the classical music and dinging floors.

When they pulled into the driveway of his grandparents' home, he could see some of the boys still throwing a baseball at the empty lot down the street. His greed for the outside world got the better of him when he eagerly rocketed out of the car before it fully stopped. Ethan slammed the door and waved as dust kicked up underneath his sneakers. The boys shouted a greeting and immediately threw him the ball. He caught it and tossed it under his leg to one of the others. The day neared dinnertime when Ethan and his friends finally settled down and rolled the ball between them. They shared things they heard about fellow children around the town.

"Sally Mae is apparently really sick, and her parents are considering letting her die." One of the boys made his eyes bigger as though the expression would make him more believable.

"They wouldn't do that," Ethan scoffed and rolled his eyes.

The boys continued to argue in the background, and Ethan laid back.

A cloud of dirt exploded around his head and coated his thick hair in a layer of dust. He cricked his neck awkwardly in a stretch. Along the horizon line, he saw several tiny black spots. He squinted.

"How hot do you think it is today?" Ethan asked.

"Not very, why?"

"Does anyone else see the black things?"

The boys followed his line of sight and gasped in horror.

"It's the Black Riders!" one of them shouted.

They leaped up and ran for their homes. They screamed loud as day about the dots racing toward them. Ethan walked home casually and watched as doors locked and curtains drew shut. His grandfather yelled for him to return, and he sped up his pace.

"What are the Black Riders?" Ethan asked as his grandpa shoved him into the garage.

"They're a group of murderers. An extremist group. The Black Riders enter towns and wipe them out to cleanse an area they believe cursed by elementalists. Stay in here."

A clatter of hooves echoed around the garage as the Black Riders arrived in the streets on horseback. His grandfather shut the door and hurried through the house.

"They're hiding, break down the doors!" someone commanded.

The shattering of a window pulled him back to Harlowton. Ethan slammed his hands over his ears. The screaming permeated his attempt to block out the memories. Something dragged across the pavement outside the garage. It bounced between houses. Something outside gave Ethan the overwhelming sense of *death*. The flip of a cloak. The Council's blood red cloaks sweeping across the ground. The beating of a battering ram against the front door. The head of the Rogue hitting the ground. The whine of metal as it wrenched apart.

The door fell with a solid thud onto the tile and shattered the entryway design. He didn't hear his grandparents' screams, but he knew they died behind the garage door. He could sense it. He held his breath and focused on the knob—waited for it to turn. A faint *click-tap, click-tap, click-tap* against the floor inside. The sound reminded him of the cowboy boots in the western movies his grandfather watched obsessively. Each step moved slow and steady across the tile. A chill ran down Ethan's spine. A long whine of the floorboard. The clink of a belt and a holster.

The door creaked open. *Click-tap, click-tap.*

The attacker brushed against the car. The alarm blared. *Click.*

The cold barrel of a gun pressed against his forehead.

Ethan whimpered in fear as the stranger's eyes met his. Silent tears left salty trails down his cheeks. He held up his hands.

"Please, please, don't shoot."

The man removed the safety with his thumb.

"Please." Ethan squeezed his eyes shut as he thrust a hand forward. A rush of power surged through his body.

The resounding crash of a heavy body hitting the wall made him open his eyes. He lowered his hands to see the threat buried in sheetrock and not breathing. Ethan didn't bother to stay around. He quickly ran through the house and threw open the sliding glass door. Within seconds, he vaulted over the backyard fence and raced toward the woods where he could hide. Once out of the town and thoroughly lost in the trees, he crumpled to the ground and cried. The roots dug into his hands and knees, and left behind their imprint, but he didn't notice.

May 27, 2311

Cape Meares, Tillamook County, Oregon, United States of America

"The stars sure are pretty tonight," a little girl said from the doorway of Ethan's room with the boys.

"You know you can't be found in the boys' room, Lulu. The Madame will be upset, and you won't get dessert."

"I know. I wanted to show you how pretty the stars are tonight."

"I'll come with you to the door, but afterward you have to promise to go to bed."

"Of course!" Lulu stretched out her hand. He took it and gently smiled at her. Once they stood at the front door, she lifted a hand to point. "See that one? It's Capricorn. The one over there is Leo, and there's the dragon Draco. I wish I could see a real dragon."

"I wish you could one day, too."

She giggled in response. "Dragons aren't real silly."

"Maybe they are up there with *them*."

"Shhh, we're not supposed to talk about them." Lulu looked around for the Madame in case they heard them whisper about the elementalists.

"They're not around." He slid his fingers through her soft brown locks. She wasn't family by blood, but he considered her a little sister since his arrival at the orphanage. "Time for bed."

"I'll see you in the morning." Lulu headed to the girls' quarters.

Ethan slid out of the open door and closed it behind him. He shivered in the chill air and located the dipper pair. The earth trembled beneath him, and he nearly fell over. The ground cracked and Ethan reached for the door, only to have it open away from him. People screamed inside as the cliff crumbled toward the ocean. It wasn't a normal earthquake—it was something elementalist.

"Ethan!"

He recognized the voice. Lulu's socked feet slid along the wood flooring. She followed the building and fell away from him, hand outstretched.

"LULU!" He dropped to the ground and reached out a hand; their fingertips brushed. With a *whoosh*, the building landed in the cold ocean.

Ethan ran into the small fishing town to search for someone to help. Seven figures walked calmly up the street in red robes. Ethan paid them no attention; he needed to help those swept away in the waves. He rushed past them and ruffled their clothes. A gloved hand jumped out and grabbed his wrist. When Ethan faced them, he knew them. The Council.

"Where are you going, young man?" the deep voice asked.

"The orphanage, it fell into the ocean. I need to find someone who can help rescue the people," Ethan huffed out.

"Tell me, is there an Ethan Silverspoon among the wreckage?"

"I'm Ethan."

"Our only charge is to collect you, but it would be a waste for the human world to lose so many children."

"But—"

They cut him off. "We will help them Ethan, but you must come with us."

"Please, find my friend Lulu. She's nine." Ethan tightened his jaw.

"We will do our best to save everyone. Now please, leave with these two."

He let them pull him away and watched from the transportation pod as the strong swimmers reached the shoreline long before the elementalists arrived.

July 1, 2316

The Council's Death Chamber, The Academy, Elementōrum Patriam

The impact never came. Ethan heard the weapons fire—but he had no open wounds. If he died, he didn't expect the afterlife to be quiet or dark with a slight tint of orange—the same color as when he closed his eyes. Ethan pried one eye open and found himself standing in the same room from moments before. The bloodstained walls stared at him, and he turned his head slowly to see if the wall behind him had a fresh stain. It didn't. *I'm not a ghost.* He looked down for good measure to make sure he still had a body. Ethan opened his other eye and glanced around the room. The same spectator box sat above him. For a moment he thought he saw a figure move behind the dark glass.

"What did you do?" The female voice sounded irate.

Ethan lifted his hands and pressed them firmly against his chest. Solid. No wounds. Behind him, he found six burn marks on the wall and six fired shells on the ground across the room. The sagittae passed through him. *Not possible.*

"I didn't do anything," Ethan said. No elementalist had the power to avoid death, yet there he stood.

"Stay there," the woman told him.

Ethan didn't know where he could go. The Council thought he caused it; he didn't remember doing anything intentional. His eyes drifted back to the shells on the ground.

"I don't understand—you saw it, didn't you?" Luana Ford leaned against one of the tinted windows overlooking the Council's death chamber. Her pale forehead pressed against the glass. When she pulled away, her skin left a smudge of oil behind. She ran her fingers through messy brown hair, adding to the static, before swinging it over her shoulder.

Luana waited for the other four in the room to catch up. Mixed expressions of shock and curiosity flickered around her. They kept their eyes trained on the Rogue below. Luana tugged at her faded green shirt with holes in the hem before reaching for the phone in her cargo pants' pocket out of reflex. She spun it between her fingers before returning it to the pocket without sending the text she desperately wanted to. She tapped her foot against the floor, and her black combat boot made a clomp against the ground, shocking the other Council members out of their stupor.

"We all saw it," Eilene Vos rolled her eyes and kicked her shoe away from its raised position on the wall. She shook her head and her blue tinged blonde locks flipped against her back. Eilene played the opposite side of Luana as often as she could—the stereotypical Water/Fire relationship, despite Water being the natural enemy of Earth. She wore highlighter colors to compliment her pixie-like features, pale skin, sharp smile, and pointed nose. The Water elementalist's cool gray eyes settled on the older woman.

"Maybe the calibration was off?" Dwayne Tebogo rubbed the light stubble on his jaw. An unfamiliar frown marred his umber skin.

"No, he did something." A low and calm voice permeated the air around them. Scott Everton leaned back on two legs of his chair, the backrest against the table and booted feet against the wall to keep his position steady.

"Even Scott has something to say about this one." Dwayne's face spread into a familiar smile and the warm dimples at the corners of his mouth appeared. "Are you planning on talking to us today?"

Everyone ignored him except Eilene, who couldn't help the *hmph* of laughter which slipped past her lips.

"I told you this would happen," said a cryptic voice from the corner. A smirk settled on the woman's tawny brown skin, and she shifted in her chair, and her Converse squeaked against the floor. She pulled her ash brown hair forward to cover her face.

"Yeah, we appreciate the warning," Eilene snapped. She closed her eyes and sighed. "Sorry, Series."

Series coughed, gave a soft hum for an official reply, and found a more comfortable spot to help her drift to sleep. Luana shifted to Scott; he would be the only one with helpful advice.

"We did plan on the contingency," she paused, "Plan X."

Scott didn't vocalize an answer, but he nodded slowly. He raised a hand to push the fringe out of his eyes and tucked it behind his ear. Scott crossed his legs at the ankle against the wall and let his neck drop back. Luana pursed her lips. The rustles of his black, leather jacket couldn't give her what she wanted— she wanted Hans there, but he currently resided in Russia with Scarlet on important Council business. She pivoted back to the window and avoided the oil stain with her eyes. She stared at Ethan. He returned her gaze, and for a moment she swore he saw her through the glass.

Luana reached for the control panel in front of her and pressed three buttons. The hidden door opened smoothly. She had to face the Rogue.

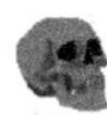

Ethan turned away from the window for a second time and touched one of the marks on the wall. The burns scared him. More than being a Rogue, something else made him *wrong* in elementalist society. He closed his eyes and leaned his forehead against the wall. The tip of his finger slid across the raised edges of the burn. A click behind him startled Ethan. The exit panel slid open, and, in the doorway, stood a Council member dressed in the familiar blood red robes. The two stared at each other for a long while. *Maybe they have a sense of humor.*

"Death finally came for me? I'd say you're too late, but I'd be lying." He couldn't see the face of the Council member behind the dark face plate, but he could feel their unsatisfied glare. *No sense of humor.*

"Come with me," they commanded.

Ethan recognized her voice from the loudspeaker. As he neared the Council member, he realized she was an average height, and he had several inches on her. If given an opportunity, if human instead, he might be able to overpower her and run—but the Council consisted of the strongest elementalists in the country. He didn't know which element she wielded.

He followed the elementalist up a set of stairs; their shoes echoed against the concrete. Ethan yawned and stuffed his hands into his pockets. A little way ahead of them, an open door waited. She led him into the room where a small collection of people without blood red robes to hide their identities waited. He pulled a hand free and slowly pointed around the room at the Council.

"You're going to die. We don't care if you know what we look like." One of the men grinned like a bobcat.

Ethan cleared his throat and sucked on his teeth in lieu of a response.

The woman who collected him yanked the robes over her head, revealing her lithe figure. She tossed the robe onto a hook, and it swung from side to side until it settled. For a moment he thought it would fall off the hanger, but it clung on by the hem. Ethan took a moment to inspect the inside of the spectator box. It looked like the pictures of VIP boxes at sporting events. The pale blue walls complemented the cream tiled floor. He felt the urge to explore the room, and use the windows to survey the death room, but one glance at the Council kept him rooted in place.

The elementalist who brought him to the room pressed herself close to the wall as she felt around for something specific. The blonde across the room reached for the control panel and triggered the button the first woman needed. A panel opened. The dark-skinned man gestured for the second to lean forward, and she obeyed. He whispered something into her ear, and her shoulders shook with laughter. Ethan wondered how the citizens of Elementōrum Patriam would react if they knew the feared Council members existed behind the scenes as adults with the same behaviors as everyone else.

When his eyes met the other male's, the wide smile on his face made the man appear younger than Ethan, but when the smile dropped, the Council member's face showed his true age.

"Ethan Silverspoon. I'm Dwayne. It's not often we get to meet people. Luana was irate," he nodded in the brunette's direction, "she doesn't like people from the Academy."

Ethan stayed quiet. His eyes drifted back to Luana, who had her elbow pressed into the side of the cubby. She twisted her arm up to her shoulder and attempted to push farther forward than her collar bone would allow.

"Who put the stupid bottles back that far?" she demanded and glared at the others.

The last male in the room let his chair fall forward onto the ground with a bang. He stood without saying anything and easily reached into the cubby space. He pulled the objects forward before he returned to his chair.

"Thanks, Scott."

She smiled, and Ethan prayed she meant it as a friendly gesture. Luana pulled the cork out of the bottle and held the drink out to him.

"Here you go."

"What is this?" Ethan sniffed it. It smelled delicious.

"Poison." She didn't sugarcoat her response. He looked down at the bottle and swallowed hard. The cold gaze the blonde woman gave him from across the room made him want to jump off a building instead.

"Got to have plenty of ways to kill people." Ethan nodded, licked his lips, and lifted the bottle. The poison ran over his tongue and down his throat—it tasted like raspberry lemonade. When he finished taking a long drink, Luana took the bottle back and replaced the cork.

"You weren't supposed to survive," Luana muttered quietly. She set the bottle on the table and watched him for signs of death.

It's not as though I tried not to die. Ethan bit his tongue. He felt, if given the chance, she'd kill him with her bare hands. Two minutes passed before the Council broke the silence.

"You're not dead yet?" Luana stepped forward and examined him closely. She gestured for Dwayne to join her, and he did so obediently. He held out a hand and a familiar green light appeared.

He's the Life elementalist, Ethan thought.

"There's no poison in his system." Dwayne's brows furrowed together as he looked closer at Ethan.

"Did you pretend to drink it?" Luana grabbed the front of his shirt.

"I drank it. It tasted like raspberry lemonade." Ethan held up his hands as a symbol of surrender.

"You can tell he drank it. The level in the bottle is lower." Eilene stepped to the table and held up the bottle. She shook it, and the contents rattled.

Scott took the bottle from her and removed the cork. He sniffed it and glanced at their leader. "It's poison."

Luana rounded on Ethan. A whip of fire formed in her hand on the turn and without hesitation she lashed it at his neck. In his mind, his head rolled like in 2302—but the fire passed through his body. For a moment, his neck lost all material form, and he couldn't breathe; in the next second it returned to normal. The Council stared at him in shock. Ethan lifted a hand slowly to his neck and felt the skin. Solid.

"Go wait in the hall." Luana pointed at the door.

"Can I take the poison?" He pointed at the bottle. Scott handed it to him, and Ethan quickly retreated from the room. The door slid shut behind him and plunged him into darkness. He picked at the label with his fingers before lifting it to his lips to drink once more.

It still tasted like lemonade. Ethan took a steady breath and leaned against the wall. He let go of the tension in his neck, and his head tilted back and slammed into the solid surface. He groaned in pain and took another drink. It would be easier if the bullets didn't pass through his body. Instead, he drank morosely over a bottle of poison. He let the pressure in his legs release, and his back slid down the wall until he sat on the floor.

Every event in Ethan's life brought him closer and closer to death, but when it finally came knocking, the door wouldn't unlock. He couldn't help feeling his survival meant he could be more than a Rogue.

"He seems fun," Series said from her corner of the room.

"What are we going to do with him?" Luana's voice cracked around the words.

Eilene shared an uneasy look with Dwayne. Luana always had the answers—she never consulted any of them on their opinion.

The other Council members could tell she was quickly approaching losing control. She ran her fingers through her hair again at a harried pace and made the short strands stand on end. Luana only acted like that when her support system left. Eilene wanted to text Hans and tell him to return immediately—but she had no authority over him. Luana functioned as the leader of the Council.

"We're going to have to do some research." Series gave up on her nap and draped herself languidly over her chair, resembling an experienced model instead of a sleepy seventeen-year-old.

"Can you not see anything about him?" Eilene used a hair tie on her wrist to pull her hair away from her neck, and the ends trailed softly against her shoulders.

"No, not anything important. I saw him survive the shooting, and I can see him lying in a cell. I've seen the library and a few books we should look in, but that's it right now." Series bit her lip and prayed the others wouldn't recognize her lie. She saw a lot regarding Ethan and the Council, but she didn't know what any of it meant. She needed to consult her dreams further before she brought the information to the Council. Scott's eyes narrowed, and his lips parted as he watched her. If anyone would notice her ticks, he would.

"What are we supposed to do with him, then?" Luana said.

"Well, Molelo," Dwayne said, "Muuyaw over here said she saw him in a cell, so I'm thinking Plan AZ."

"AZ?" Eilene recoiled and crinkled her eyebrows.

"It's the last plan for killing an elementalist in the book. Probably the least humane." Luana pursed her lips. "We'll do it. Starve him to death in a cell. It makes sense. Bring Ethan in."

CHAPTER THREE
Dissolution

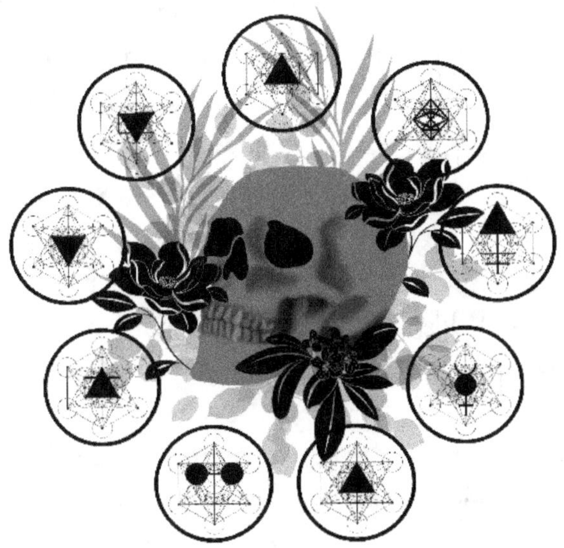

"Hold up." Dwayne raised a hand to stop them. He leaned forward on the chair and rested his elbows on his knees. He pressed his tongue against his teeth, and his eyebrows crinkled together. The expression painful; he rarely looked concerned. "How long has it been since the Council initiated AZ?"

"Since the end of the Second World War," Series said.

"Is that sanitary?" Dwayne said.

"I'll go blast one out while you drag him in." Eilene rolled her eyes and stretched. She used her elbow to hit a button on the wall behind her, and the hidden door opened. Her thin form vanished into the dark hallway, and the door melded into the wall.

"Are we going to try and keep him alive?" Series stretched her arms and let her jaw fall open in a wide yawn. Her elbows cracked under pressure, and she dropped her arms back into her lap. Scott shook his head, but he looked to Luana for the final say. Her mouth twitched as she lifted her shoulder into a half shrug.

They had no logical reason to keep Ethan alive.

Luana pressed her lips into a thin line. "We need to investigate why he survived. Any ideas Dwayne? Maybe a bug?"

"You seriously think there's an elementalist disease that saves people from drinking poison and being shot?" Series' voice and left eyebrow lilted together.

"It can't be a disease. The line stops there. Rather than a disease it's like a cure for Rogue's—something that makes them a Rogue, but as a side effect it creates a race of people who can't be killed by conventional means." As the Life elementalist for the Council, Dwayne knew the most about diseases. His element demanded he study medicine, and there wasn't a single cluster of symptoms he couldn't identify. They needed to identify where the new mutation came from if, like Dwayne predicted, it became a *cure*. "The Uns are experimenting lately. Could they have resources to create a cure that malfunctioned?"

"Why would the Uns want to create a cure for Rogues?"

"They've been restless, Luana, haven't you seen it in the news? Everyone is wondering what we're going to do about it since we haven't addressed the issue yet." Series stood up from her chair and wandered over to the one-way window. "I'm sure a select handful might have the resources. We can't manage everything that goes in, and we don't know what the land provides."

"It can't possibly provide anything, it's a desert," Dwayne said.

"This isn't getting us anywhere right now." Luana held up a hand. "We need to escort Ethan to the cell then we can dive into research. We'll meet in the library after lunch."

"I hate the library." Dwayne's voice lowered in a groan, and he placed his hands over his face to rub at his temples.

"How do *you* hate the library? Your room is full of books." Series turned away from the window. Her eyebrows drew together, and she suppressed a laugh with her hand.

"I like *good* books, not the history and technical texts we keep in the spider infested shelves." Dwayne narrowed his eyes. A smile crept onto his face. "Don't you like books, though? Your name is *Series*."

"I thought my name is Muuyaw, coming from you," she returned softly.

Her vision swam shakily. Everything went dark, and she felt herself falling. Something flashed in front of her vision, but it wasn't visible.

"Muuyaw?" Dwayne called. She jumped, her whole body careened back into the glass, and she rubbed her shoulder to take away the momentary pain. "Did you hear what I said?"

"Sorry, I spaced out for a second." Her lips curved into a broken smile and bled into her apology.

"Did you see anything?" Luana asked.

Series opened her mouth, closed it, then opened it again.

"More books," she lied.

"We'll need all the help we can get." Luana cleared her throat and tugged at her shirt. "Dwayne, go get the *thing* from the hall."

"Rogues are '*things*' now?" Dwayne lifted a single eyebrow and stood.

"Dwayne," Luana's voice deepened several tones as he quickened his pace to the door.

"I'm going, I'm going, dear kgosi."

"Stop using Tswana to address me. I don't know what it means."

"I will never stop using Tswana, Molelo. Kgosi means king." He bared his teeth as he spoke—the only form of back talk he could get away with. The door opened with a quiet *thud*. He turned into the hallway, and his voice rose. "You drank the whole bottle?"

"To be fair, it was only three-fourths full when you handed it to me."

"It's time for you to come back in." Dwayne gestured. Ethan stood and rubbed the palms of his hands against his jeans. Dwayne was a little taller than him, but Ethan refused to think he hit his height peak yet. He wondered how tall he would be if he didn't die.

"What are you going to do to me?"

"We're putting you in a holding cell." Luana barely glanced at him when he reentered the room. "Eilene has gone to do some cleaning. Series will take you down."

Series pushed away from the window. She ran her fingers along her jaw and swiped at her dark hair; with a large smile, she said, "Hi."

Ethan examined the way she walked. Her feet barely touched the floor before she moved to the next step. Series was like a lazy cat who only looks for food and sleep. Each breath aligned with her steps, and her body rose and fell in a never-ending dance. He let a small smile creep onto his face as she put a hand on his shoulder and guided him to the open doorway.

"How long have you been a member of the Council?" Ethan asked once the wall shut firmly behind them.

"Ever since I finished my training—I was fourteen." Her tone was sharp and uninterested.

They reached the doorway to the cells in silence, but Ethan felt increasingly awkward the longer they didn't speak. He ran a hand through his hair; the individual strands stood on end. He stuffed his hands into his pockets and let out a slow breath before cringing on the inhale. His lungs took in the putrid air and nearly made him choke. It smelled like rot. He pretended it was vegetable rot.

Series peered between every row of new cells to find Eilene. At the end of a long row, the woman stood in front of a closed door. Series grabbed Ethan's elbow and directed him down the hall.

"I was thinking," he said, "if you ever get lonely or something, you could come visit me. Before you have to drag my body out."

"You want me to visit you?" Her eyebrows rose and her melodic steps stuttered across the floor. "That might be fun."

"Great."

She moved away, and he obediently followed.

Eilene pushed open the door—a large piece of wood with a small viewing window—and gestured for Ethan to enter. The room, unlike the rest of the dungeons, was free of the "vegetable" smell, and the surfaces glistened with drops of water from recent cleaning. A couple of laundered blankets and a pillow rested on a stone slab against the right wall. His feet padded across the same concrete block floor, and no windows occupied the walls. One electric light hung from the ceiling. The suspension chord swung back and forth and made the light patches dance across the walls in uneven patterns. Shadows crossed Ethan's face and amplified the sadness in his eyes; he terrified them.

"Nicer than I expected," Ethan said brightly.

"At least you can't say the Council doesn't take care of their prisoners." Eilene kept her gaze away from his eyes.

"Definitely one thing I won't be telling people." Ethan stepped inside and turned back around to face the women. "Thank you—for the blankets."

Luana staggered down the corridor toward her room. She tangled one hand into her hair and pulled at the knots. She needed to rage—to set things on fire; the one person she could talk to couldn't come to her aid. Luana wished she never sent him.

She felt the wall in front of her for the hidden button and stepped into the bedroom. The decorations confused her. A bed in the same place as her bedroom, but she didn't remember choosing green quilts. It smelled of fresh dust and cologne. Musk rested over the pale blue walls and hardwood floor with a hint of ryazhenka in the stale air.

She stepped slowly to the lamp on the nightstand and clicked it. The bulb stayed stubbornly off. Her mouth curved into a frown. She sat on the edge of the bed in the dark. She picked up a gold picture frame propped on the stand and used her phone to illuminate the photo. Luana nearly dropped the fragile object when she saw the people in the picture.

"Hans," her mouth formed the name before she could stop herself. It wasn't her room.

The boy in the picture was no more than five-years-old. She hardly recognized him, but she could see the familiarity of his features in his parents. His firm jaw line and lean build came from his father, but his eyes and hair resembled his mother. She looked happy in the photo, but Luana knew she had little joy left. She wrapped her arms around her two boys, Hans and Maxim. Maxim joined the Uns a few months after the photo was commissioned. Odessa, Hans' sister, stood next to her father holding up her acceptance letter to the Academy. Luana remembered killing Odessa in 2306. She took a slow breath in and replaced the picture on the stand.

Her eyes trailed to the desk on the opposite wall. The chair still sat away from the desk. She remembered spinning on it while they worked the night before he left. Her red sweater hung over the back. She left it in his room by accident. Luana didn't bother to collect it.

She let her head hit the pillow on the bed. She rolled until she rested on her left side. Luana ran her fingers over the quilt and fisted her hand in the fabric. The pillow smelled of kolbasa and dirt. It smelled like Hans. A tear leaked from the corner of her eye and dampened the pillow where her cheek rested.

She whispered unintelligible words into the sheets.

They didn't answer.

July 3, 2316

Presnensky District, Moscow, Russian Federation

Scarlet Lí raised her hands over her head and stretched dramatically. She groaned to add to the movement, and her partner in the workspace turned his head over his shoulder. Her black hair faded into an ombre of bleached blonde which shone under the light from the lamp on her desk; her slim shadow cast across her companion.

"Tired?" Hans Aliyev asked in Russian. His accent grew thicker since the return to his parents' homeland. He didn't normally speak the language daily. Scarlet found herself glad she had him by her side. She spoke Russian as a third language and missed things at times. Hans explained them to her in English, her second language. Hans had no communication skills in Mandarin; he tried once and failed miserably. To help Scarlet build her Russian acquisition, they always spoke it when in each other's private company, even in their hotel room.

"Just a little." Scarlet's voice sounded rough from little use over the last several hours. Hans stood and drifted over to the window for a break from work. He stared up at the sky, and the rays of light made his dark hair turn several shades lighter. The stubble across his chin, he hadn't shaved for their duration in Russia, glistened blond. For a moment, the image captivated Scarlet. On the corner of one of the pages of spare paper on Hans' desk, Hans had doodled Luana's name in fancy script before he scribbled it out. A frown formed on her lips.

"Do you miss Luana?" Scarlet asked.

"What?"

"Do you miss her? This is the longest you've been separated since you joined the Council, right?"

"It is hard to separate the Council. Of course, I miss our leader."

"That is not what I meant."

"I don't know what you mean, then."

Hans moved away from the window and into one of the bedrooms connected to the main sitting room. The yellow and cream of the walls and furniture in the hotel room made the atmosphere bright and quiet. "When are you ready to return to the meeting?"

"Give me a few minutes to finish this paper and grab my sweater."

"No problem." Hans tossed his blue windbreaker onto the arm of the couch and settled into the pillows.

Scarlet's pen scratched across her tablet screen. A flash of orange light startled her. Hans' phone flashed with an official Council message on his work desk. She recognized the name on the notification. Scarlet called to him, "Luana messaged you."

Hans threw his body across the room. He grabbed the piece of glass with such force the desk started to tip. He quickly righted the furniture with a soft *bang* against the wall.

Scarlet grinned. "Tell me again how *not* in love you are with our leader?"

"I'm not in love with Luana."

"Uh-huh."

"I'm not." His voice dropped on the last syllable.

Scarlet made a loud click with her tongue. The noise annoyed Hans, but she returned to her work. "So, what does lover woman have to say?"

"There's a situation they need help researching. We need to try to clear up the last of our issues today, so we can return to the Academy."

"Let's go now. I'll write in the taxi." Scarlet pushed all her loose papers into her briefcase and locked it. She grabbed Hans' arm and steered him toward the door. He barely managed to remember to grab his jacket off the couch.

July 4, 2316

The Council Chambers, The Academy, Elementōrum Patriam

Luana spent one rough day waiting for Hans to return home with Scarlet. She remained in Hans' room, curled up with her sweater on top of his covers. On her second night in the room, she fell fitfully into lucid dreams which turned into memories. She stood in the corner of the living room in her childhood home and watched her five-year-old self run into the room. The TV faintly played an old television show.

The room smelled like cigarette smoke, and young Luana lifted her fingers to pinch her nose. "Daddy?"

"Foolish child, your father shipped out to Kazakhstan yesterday. Surely you remembered that? You saw him off at the airport." Mrs. Portsmith snapped at her from her relaxed position on the couch. A duster sat on the floor nearby in a pitiable attempt to make it look like she did her job. Mrs. Portsmith lifted her hand away from her mouth and let a stream of smoke leave her lips. Luana's dad didn't know she smoked. The woman had a talent with getting rid of the smell before he returned home.

"I just—I thought he might—"

"Might choose to return home to you? No one wants to be with a brat like you."

Luana's small hands jumped to the dog tags around her neck. One of her dad's decommissioned sets; he helped her glue green, plastic gems to the unmarked side of them.

Luana jolted awake on Hans' bed; the pillow wet with her tears. Her right hand gripped the dog tags like in her dream. She flipped the pillow over. When she rolled over, the alarm clock showed three in the morning. Annoyed with herself, she pulled the sweater over her hands to stay warm. It didn't help.

On their return to the Council quarters, Hans and Scarlet met with the others—Eilene whisked Scarlet away to give her a rundown of the situation, but Hans continued to his room.

He opened the door and made to call out; he knew Luana would be there, but he stopped when he saw her sleeping on his bed. She kept to the left-hand side, closest to the door, and her brown hair spilled over the pillow. He took calculated steps across the floor to the other side. Hans sat down and hoped the dip in the bed wouldn't be enough to wake her. He slipped his shoes off and joined her on top of the covers.

"Lu," his hand touched her shoulder and gently rolled her toward him. She groaned and tried to turn away from his touch. Her mouth opened in a slow yawn, and her eyes cracked open to his prone form.

"Hans," Luana breathed. She reached out for him and wrapped her arms around his torso. She breathed in his smell and took comfort in the earthy cologne and Russian food. He pulled her tighter to him and took a steadying breath.

"What's going on?"

"It's this—I don't even know how to explain it," she whispered. "It's an anomaly."

"Can you show me?"

"Yeah." She slid from his grip and off the bed. Her bare feet padded across the floor.

"Do you need shoes?" he asked.

"No, I'll be fine. It's a short trip."

"Where are we going?"

"To the jail cells."

Luana and Hans walked in comfortable silence for a stretch through the dark halls; they didn't often use the hallway light. They knew the halls well and didn't need to check the map on their phones to navigate.

"What are you keeping down here?" Hans said.

"A Rogue."

"Why are you keeping a Rogue?"

"We aren't able to kill him." Luana shrugged.

"Momentary lapse of will?" Hans' brows pinched in the middle. "I don't believe it of you."

"We shot him six times. He drank a bottle of poison. I tried to behead him—he's still alive." She opened the door to the cell area and led him through the winding paths. "We put him in a cell down here in order to attempt AZ."

"Are you sure he's still alive?"

"Yes? We're looking into his case. I needed you here with me." Luana kicked the ground with her toes. A warm hand landed on her shoulder, and she met Hans' green eyes. He provided a soft smile, cracking his hard features. She placed her left hand on top of his before they continued.

They approached a cell at the end of a hallway, and she called out, "Ethan?"

"Hey, did you know you guys gave me a piece of wood in the blankets on accident?"

"No, I wasn't aware," she paused for a moment, "I brought another Council member to meet you."

"I tried to make a shank," he said at the same time. "Oh, uh, sorry."

Ethan's red hair peeked into the view plate of the door, and he stood on his tiptoes to look out. "Hey, I'm Ethan Silverspoon."

Hans took in the Rogue slowly. "Hans Aliyev."

"Why'd you make a shank?" Luana asked.

"Thought I might be able to kill myself with the shank, but I ran into an issue." He went quiet, and he shuffled around the cell space.

"Which is?" Hans prompted lowly.

"Hold on." He reappeared in the open hole and held his hands through the space.

In his left hand, he held a rough piece of wood. Ethan bent his right wrist back, so the main vein stuck out. He stabbed himself with the point. Luana managed to push a short scream down. The shank stuck through from one side to the other, but his arm no longer existed where he stabbed. Gray smoke filled the space, and despite the disconnect between his forearm and hand, he wiggled his fingers.

"It doesn't do anything."

Luana cleared her throat. "That'll give us more information to work with. I came down here to introduce Hans to you since he just got back. Have you met Scarlet?"

"Yeah. She came down with Eilene earlier."

"Good." Luana didn't bother to say anything else before she walked away. Hans followed her obediently.

"Research? About why he's alive?"

"You're going to have to stop asking questions, Hans."

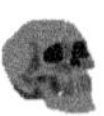

July 20, 2316

The Council Chambers, The Academy, Elementōrum Patriam

"This is exhausting," Dwayne's head hit the table. A faint gold glow surrounded him and the other Council members. Series' ability at work to give them luck in searching. Several books fell off the end of the desk, and Eilene glared at him. "We're starving Ethan to death, anyway, does it matter if we figure out what's going on?"

"Dwayne poses a good question." Series' voice muffled from the number of shelves separating her from the rest of the group. The rest of the Council previously assumed she fell asleep.

"Muuyaw agrees with me?"

"That name is going to haunt me forever." Series stepped into the middle aisle with a pile of books.

"The nicknames aren't bad," Dwayne defended. He pulled a ladder into position, so he could reach the higher shelves. With most documents moving to digital, they kept the library small width and length wise, fifty feet by twenty feet. One path cut the room in half with rows of perpendicular shelves lining either side; the shelves rose twenty feet and touched the ceiling.

"I find them endearing." Eilene pulled a face at the book she held in her hands. The book closed with a snap and an unwarranted cloud of dust. She pushed it onto the shelf.

Scott grunted from his row of books, the darkest row in the room.

"I agree with Scott." Luana appeared in the doorway of the library with Hans.

Dwayne shifted his weight on the ladder, sliding to the end of the row with a snap. He peered around the corner at their leader; a smile plastered on his face.

"I suppose you could come up with better nicknames, Molelo."

"I don't even know what that means," Luana said.

Dwayne rolled his eyes. "Because you haven't tried to learn any other languages. You already know English, so why bother, right?"

Luana opened her mouth to argue, but Hans stopped her by pulling a book off the shelf. He held it out to her, and their leader took it hesitantly. She stared at the cover. "Setswana to English Dictionary."

She flipped through the pages with greed until she found the word Dwayne kept calling her.

"Molelo means fire," Luana breathed. "That's actually sweet of you."

"Idiot," Hans muttered under his breath. She ignored him. He knew he would be the only one who could get away with the insult.

"As if I'd give any of you truly insulting nicknames. Mosupologo agrees with me."

Scott walked through the shelves to return several books and collect new ones without replying. Eilene watched him before her eyes fell back to her next dense text of Elements in the natural world.

Luana flipped a few pages in the dictionary. "You call Scott, Monday?"

"He reminds me of the day. Ornery and cold," Dwayne said.

"Since when have I been cold?" Scott asked.

"Oh, it speaks!" Dwayne pointed at Scott like a specimen in a zoo. "Say something else."

"Leave him alone," Series said from the corner.

"Whatever you wish, Muuyaw." Dwayne gave her a playful bow.

"With that book we could know what month you were born in." Series' expression lit up as she rounded the corner and took the book from Luana.

"I am not telling you it again with that book anywhere near you. I don't like celebrating my birthday." Dwayne's jovial smile disappeared. He glared at the Setswana to English dictionary. "What I wouldn't give to be a Fire elementalist right now. *Poof.*"

"If Dwayne insists on giving us nicknames, we should give him one."

Eilene placed a book on the table of useful texts before returning to the shelves.

"That is my thing, Dickens." He used his first two fingers to point at his own eyes before he turned the gesture on Eilene. She snickered.

"Any good books so far?" Luana threw herself into one of the chairs at the main table where they kept the potentially useful books. She pulled one from the top of the pile. Hans assisted the others in putting away the useless texts. Dwayne held a book out to Luana. The brown cover had letters on the front in gold leaf foil, a medical instruction manual.

"This one has some interesting information on curing humans of illnesses we're immune to," Dwayne shuffled the pile for another book with a cracked spine, "and this one discusses the health risks with life spans in humans and elementalists who lived over a hundred years. Honestly, the research made me glad we die around sixty. Sounded like a horrible time in history."

"That's not what we're looking for." Luana let her head hit the table and she narrowly missed the corner with her eye. Hans flinched.

"You asked if we found anything good, it is a good read." Dwayne grinned.

"Scott, please tell me you have something," Luana said.

Scott shook his head and propped a history book onto a stack of other books, so he could read.

"Anyone up for ice-cream in London tonight?" Eilene yawned.

"It's almost nine o'clock there. We'll never make it in time," Luana said.

"Then let's plan it for tomorrow night, or over the next couple of days. We have to get out of the library to give our minds a break."

"We can't leave Ethan alone."

Dwayne cleared his throat to break the tension growing between the two women. He scratched his nose. None of them wanted a fight.

"We're starving him anyway. If we leave for three days, it's not going to change anything." Series tipped another book onto the desk next to her. "If you're insistent about research we can spend some time in the British Library. While our library is extensive, they might have something we don't that will give us a clue. Afterall, everyone here is blessed with luck." She waved her fingers through the air.

"Alright, but only for a few days," Luana said.

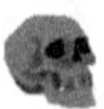

Ethan sat on the stone slab bed and leaned against the wall. He stared into the dark corner. If he looked at it right, another figure appeared in the space. It resembled his mother.

"When it gets quiet, I wish I would just die." He bounced his leg against the concrete. "You know what I mean, mom?"

The whistle of cold air through the cells responded. The breeze brought the smell of the other cells with it. He coughed and pinched his nose. He couldn't tell how many days passed since Hans and Luana visited him. His stomach growled, and he let his body fall against the bed for another nap. Sleep always staved off the hunger for a while longer.

He didn't want to keep holding on. Memories blurred across his eyelids. The first bad decision in Ethan's dream would be tumbling over the edge of the waterfall. He fell through the air. Lulu reached out from the branch of a tree for him. Her pigtails blew in the wind and floated around her head like a halo. He put out his hand for hers, but his fingers slippery with water made sure her grip didn't hold.

He crashed painfully into the water at the base of the fall. He writhed in the twisting currents. He couldn't breathe. Ethan couldn't tell where he needed to swim to get air. He couldn't grab any of the rocks to pull himself free from the current as the water swallowed his body. The waves spat Ethan onto a sandy shore where seven people sat on a picnic blanket. They appeared in black and white and wore clothes which reminded him of old 1950s films. The four women sat with their poodle skirts fanned out. The men adjusted their polo shirt collars and flexed their muscles to impose their dominance.

"Ah Ethan, we've been expecting you," Luana said with a smile. She lifted a teacup and took a dainty sip.

Ethan glanced at the waterfall and into the trees which grew at its edge. "What happened to Lulu?"

"You will see her again if you cooperate." The group laughed as one. "Answer three of our riddles and you're free to go to Lulu."

"What if I don't want to answer them?"

"Then you'll never see Lulu again." Somewhere in the back of his mind he registered Lulu died—he saw the orphanage crash into the ocean. At the same time, he didn't want to take the risk and lose her a second time. "Here is the first riddle: with thieves I consort, with the vilest, in short. I`m quite at my ease in depravity; Yet all divines use me, and savants cannot lose me. For I am the center of gravity. What am I?"

Ethan's mind raced as he tried to muddle through the words. Luana repeated it a second time for him when he didn't reply. Ethan closed his eyes and focused. The second to last line stood out to him. *The center of gravity.*

"V!" he shouted.

The black and white setting faded along with the Council. Ethan tumbled through the sky. He wanted to scream, but it caught in his throat. He only answered one riddle. He landed on a soft mattress, a large king-sized bed with too many pillows; it bowed under his sudden weight. He rolled over and pushed himself out of bed. When he opened the door on the far-right wall, he could hear two female voices call for him.

Gold sconces decorated the walls of the hallway alongside crimson curtains and bloody carpets. Ethan ran after the sound, and he came to a fork in the long hallway. Down the left side stood Lulu and, on the right, his mother. He pivoted between them. They vanished.

"Choose," a harsh voice whispered in his ear.

He took the left path. Behind him he heard the scuttling of something with too many legs. He didn't dare turn around. As he caught up to Lulu's figure, a large, wet something wrapped around his ankle. He hit the carpet and burned his chin. Ethan twisted around and saw a large centipede demon reared over him. It's long snake-like tongue flicked out, and the demon hissed. Ethan tried to scramble back, but he couldn't gain any traction on the carpet, slick with blood. The demon opened its jaw filled with rows of sharp needle teeth and dove.

Ethan jolted awake and fell off the stone slab. Pain ricocheted through his bones. He grunted and pulled his hands in front of him, but he had no strength to push himself off the stone floor. Ethan's chin hit the floor, and liquid ran across his chin. Blood. A sarcastic grin settled onto his lips and caused them to crack and bleed, too. Ethan found enough energy to reach up for the wood shank. He cracked it weakly against the ground until he had a sharp splinter.

He pressed the splinter into his finger, and he didn't startle when a red bead formed at the puncture point. Ethan rolled over onto his back and a mirthless laugh burst from his lips.

The Council won.

CHAPTER FOUR
Undoing

July 21, 2316

London, Greater London, England, The United Kingdom

Eilene stretched as she stepped out of the transportation pod. Scott and Dwayne exited on her heels. The trio's tall frames made the space cramped. Dwayne rolled his shoulders to release the pressure in his joints and let out a low groan. The foursome from the first pod exited slower as they woke from their naps. With their identities hidden as the Council—when they visited the human world for short trips where they didn't meet with other dignitaries— they didn't have to wear their robes. They hid the robes in the storage compartment of the pods, so it wouldn't tip off passerby if they happened to glance inside.

Series touched each of the Council members on the shoulder before they separated in the library. Luck flowed through their veins as they approached each shelf.

Dwayne knew he should look for information on their people, but the letters burned a hole in his pocket. He didn't know why he grabbed them off his desk before they left for London. He didn't have an address to send them. Rather, he didn't know if the recipients still lived.

He sunk into a chair at one of the study tables and removed the folded envelopes. They uncurled when he tossed them on the desk. Dwayne grabbed the first one and pulled the sheets of paper loose from the unsealed envelope. The papers were folded into messy thirds and some of the previously wet ink stuck to the clean sides of the paper. When he opened the pages, several words became illegible. Dwayne bit his lip and wondered if he should write them in Setswana instead of English.

He stood and asked the front desk for some paper and a pen. Back at the desk, he turned the table lamp to the clean printer paper and started a scrawl across the page in his heritage language.

Thisipuni:

It's been a while since Tsaya Ya Mogale Orphanage. Sometimes I wonder what happened to you and Drummer. Were you informed I died? The Council is good at hunting people down and letting them know when that happens—but I don't know if they could find you. I heard in passing, before we separated, they adopted you for factory work. I hope you remain safe with all those machines. I'm scared to go near them as an adult. You were always braver than me.

Sometimes I think about how you'd be in your thirties now. In my dreams, I see you with a loving husband and several children. All are cared for and loved. Your children get along with each other, unlike us three. I'd be a doting uncle and buy them too many toys and sweets. You'd be mad at me; I'd never call any of them by their real names.

Do you still live in Botswana? I still don't like celebrating my birthday. I'm twenty-seven now. I hope you remember my age without the reminder.

I'm sorry we couldn't stay together as a family. I don't know if things would've been any different. I'm the oldest member on the Council here. I'm not the main kgosi though. That's Molelo. She's been on the Council the longest of any of us.

I miss you, Thisipuni. I plan on seeing you again before I die. Maybe in your early forties. Wait for me, wherever you are.
Dwayne Tebogo

He was more confident in his second draft. It would never leave his hands because he'd burn it when he returned home. Dwayne tucked the new papers into the envelope and folded the old into a tight square before returning the set to his pocket. One more letter to go.

Drummer:

Have you ever thought about how strange our names are when our parents ended up dropping us off at an orphanage? Of course, I'm thinking more along the lines of yours and Thisipuni's names. I think they gave up on mine.

Abeje means our parents asked to have our sister, and you—Chimelu—were what God created. Why did we end up where we are?

I heard the nice man in the suit was a slave trader. It's hard to think this stuff still goes on today. I don't know where you ended up. I hope you're making music wherever you are. I loved listening to the songs you wrote. The beats still pound in my head at night when I can't fall asleep. It sounds like home.

A few years ago, I might've told you I didn't know where home is. Perhaps I still don't know. I like to think I have two homes... I have a home at the orphanage with you. The other is in Elementōrum Patriam. It's on the third floor behind the locked door. I don't think you know the one I speak of. Everyone here does. They're terrified of it.

I'm a little scared of it, too.

There's seven of us here. Dickens is my best friend. She's great. I think you'd like her if you ever met her.

If we both make it out alive of whatever comes next, I'd

love to see you one last time. I hope you escaped and have a family now. I want you to be safe. Perhaps I worry over you and Thisipuni more than I should as the youngest sibling.

I'll give myself a deadline. I'll see you in the next five years, and you'll be happy. I know it. You can't deny it.

Dwayne Tebogo

He didn't like his letter to Chimelu. He always found his brother harder to talk to. He shoved the pages and envelope back into his pocket without neatly folding them. The letter needed serious work—even if Luana wouldn't let him send it. Dwayne leaned back in his chair and grabbed the first book he found off the shelf. A chill ran up his spine. Luana watched him closely from across the study area. He shuddered and immediately went to work.

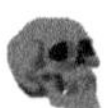

Eilene wandered into the history section by herself and started toward the aisle with a plastic sign advertising it as the elementalist section. She reached the end of the row and stared at the long columns of books. Eilene skimmed her fingers past the ones she recognized from their home library and pulled the others down onto the middle table between the rows.

One text caught her attention among the worn, dusty, brown, and gray covers. Wine colored with gold filament accents. Eilene pulled at the top of the spine and the book fell into her hand. She held it in her open hand and ran a finger across the cover. *Elementalists Across the Ages.* They didn't have the book in their personal collection.

Eilene opened the cover and heard the binding crack. She flipped the pages softly. The book was made from heavy-weight paper, but the text didn't look dense. She could see the places where the restoration team repaired the book a few times—new binding and tape on the inside cover. The publisher stylized the book to imitate old bibles with a large, calligraphy based, ornately drawn first letter at the beginning of every chapter; the rest of the text kept a single column of serif style lettering. Eilene thumbed the first few esthetic pages of the book until she located the table of contents.

One of the chapters listed a breakdown of each element and she turned to page ninety-two. The chapter had a boldface font at the top with decorative pieces above and below the title. Eilene stared at the page. Nine elements, not seven. She slammed the book down onto the table and several other patrons glared at her. *Ethan is an elementalist.*

Excerpts from *Elementalists Across the Ages: British Library Collection*, Published 1946

SCIENTIFIC RESEARCH

Elementalists (*Homo elementa*) are a group of people who emerged from a genetic mutation on the thirteenth chromosome. The mutation allows them control one of the natural elements of the world. There are certain limitations to the mutation. While elementalists run at a higher core temperature and thin air doesn't affect them the same as it does *Homo sapiens*, their body is quick to break down when it receives damage from external sources.

External sources include tobacco products, which damage the lungs, and alcohol, which is known to destroy the liver. While these can cause irreversible problems in humans, for the elementalists, it kills them. One cigarette breaks down the lungs capacity and erodes the mutation in their lungs which adjusts to the elevation. A single sip of beer (or any stronger form of liquor) performs the same action in their liver, and their organs shut down accordingly.

One orientation of the mutation causes what the elementalists label as a **glitch**. The glitch occurs when the nucleotide Thymine (T) lines up with a Cytosine (C). The combination is rare and causes a malfunction in the elementalist's body which doesn't allow them to fully control one element—they can use pieces of all the elements. The elementalists call this mutation "Rogue".

In comparison, children without the genetic mutation

can be born to elementalist parents. Instead of the term human, the elementalists labeled the "demutation" as Un.

...

HISTORY OF SEPARATION

The first Council formed after strenuous warfare across Pangea. There are few records which indicate what happened at that time. A lot of the history for the forming of the eight main continents, with only seven on the Earth's water level surface, comes from speculation. The original Council created Elementōrum Patriam. The oldest cities in the country are named after the original nine Council members.

The nine Council members created nine cities on Pangea before tearing the world apart. During the first war between humans and elementalists, all nine cities—Moscow, Jerusalem, Ekurhuleni, Venice, Hong Kong, Shikaakwa, Kaerlud, Pompeii, and Cochabamba—were destroyed. The remnants remained. Humans built new cities on the foundations, and those nine cities remain safe havens, or harbor cities, for elementalists today.

Vasha is credited with tearing Pangea into the seven lower continents. According to historians, she died during the process—but the elementalists never ruled the event as accidental.

...

ELEMENTALIST PRESENTATION

Elementalist researchers report ten possible mutations on the thirteenth chromosome which result in someone with elementalist genetics.

The tenth mutation is the Rogue, while the eighth and ninth are two elements in addition to the widely known seven. These two elements report regular dips in presentation and typically have less overall representation among the elementalists.

The last recorded population spike of these elements occurred in the early 1900s. During the world wars, young elementalists with the eighth and ninth mutations were recorded as great warriors on the field. Their elements made formidable enemies. Many accounts report one of the mutations allowed an elementalist to cross no-man's land in seconds. They could avoid bullets and act as sting operations behind the opposition's backs. Some reports include a gas-like substance emitting from one of the elementalists and killing everyone in the trenches.

These stories discuss the eighth and ninth types of elementalist, the Supernatural and Death elements.

...

A BREAKDOWN OF THE NINE ELEMENTS

Among the nine elements, there are histories of power struggles. Some elements are built to fare better against others to keep their power in check. It is a natural system of checks and balances.

Fire

They can control flames created by friction, spark, or their body. Fire is versatile for these elementalists. Many train to create specific shapes. Fire is best combated by those who control the element of Earth.

The first Council member: Messina of Pompeii.

Water

Water is not limited to the liquid form; it includes the gas vapors and frozen forms. Many water elementalists can create boiling water at will. Water elementalists are best combated by those who control the Air element.

The first Council Member: Ricci of Venice.

Earth

Earth elementalists can form precious jewels, control

mud and quicksand, and even create new land formations. They are weakest to those who control Water—as seen in the natural wonders of the world.

The first Council member: Vasha of Moscow.

Air

Air elementalists can make air thinner and harder to breathe, remove oxygen in a small zone, and manipulate air currents to fly. Those who control Air are most vulnerable to Death.

The first Council member: Victor of Cochabamba.

Storm

Storm elementalists are better described as Natural Disaster elementalists. They are known to generate tornados, earthquakes, tsunamis, and other natural disasters. Storm elementalists are best combated by Life.

The first Council member: Brooks of Kaerlud.

Fortune

Fortune elementalists see the future and affect the good and bad luck of those around them. Studies found that Fortune elementalists only see the future when they are asleep. Fortune elementalists are weakest against Supernatural.

The first Council member: Xia of Hong Kong.

Supernatural

Supernatural elementalists control space and time; they can speedily expand the universe or stop time on Earth while they move at full speed. The Supernatural elementalists are best combated by Fire.

The first Council member: Wabaunsee of Shikaakwa.

Life

Life elementalist powers have a wide range. They can heal any illness (unless it is a genetic mutation). If a Life elementalist isn't inclined to follow the path of doctor, they often work in agriculture. Life is weakest against Fortune.

The first Council member: Yahav of Jerusalem.

Death

Death elementalists appear immune to death as they are difficult to injure or kill. Researchers found they can be weakened (starvation, exhaustion) and injured by any item. They are best combatted by those who control Storms.

The first Council member: Ubuntu of Ekurhuleni.

Eilene snatched her phone from her pocket and lifted the slim piece of glass close to her face. Her thumbs tapped hurriedly on the screen. The message to the other Council members contained numerous errors. She hoped the garble of letters on her screen would be coherent. Eilene pressed send and heard six text tones in rapid succession like gunfire. Patrons grumbled around her about the excessive noise in the study area, but Eilene paid them no mind. She opened another app on her phone, allowing her to scan the entire text of the book. She moved to a better lit study table and set her phone on top of the cover.

"Found something good?" Dwayne came up behind her and rested his chin on her shoulder. She prayed he couldn't see the flushed color spread across her face from his angle. "Your message is barely coherent. Something about Ethan being an elementalist."

"There's nine elements, not seven. It's why there are nine Council members originally," Eilene whispered. "According to this book, the Supernatural and Death elements have low numbers. Based on the descriptions on page ninety-two, I would guess Ethan is of the Death element. There's a theory that ties the elements to times of war, but I'm not sure it's true. However, if Ethan is a Death elementalist, someone out there is going to be a Supernatural elementalist."

"Even if Ethan is a Death elementalist, we have another problem to solve," Scott said, walking to the other side of the table.

Eilene's phone showed a progress bar halfway through scanning the book into their electronic database.

"He hasn't eaten anything in weeks, he might be dead," Series finished his thought.

Luana drew attention to herself as she marched across the library toward them. Her feet hit the floor hard with every step, Hans followed obediently on her heels. She shoved her phone into Eilene's face. "Ethan is not one of the seven."

"He's one of the nine, Luana," Eilene said.

"There's not nine—"

"There is." Series' eyes widened. "Whenever there is a trial for a new Council member, there are nine doorways. We ignored the other doorways because the crystal colors never matched up with our own element. We even have two rooms we never used because the Council chambers housed all seven elements we knew."

"They built the rooms for Death and Supernatural." Dwayne nodded. He snatched the book away from Eilene's phone when it finished scanning. He opened to the page Eilene specified earlier and read through the section on the Death element. "If we don't get to Ethan now, we might have another problem on our hands."

"What is it?" Scarlet tried to read over his shoulder. He set the book on the table and pointed at the specific line.

"In a weakened state, he can be injured and killed by anything."

"If you have it in you, Series," Luana started, their eyes met, "we're going to need a lot of good luck."

Transportation Pod #1

Eilene forwarded the book document to them once inside the transportation pods. Each of them remained silent as they read through some of the information on the two unknown elements.

"How many of them have I killed?" Luana whispered.

"'*We*', Luana. You weren't the only one involved," Hans said. "You can rule out the Death elementalists. After seeing Ethan, it's clear we've never come across them before."

"But the Supernatural—"

"We have no way of knowing. The fault is on the previous Council's heads because we did not know." Hans placed a warm hand over hers. "It's been over three-hundred years since the last known record of Supernatural and Death elements. Our history is lacking. It was a mistake."

"Over three-hundred and fifty," Series corrected in a soft mumble.

"No need to be pedantic, Series." Scarlet rolled her eyes.

"It's been too long for us to say we killed them knowingly. It's not a big deal. If Ethan is here, it means other Death elementalists will arrive again, too. So will Supernatural. We'll have to figure out a test for them to take based on the information in this book." Series waved her phone in the air. "No problems going forward."

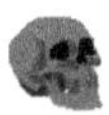

July 22, 2316

Transportation Pod #2

As the resident Life elementalist, Dwayne became their only healer for the group. He held no fondness for the doctoring profession and often complained in private about the duties he filled. In moments like these, he prepared in the only way he could. He slept. The only one in their pod to sleep. He needed his strength for the battle waiting for him at the Academy. No other elementalist could rival his knowledge and skill. No matter how much he hated the job. Ethan would be in bad shape, and they'd leave it up to him to make sure he remained okay. Eilene picked up her phone and typed a quick message to Series in the other car.

> **Hey, you should probably sleep, too. Dwayne's passed out. I'm sure he'll need your help maintaining a good atmosphere.**

She didn't receive a reply, and Eilene prayed it meant Series already slept. Scott bumped her with his elbow. He offered his shoulder for her to rest on.

Eilene shook her head. "I'll be fine. I don't need to sleep."

"Sleep anyway," he said.

"Alright." Her head dropped to the left side of her body and rested against Scott's bony shoulder. Her eyes settled on Dwayne.

When she first met him after joining the Council, she lashed out at him when he touched her shoulder. A reaction caused by the trauma from her uncle. It took months before she realized they could be friends, and he wanted to get to know her as a genuine person.

October 5, 2312

The Council Chambers, The Academy, Elementōrum Patriam

"What do you like doing for fun?" Dwayne nudged her with his knee as they sat in the video game room. Twenty-year-old Eilene felt like napping over playing games.

"Reading—it lets me avoid people."

"What do you read?"

"Classics, online comics." She shrugged. Her hair spilled across the back of the couch. She scooted down the cushion until her butt hung off the edge and all her weight rested on the small of her back. "What do you do in this pit of politics?"

"Whenever I can escape kgosi, I hide out here or in my room. I like video games and music."

"What kind of music?" Eilene asked.

"Old music, a classic. I'm talking like three-hundred years old at least."

"Lame." She covered her mouth. "I've wanted to ask for a while—why do you call Anika, kgosi?"

"It means 'king' in Tswana. Since she's currently the head of the Council by seniority, I gave her that title. It'll transfer to whoever is the next senior member."

"You speak Tswana?"

"I'm from Botswana," Dwayne chuckled. "The elementalists pulled me from an orphanage in Maun. Where do you come from?"

"City of Barren, long line of elementalists."

"Impressive."

"My death ruined their line though," she snorted.

"Better you than anyone else. Anika likes having you here so far."

"She's like a mom to the rest of the Council," Eilene said. After her trial to join the Council, Anika helped her transition the most.

"She's forty-nine, though."

"Disappointing." Eilene chucked the controller for the game onto the coffee table in front of them. Humans and elementalists alike had short lifespans. Most barely lived to see a day above sixty. "See you later, Dwayne."

"Thanks for hanging out with me."

Eilene walked out of the room and down the hall. A door cracked open, and she pushed it further. The room had a desk light on in the corner, but it didn't give enough light to see who occupied the room. Eilene pressed the button for the lights and stared at the body on the floor. Anika stared back at her with eyes glossed over. Bile rose in her throat.

July 22, 2316

Transportation Pod #2

"Hey, Dickens, time to wake up." The voice sounded familiar; she groaned. "You too, Mosupologo."

"You're supposed to be the one sleeping." Eilene pushed herself off Scott's shoulder.

"I woke up to eat food. We're approaching the northeast coast of America. We'll be home soon." He pressed a sandwich and a bag of chips into her hands.

"Thanks Dwayne. You should sleep more."

Dwayne shook his head. "If I sleep anymore, I'll be of no use. I need to be awake to think about medical things properly. I hate to admit it, but I'm a bit rusty."

"I'm sure you'll do fine," Scott reassured him. He took a bite of his sandwich, and the pair watched him closely. "What?"

"If Scott's telling you 'You're fine', then you're fine." Eilene pulled at the seam of the chip bag, and it popped open. She leaned into the smell. "Nacho cheese."

They ate in silence for a while and a frown marred Dwayne's face. Eilene pressed her foot against his on the floor until he looked at her.

"You look like something's bugging you," Eilene said.

"Did either of you have siblings before coming to the Academy?" Dwayne asked.

"Little sister." Scott reached for one of the water bottles.

"Two older sisters and an older brother," Eilene said.

"I had an older brother and sister. I've been thinking about them lately. I don't know much about them outside of where they were taken after the orphanage." A frown slid across Dwayne's face.

"My sister died from pneumonia. She got sick trying to take care of my father, and he didn't notice," Scott said.

Eilene placed a hand on top of Scott's. He looked at her under heavy eyelids. She lifted her free hand and swept some of the hair out of his eye. His breath quickened, and Dwayne narrowed his eyes from across the pod.

"You look tired. Go back to sleep for an hour or so. We'll wake you at the ascent."

Scott managed a nod before he leaned against the seat cushion again.

"I wrote letters for my siblings," Dwayne confessed.

"It helps, doesn't it?"

"I didn't realize it had, until now."

"I wrote a letter to my parents once. Asked Luana to burn it. She can be helpful sometimes." A laugh crept past her chapped lips. "Do you think you'll be able to save Ethan?"

"I don't know," he said. "I'm going to try my hardest. I haven't had a patient die on me yet, but I don't know his case."

"The book says he can be weakened by starvation and exhaustion. I wouldn't be surprised if he had both."

"I wouldn't either." His brows crinkled together. "Will I be able to use medical instruments on him?"

"If he's in that state. If he's not, I'm not sure." She opened the application on her phone and scrolled at a rapid pace down the screen. "I don't see anything."

"I don't know if we'll get there in time."

"We can at least try."

"Scott."

A hand shook his shoulder, and he pulled away. He tried to roll over, but his legs collided with someone else's. His eyes shot open. Scott didn't remember sharing a bed with anyone. Eilene crouched over him in the transportation pod.

"We're about a half-hour away from home. We thought you'd want to be fully coherent. Luana sent out a text, she plans to run since it's an emergency."

"We're gonna scare the entire population of our country running through the Academy for our base of operations," Dwayne laughed. "I don't know what Molelo's thinking."

"After this ordeal we might need to call in a Code Birthday." Eilene winked at her best friend.

"I could go for a Code Birthday. I'll put on my vintage music."

"No. It's gonna be Snow Patrol again." She hit her head against the glass of the door.

"They happen to be a wonderful band from three-hundred years ago."

"They're so old." She fell into a fit of laughter, and her head landed on Scott's shoulder unsolicited. He stiffened. "Sorry, Scott."

"I'm afraid to ask." He pointed between the pair.

"Code Birthday?" Dwayne cocked his head to the side. "Yeah, it's a top-secret thing for us."

"It's not that big of a deal." Eilene rolled her eyes.

"I beg to differ. It's an especially important time where I am allowed to wallow in my ancient music and not do my job. Alongside a pretty lady, I might add."

"If I called the Code Birthday, then I get to pick the music."

"You're ruining the mood, Dickens."

CHAPTER FIVE
Tomb

July 22, 2316

Council Holding Cells, The Academy, Elementōrum Patriam

Ethan's body burned. Days passed since he first injured himself and the symptoms grew furiously worse. Rashes raged across his skin. When he scratched them, his skin peeled and made him bleed. He drifted in and out of shock as his body tried to stay alive. His heart pounded, and an ache rested in the base of his skull—it never went away. Ethan's body jolted on the bed and sent him spiraling onto the hard ground. His blood pooled around him, and he pressed himself into the momentary warmth it provided. He coughed, and a new spattering of red joined the rest.

A whimper escaped his lips. He covered his mouth with his hand. He didn't know if the Council watched—he didn't want to show any weakness as death approached. His body convulsed into another round of coughs. He gathered the last of his energy and placed a hand against the edge of the stone bed. Ethan pulled himself onto the slab and breathed laboriously from the exertion. Sicker than he felt before, he rolled to the side and puked. The mess joined his blood on the floor. The rancid smell swirled around him till it enticed another round, but he couldn't do anything about it.

Ethan curled into a fetal position on the stone and willed the tears to stay locked behind his eyelids. He lost hope the Council would come for him. His body couldn't keep up the fight for his life much longer.

The cell blurred and Ethan squeezed his eyes shut. The vertigo from these moments usually sent him into long periods of vomiting. He let his breathing slow into a steady pace.

Hans yanked Luana's robes over her before they pulled into the parking garage of the Academy. She didn't want to deal with the stuffy robes, but these were Council designated pods, and they couldn't risk anyone discovering their true identities. He kept a steady hand on her shoulder as they walked across the short space to the Academy doors. They couldn't run in the parking area because it would send people into mass hysteria. The Council had to wait until they were in the less crowded corridor outside the garage.

They broke through the double doors and ran. They bumped into the corners of walls when they took turns too sharp, but they couldn't bother with the momentary shock of pain. Their steps whirled up and down staircases and in circle patterns around the Academy. The intent to keep the Council room hard to access created barriers in times of trouble.

During their harried course, they passed several students. The elementalists jumped out of the way and tried to hide their terrified expressions. The Council didn't care enough to assuage their worries.

Luana slipped on the polished floor as they rounded the final corner. She tumbled into the other wall with a sharp crack. Dwayne continued running for the Council door, Eilene and Series kept pace just steps behind him. Series left a trail of glittering gold behind her as she managed to just touch Dwayne's back. The other three stopped to check on Luana. She shoved them away and tried to push herself off the floor. The robes caught around her feet and brought her down a second time. She let out a guttural growl and burst into flames. Hans made sure no one would see her outside her robe before they tried to catch up to the Life elementalist. Luana left a trail of ash behind them.

With Dwayne's head start, the main door waited wide open. Scott, the last through the door, made sure to shut and lock it before following the rest. Luana's form lit the way as they continued their trek through the mess of halls to the containment cells. Each of them tore off their robes and left them in unusable shambles through the dark corridor. Hans lifted a hand and sent several pieces of rock hurtling through the air to activate doors ahead. Scarlet caught up with Dwayne first. Eilene passed him the key to Ethan's cell. He fumbled it as they ran. It dropped through the air but didn't hit the ground. Scott caught it with a sharp blast of wind and pushed it firmly into Dwayne's fingers.

"Ethan!" Scarlet called through the cells. No response came from his sector. Their mouths curved into frowns as they considered the worst.

Dwayne nearly ran into the wall when he couldn't make his legs stop. With his left hand, he managed the key, fumbling to get it into the lock. One successful turn later, Eilene yanked the door open. The rusted hinges screamed under the weight of the door.

"Ethan?" Dwayne hurried into the room, still glowing gold, and nearly slipped on the large puddle of sick spread across the floor. Scott covered his mouth and tried to choke down his own bile. Unable to hedge around the vomit, Dwayne took the most direct route and immediately put out his hand for a scan. He used two fingers to trace Ethan's pulse through his neck. "He's still alive, but barely."

"Someone run ahead and prepare the medical room," Hans said. Scarlet took Series with her.

Dwayne tried to pick up Ethan by grabbing his arms, but the skin cracked and tore under his grip; rivulets of blood stained his dark skin.

"Damn it," Dwayne shook several drips of blood from his fingers.

The elementalist flung the arm over his shoulder instead, blood soaked the light cotton fabric, and picked Ethan up bridal style. The Council cleared the way as he walked to the infirmary with their charge. Dwayne kept a steady, fast pace and tried not to jostle Ethan too much because he knew the jolts would cause more damage.

Scarlet and Series dutifully prepared for their emergency. When they walked into the room the pair organized a few tools onto a surgical table. Dwayne deposited Ethan's body onto the clean, white sheets, and the skin that tore from his limbs stained the cloth.

"Dickens, grab that table." Dwayne pointed to a small metal box in the corner. He walked to the far wall and opened the cupboards and drawers. From each he pulled out IV bags, tubes, and needles—the objects were placed in a haphazard pile on the sterile counter. He raided the fridge next and placed several bottles of medicine next to the drips.

Series rolled a silver IV tree to the counter. She tied the needles, attached to their tubes, together with an elastic band and slung them up to remain sterile. Scarlet placed table straps next to Ethan on the bed. Dwayne walked to Ethan's side. Eilene wheeled the tray to him, and Series held out one of the needles on the IV tree.

The Life elementalist prepared to attach a blue catheter into Ethan's vein, but the skin pulled away under his hand and blood soaked the sheets. Hans quickly wheeled a trash can closer to the medical station and Dwayne deposited the skin into it.

Scott was the first one to meet him with gauze, bandages, and self-adhesive tape. He quickly wrapped the injured arm, catching some of the blood. He placed Eilene in charge of stopping the flow and changing the bandaging while he worked. Scarlet handed Dwayne a towel that he used to help handle Ethan's delicate condition. Once he had the IV placed safely in the teen's other arm, he set up the line for multiple infusions.

He returned to the other side of the bed and used a vein in Ethan's upper arm to collect a sample of blood. Hans took the vial from him and placed it in the Chemistry Analyzer. It beeped every few seconds to read off a new stat and file it into the patient's information. Dwayne pushed the straps to the end of the bed, and Scarlet returned them to their home—they were unusable.

Ethan's body racked with chills, and Series grabbed the shock blanket from a towel rack in the corner. She pulled it over him without disturbing his arms or any areas Dwayne needed to access.

With the medical basics under control, Dwayne allowed himself to examine Ethan's condition. One hand hovered over the still body, a green light between them. Dwayne typed furiously into a small computer. The larger screen in the corner flickered with updates. Dwayne stepped over to the larger computer and organized the information into a suitable format. Adrenaline rushed through his veins as he caught sight of a startling number in Ethan's information.

"His temperature is too low. Dickens, grab the bottle from the fridge—the white one. We have to shock his body into elementalist territory, or we'll lose him."

Eilene lifted the bottle from the shelf and used a whip of water to push it directly into Dwayne's hand. He twisted off the lid and used it as a measuring cup for the drug. The medicine looked like milk, but it had the consistency of deep base paint and smelled like stale vomit. Several of the others covered their mouths to mask the smell, but it didn't help. Like when performing CPR, Dwayne pushed Ethan's head against the pillow and opened Ethan's mouth. He dumped the medication in and held his jaw shut. Ethan's body spasmed against the bed. The blanket pulled away and took his skin with it.

"Hold him down," Dwayne ordered.

Hans and Scott grabbed his legs. Eilene and Scarlet threw themselves onto his arms and shoulders. Ethan's back arched against the bed, and he made a muffled gurgling noise as his body refused to swallow. His brown eyes shot open and stared blankly at the ceiling. For a moment, his eyes flashed around the room before they closed, and his body fell heavy against the bed. Dwayne took an uneasy breath and returned to the diagnostics screen.

"His vitals are normalizing. We should be good for now."

He was certain Ethan would be okay, so he stepped away and thoroughly washed his hands at the small sink. Dwayne splashed water on his face to clear his thoughts. With the towel in his hands, he faced the others. Luana stood still in the corner with eyes the size of dinner plates and a hand over her mouth. She didn't move since they entered the room with Ethan. Her back pressed firmly against the wall, tears gathering at the corners of her eyes.

"You okay, Molelo?"

Luana's eyes shot to him before she darted from the room.

"Sorry." He pat his face dry with the towel and ran a hand over the stubble on his head.

Hans started to say something, but the words failed. He paused and tried again. "She needs time to herself."

"Alright ladies, we're changing clothes and dressing wounds. If you don't want to see our friend here naked, you should leave now," Dwayne said.

Series pretended to blanch, making the men smirk.

"Thanks." Eilene stood on her tiptoes and pressed a quick kiss to his cheek. He ruffled her hair in response, and she glared at him because she had to fix the strands around her side part. Dwayne chose to ignore the pair of cool blue eyes that settled on him with less than desirable intentions.

The door shut behind the three women, and Dwayne returned to his compatriots. His expression fell from his familiar smile into a grim frown. He reached into one of the drawers and tossed a set of medical-grade latex gloves at Hans and Scott. They caught them easily and snapped them into place.

"We're cutting off clothes because it'll be easier for his body in this state." Hans threw two pairs of scissors to the other men from a drawer.

Ethan drowned in a sea of black. He groaned and lifted a hand to his head. His red hair tangled as he rolled over in the darkness. A faint orange glow urged him to open his eyes. He drew in several deep breaths and squinted until his pupils constricted in the excess light. Once his eyesight returned, his other senses clicked in one at a time. He felt the grit and individual grains of sand against his hands and neck. A dry wind blew through a forest far behind him. Large waves crashed against the sand and the smell of sea salt made Ethan's stomach churn. An unnatural dryness filled his mouth, and Ethan hoped he didn't swallow too much sea water. He blinked rapidly and propped himself on his elbows. He lifted one arm and swiped at the sand clinging to the back of his neck and hair.

Ethan didn't think the Council would place him on an island, but it didn't feel the same as his other dreams. He remembered laying on the concrete slab—dying. Pain from his memories in the cell still plagued him. He tried not to let it show as he rolled onto his stomach. He forced himself into a crawl and tried to move forward a few paces. His stomach rolled, and a cough turned into violent vomiting. Ethan managed to push himself into a standing position. He stumbled toward the line of trees.

The dark spaces between them hinted at the depth of the island. His hand hit the first jungle wood trunk and provided support. He lost his footing when a short, child-like giggle sounded behind him. Across the sand, a second person stood on the beach—a girl, no more than eight-years-old. Her black hair pulled into a high ponytail, and she wore a white dress contrasting her dark skin. Instead of hugging her frame, the dress floated around her. As she stepped across the wet sand to Ethan, she left no footprints. The wind didn't disturb her hair as a particularly strong gust picked up. He gathered his growing strength and took several steps toward her. His body listed as the sand gave way under his feet.

She turned on her heels and skipped in a zig-zag pattern through the cresting waves. Ethan knew the child, but no name came to him. He followed her through the waves and reveled in the sea bubbles around his ankles. A pier with large carnival rides, long abandoned, waited far from where Ethan washed ashore. The paint chipped on the carousel animals, and the Ferris wheel tilted dangerously to the side where several support beams gave out. The girl turned at the start of the dock and stared into his eyes, unblinking.

"What's your name?"

The girl hissed, and Ethan took a single step back. "You've defiled your own memories and destroyed everything you've touched."

"What?"

She blinked for the first time and her eye color changed from brown to blue. Memories flashed in front of his eyes, and he recognized her as one of many casualties from the orphanage.

"Your time is coming, Ethan Silverspoon." Her voice changed to chorus all genders. They cried out his name and called for his help. Ethan watched as her eyes changed colors at a rapid pace. Her skin turned splotchy as it mimicked the colors of those who died in Ethan's presence. "Your death is foreseen. We should not have died. It was YOUR FAULT."

Her last two words echoed. Ethan took several steps backward. His heel caught on a loose plank of wood, and he fell. He used his hands to push himself. The apparition's back hunched. Its skin melted into a humanoid blob of black tar. The creature took another step toward Ethan and opened its mouth. Tar strung between its lips and sprayed toward him as it spoke.

"We want your blood as recompense." It lunged for him—hands wrapped around his neck.

Ethan jolted awake to the smell of antiseptic. His mouth held firmly shut by something heavy. He tried to lift his hands to pull at the force—memories of the tar monster still pulled at his consciousness—but others in the room held him down. The taste of spoiled milk rested on his tongue and tickled the back of his throat. A familiar face hovered over him, but he couldn't place where he knew the dark skin from. He didn't recognize the language he spoke, but he knew he should. The man's face moved away and pointed to something else. Ethan's mind stumbled to comprehend, and he slipped into sleep again.

The next time he awoke, he lay in a dark room on a stiff mattress.

Ethan blinked several times. His change of temporal locations made it impossible for him to make out reality. Memories of the disgusting taste in his mouth from the white room pushed him out of bed to find some water. His feet touched the cold stone floor, and he nearly jumped back under the quilts. Ethan pushed himself to walk across the room to the ornate wash table. He poured water from the silver pitcher into a ceramic cup over the bowl and took a drink. The style of the room reminded him of the late eighteenth century. Ethan pulled the heavy curtains from one of the windows and used the moonlight to help him find a candle and a box of matches on the bedside table. He traipsed across the room to locate the way out.

On the far-left wall in a dark corner, a large double oak door waited. It required all of Ethan's strength to pull it open. Three-pronged candelabras lit the hall between each new doorway. A large red rug with gold filaments decorated the floor. The set-up reminded him of his dream in the cell when he chased after Lulu and was attacked by the centipede monster. Ethan decided to bring the small candle from his room even if he didn't need it. He started down the hall and another heavy door squeaked as it opened. He tried to locate the direction, but the echo of the hallway prevented him.

"Who's there?" Ethan didn't want it to be the thing from the beach.

"Ethan?"

He knew the voice. A small girl with a familiar smile and twin ponytails spiraling onto her shoulders peeked around the corner from one of the doorways with big baby blues. The small freckles across her nose caught the light of the candelabras and glowed like embers.

"Lulu," he breathed. Ethan dropped the candle and reached to pull her into a swift hug. She hadn't changed a day. He missed his pseudo little sister.

"Ethan, you set the rug on fire," Lulu whispered.

He grabbed the candle cradle and set it away from the fire; he used another section of the rug to smother the flame. Lulu disappeared.

Ethan called out to her. No response. Fifty feet away, a grand staircase descended into a large atrium. When Ethan reached the top of the stairs, he spotted Lulu at the bottom. Ethan took hold of the wood railing and ran after her. Halfway down the stairs, his foot caught in the boot cut hem of his jeans, and he lost his balance. Ethan hit the stairs hard and rolled painfully down the steps. He failed to protect his head with each roll, and when he hit the corner of the railing at the bottom of the staircase, everything went black.

July 23, 2316

Farae Forest, City of Yahav, Elementōrum Patriam

Luana moved swiftly through the thick vegetation of Farae Forest in the northcentral sector of Yahav. None of the Council chose to follow her—none of them knew where she went. She left the Academy without her robe, a risk to the sacredness of their role. Without it, some of her friends before she joined the Council might recognize her. Council members were supposed to be dead—dead to loved ones, dead to their people, dead to emotion. Emotion made them weak. They were all powerful. That's what the Council taught Luana. They lived only for each other. Ceremonial and carrying out duties as laws dictated. They maintained peace.

Luana followed the hiking trail into a clearing. The edge of the clearing fell away into a steep cliff. A gazebo overlooked a stunning vista of waterfalls and jungle. The chirping of birds and hums of insects died away. She tripped on a root and landed at the foot of one of two sets of stairs leading into the gazebo. The structure wore a mossy bonnet over fine marble Doric columns. Small railings blocked the spaces between the six pillars, and a single loveseat bench overlooked the cliff.

Luana slipped between the vines, climbing the columns, and ran a hand over the railing. She slid her hand up the middle column facing the cliff and hesitated when her finger found the button. Luana pressed it, and an LED screen slid out. She entered the password on the small keyboard. A door opened near her feet. She put her foot on the first step. A stick cracked nearby.

Luana's heart raced. She couldn't let the unknown person know about their secret. She darted down the short staircase to the other LED screen where she closed the doorway seconds before the person stepped out of the trees. A visitor dangerously close to a Council guarded secret. Using the security screen, she analyzed the visitor. A young hiker with brown hair in a ponytail. She guessed somewhere around the age of fourteen. Luana left the screen to shuffle down the winding passageways in the cliffside.

She passed several empty and open half-circle spaces stacked five high and seven wide. Her footsteps echoed in the empty halls. She felt eyes following her. Luana shuddered and gathered a ball of fire in her palms as a warning. Farther into the catacombs, the doorways no longer waited empty. The smooth stone surfaces carried names. She didn't stop to look at them. She only wanted to visit one person.

At the end of one of the longer corridors, several floors down, she stopped her progress and stared at the tomb. Luana trailed her fingers across the engraving. The seal glittered gold in proximity with her flames, and she put them out. RUBEN ANTONIO PORTILLO-BENITEZ. WATER.

Luana fell to her knees in front of the second grave for the ex-Council member and pressed her forehead against the marble. For a moment, she wanted to cut through the mortar to lay her hands on the person inside.

"I need your help, Ruben. I must know what you'd do in my situation. I can't lead the Council like this." Luana took a shaky breath. "Give me your wisdom. Everything is getting worse, and I don't know what is right anymore. Please, please send someone to help me."

Luana fell against the wall of catacombs. She cried until she fell asleep in the stale air.

Hans waited on the north side of the gazebo for the unknown brunette to leave on the south hiking trail. He knew from the beginning Luana went to the catacombs after she left the hospital room. Luana needed space after the shocking events, and he waited an extended time before he went after her. Hans draped her Council cloak over his arm alongside his. The teen finally left on the southern trail, and Hans slid out of his hiding place behind the trees.

It took several minutes for him to walk through the catacomb space to Luana's location. He found her asleep in front of Ruben's second grave. Hans set the red robes to the side. He helped her stand in a half-asleep state and dressed her in the Council outfit. Hans dressed himself in his own robe and lifted Luana into his arms. He wrapped her legs around his waist to make carrying her easier. Before he opened the hatch, Hans checked the security cameras. Luana remained asleep on their hike even after he tripped over a tree root.

On the platform to catch the Bullet, elementalists shuffled out of their way. Hans ignored his curious people and chose one of the unoccupied seats of four in the back of a train car. The train stopped on a dime in Vasha, and Luana stirred. She groaned when the train picked up again and pushed away from her companion. A momentary content noise slipped past her lips, but neither mentioned it.

"Where are we?"

"Leaving Vasha on the Bullet," he whispered.

Luana examined the train car before she moved herself softly from his lap and settled into the seat next to him.

"Thank you for coming and getting me." She burrowed into her cloak to reclaim the warmth Hans' body provided.

"I would never leave you alone." He hoped she didn't understand the true meaning behind his words. They spent the rest of their return home in companionable silence.

July 24, 2316

Eilene let out a loud and low growl as she threw herself onto the large u-shaped couch of the reading room. Scott lounged in one of the large two seaters against one of the walls. He held a book in his hands; the cover had a blonde woman dressed in a pink prom dress cradled by a man in black. He clicked his tongue and put his attention back on the book. Eilene propped herself so she could spy on him over the back of the couch.

"Have you ever felt trapped on the Council?" she asked, her gray eyes penetrating Scott.

He groaned internally and closed his book. Scott weakly glared through his eyelashes.

"Right, you don't talk," she said.

"I talk when I find it necessary. People read books for a reason." He lifted the novel.

Eilene grinned. "Now I have your attention and know that you'll speak to me—have you ever felt trapped by the Council rules? I mean, no one can know who we are. It takes away the entire possibility of ever having our own families." She paused and disappeared into the cushions. "What would you do if you liked someone? Someone you consider to be a good friend. I don't mean the kind of liking in which you consider them a nice person either. Yet, they're your friend, a close friend, and you have a relationship which is already important to you."

Scott wished she had stopped talking after the first question. He knew enough, and something sharp twisted in his gut. He considered what she asked. Scott kept his relationship with the other Council members at a strict distance. He felt inadequate for the position on more than one occasion—particularly in a place where morals and logical decisions didn't cross. Ever.

He understood what she asked. It took him forever to realize why the relationship he had with Eilene felt different to the ones he shared with Series, Scarlet, and Luana. Despite the distance he placed between himself and others, he couldn't help falling for her. Romantically. Sexually. Everything in between. He also knew how she felt about Dwayne. Dwayne ensured she felt protected and cared for. Scott envied him because he was her foundation. He hated how he relied on Dwayne to keep Eilene happy.

In the extended silence, he knew he needed to give her a proper answer and once again sacrifice his own happiness for her.

Eilene sat on the edge of the couch and bit her lip as she glanced between him and the door. Scott cleared his throat to catch her attention. Their eyes met.

"Tell them," Scott managed to choke out.

"What?"

He knew she heard, so he didn't say anything. A coward hiding behind his own advice.

"And if I'm rejected?"

"It's better to know than cling to false hope." He cracked his book open. Eilene stood. Quiet footsteps crossed the room. She stood in front of him. His Adam's apple bobbed as she leaned in.

"Thank you, Scott." Eilene pressed a quick kiss to his exposed cheek and left the room in a lonely silence.

CHAPTER SIX
Inanimate

July 25, 2316

Ethan explored Wonderland. He fell down hole after hole, chasing the mysterious white rabbit—or rather a young girl. Each time he dropped in and out of consciousness, he saw her methodically tapping a large, gold pocket watch. Time ran down, but he was no closer to finding her than the night she died. He hoped to see some of the floating stationary objects from Alice's fall, to at least meet the Cheshire Cat, but nothing appeared in the never-ending darkness.

"Not even a piano?" he asked irritably. He hit the ground hard and lay under a blanket in a white room.

"What's this about a piano?" Dwayne stood at the shiny metal counter in the room and dried his hands with a paper towel. A large smile rested on his face.

There's the Cheshire Cat, Ethan thought.

Absalom and the Red Queen were suddenly far preferable to the Cheshire

Cat. Unless Luana played the Red Queen—then he'd choose to be stuck in perpetual teatime with the Mad Hatter...

"Where am I?" Ethan asked, his brain stuck half-way in dreamland.

"Council medical room—fully stocked for our use in case of emergencies. All materials and data remain hidden to anyone but us," he paused. Dwayne laughed. "I'm your doctor, Dwayne Tebogo, if you don't remember. Are there any places where it hurts?"

"What happened to the holding cell?"

"We have a lot to explain." The smile dropped from Dwayne's face. "Molelo is really worried about you. I haven't seen her that scared before."

"Who's Molelo? And weren't you trying to kill me?"

"'*Were*' being the operative." Dwayne pursed his lips. "We *were* trying to kill you until we did some research in London and discovered a discrepancy in our records. I've spent the last couple weeks stabilizing your vitals and waiting for you to wake up. You're on the fast-track healing process and should be good to go in the next while. As for Molelo—she is the leader of the Council."

"Why did you bring me back?"

"I'd much rather have Molelo, and the others explain it to you. I haven't had a chance to explore the research myself. Dickens would be a good choice since she found the information." The door opened. "Ah, Ethan, let me introduce you to Muuyaw and Mulan."

"Hey Ethan," Scarlet said. "In case you don't remember my name, I'm Lí Scarlet. Dwayne calls me Mulan."

"I remember you. We met through the door of my cell," Ethan said.

"We did. Your ability is quite interesting—especially since Eilene and I looked over the missing data." She held the clipboard from her hands toward Dwayne, and he took it. Ethan watched him input the information into the Council specific database. He couldn't make sense of all the numbers.

Instead, he said, "I've noticed Dwayne has a nickname for everyone."

Series laughed under her breath. "It's his personality quirk. Kind of endearing once you know him. He's generally nice enough to not call anyone anything they're uncomfortable with."

"Series and I chose our nicknames," Scarlet said. A smile slid across her lips.

"I always looked up to the legend of Mulan." She closed her eyes and took a deep breath. "Her strength is inspiring, so Dwayne adopted the name for me. It reminds me of what I want to become."

Ethan looked at Series expectantly before prompting, "And yours?"

Series bit her lip. "It comes from a Hopi story. The first light in the world was the moon. Since my powers are the most powerful at night when I'm sleeping, I feel a certain connection to the moon." She held out her hand, and a gold glow spread from her fingertips up her arm, over her head, and down to her toes. Under the fierce LED lighting, the gold barely reached past her stocky frame. "My power reminds me of the moon—fighting to shine bright enough for others to see by. Muuyaw means moon."

Ethan bit his lower lip. "How'd the others get theirs?" he asked.

"Well," Series' brows pinched in thought, "Eilene loves Charles Dickens, so that is obvious."

"From what I understand, Hans' is a joke relating to something from history. I'm not quite sure what it is, but Dwayne likes antique music and television," Scarlet said. "Scott doesn't complain about much, and he's hard to get to know, so I know why Dwayne chose his nickname. Luana's nickname means fire in Tswana. Straightforward." She shrugged. "How are you feeling after everything?"

"Confused. But not about the names. Mostly about what I am and why I'm here," Ethan said.

"Is Ethan awake?" Luana poked her solemn face inside the room. Bags rested under her eyes. Hans shuffled into the room ahead of her.

"Hey, Solo," Dwayne said. Hans nodded politely. To Luana, he said, "He's awake and swapping stories about my wonderfulness."

"That sounds like a lie," Hans muttered with a small lilt on his lips.

"Hi, Luana." Ethan lifted his IV riddled hand and waved. "Dwayne said you could explain what's going on with me?"

Her brown eyes wavered as they looked at him. "There was some important information regarding elementalist history which disappeared from our personal and extensive library. We're unsure if it was removed on purpose or unrecorded because it was believed these two elements had more of a permanent place in our society. Due to this error, our current Council was not aware of the existence of two elements with low population. There's supposed to be nine elements. While we can identify you as a Death elementalist, we're uncertain about the ninth element. It's possible in the last few years we identified them as Rogues and—" Luana couldn't finish her sentence.

"Always the politician," Series muttered under her breath.

"Death elementalist?" Ethan shifted his hip.

"Yes, the element which is commonly paired with Dwayne's in the human world. They have little connection in our understanding of the cycles of elementalists," Luana paused, "Do you like reading much?"

"Yeah. I once survived a raging fire in an orphanage while distracted reading."

"Do I want to be friends with him? He attracts death." Dwayne took the pulse oximeter off Ethan's finger and readjusted part of the configuration.

Ethan cleared his throat. "Death element makes sense. What do you have for me to read?"

"Eilene is working on binding an official reprint copy now." Luana pondered her next words. "It goes into detail about the nine elements. We assume the short life spans of humans and elementalists attributed to the cutoff and loss of information. As I said before, it's possible the elements tried to resurface before, but those before us, and even us now, killed them without awareness."

"Only if they are of the Supernatural element," Eilene corrected as she stepped into the room. In her arms rested two copies of newly bound books with blue velvet covers. She set her left hand on her hip and tried to use her head to flip her hair back, but it didn't react as she wanted. Dwayne stepped over and pulled it behind her back. "Thanks, Dwayne. Those of the Death element, like Ethan, can't be killed unless certain requirements are met. The book outlines a little more than a handful, but I would assume there are more viable options as well. I assume lack of a list results from a loss of test subjects which is an appropriate way to end a list. One of the ways the book outlines is our Plan AZ which we used on Ethan a month ago."

The beeping of Ethan's heart monitor filled the quiet. He broke the silence with, "I really lost track of time. I thought I was only in there for a few days."

"It's July twenty-fifth," Scarlet whispered.

"I have to reset my brain," Ethan said.

"Your vitals are back to normal, so nothing to worry about." Dwayne lifted Ethan's left arm to unwrap the bandages.

"Why am I this heavily bandaged?"

"You peeled like week old roadkill," Eilene said as Scott joined them in the room. His steps paused long enough for him to give her a puzzled look before he settled into the corner.

"Roadkill, Dickens?" A grin settled back onto Dwayne's lips, and a warm chuckle bubbled in the back of his throat.

"I think I'm going to be sick." Ethan tried to roll over on his side, but a strap around his waist kept him down.

"Need a trash can?" Scarlet waved at the overflowing biohazard bin by the door filled with old IV needles, empty blood and medical bags, bandages, and medicine bottles.

"It looks worse than me."

"That's what life looks like." Eilene walked over to his bed and placed one of the books next to him where it wouldn't disturb any of his medical lines.

"Dickens is insulting me again."

"I'm not insulting you. Life is messy and having a mess like the one in the trash proves people fought a battle for a singular life. It's proof we need to keep the precious people in our life living if we can. Death will only ever be a dead body—proof of failure."

"I was the one being insulted." Ethan winked at her.

"Wow, Eilene managed to say something profound for once," Luana said. Eilene opened her mouth to retort, but Dwayne cut them off.

"If you want to argue, take it to the hall. I won't have any of it in front of my patient." Dwayne straightened his slouching posture. When he breathed in, his bulk added a new layer of intimidation. Everyone shuffled out of the room, and the man mumbled several words in Setswana. Ethan settled into the pillows for more sleep while Dwayne worked.

Hans took a seat at his desk and pressed a button on the front. A panel slid open, and a computer screen emerged. It projected a keyboard and trackpad onto the desk, and he used the trackpad to pull up the legal documents for review.

Luana, who trailed his heels from the infirmary, took a seat on the bed behind him and didn't say anything. She had the other copy of the book they found in London in her hands and a notebook clipboard combination. She borrowed one of the pens from his desk while he opened the first letter.

He worked in silence until he sent the final draft of the document to the Council law department. Hans spun around in his chair to find Luana face down on his bed in a starfish position. The book rested against his double pillows, and notes scattered around her on the duvet and floor.

"Are you living in my room now?"

Luana took a long time to reply—her voice muffled. "Maybe."

"Where do you expect me to sleep tonight?"

"Don't know, don't care."

"Your room?"

"No."

"Alright."

Content with his break, Hans adjusted his posture and turned back to the desk. The chair creaked. He checked their email account for any urgent issues. He spent ten minutes sifting through the work and compiling it into flagged folders for completion on specific dates. Another contract renewal application filtered into the cleared inbox. Hans gave up on completing any more work for the day. He stood and stretched his arms above his head.

Hans walked to the bed and sat in one of the empty spaces between Luana's limbs. She jumped at the sudden shift in the mattress and pulled away from the source. Hans squeezed into the smallest space on the bed he could find.

"What are you doing?"

"Laying, on *my* bed."

Luana huffed at his sarcastic tone and ended her impression of a starfish. Hans took the opportunity to stretch out properly next to her.

"What's bothering you?"

"You already know."

"You've never regretted killing people before. Not in your nature," he said, staring at the ceiling depiction of a lazy cloud drifting through a clear blue sky.

"It's different this time. We almost didn't save the renewal of one of the two missing elements. I'm worried that in the last few years I might've been the one to order a Supernatural elementalist to be killed. I can't ever bring that person back." She wiggled on the bed and hung her head over the edge where he could hear her easier. The blood rushed to her brain and cleared her thoughts.

"Lu, it wasn't you who made the law to kill Rogues. You also weren't the one who chose not to record the Death and Supernatural elements. None of this is your fault. It's true our records are lacking, but we can't move forward and change our people for the better if we dwell on the 'what ifs' of the past. We saved Ethan, and that is repayment for all our mistakes."

"But—"

He interrupted her. "No, it is time you look to the future. We need to take initiative and give a directive to our people. We need to educate them with our new knowledge."

"When did you get so wise?"

"I've always been this wise." Hans winked.

"How are we going to tell the nation about this?"

"Delegate it to Eilene and Scarlet. They know what they're doing when it comes to these things." He rolled over on his right side to look at her. "You can put your trust in the rest of the Council. You are one of the people who helped choose us for this position—you know what we're capable of."

August 25, 2316

Council members had a lot more downtime than many assumed. While they resembled a Constitutional Monarchy in terms of responsibilities, they weren't seen consistently outside their chambers. Unless they had a pressing issue to attend to, they would find other ways to entertain themselves.

Dwayne and Eilene preferred video games. Something about video games made them feel a little more normal amid the chaos.

They played a few rounds of virtual table tennis and virtual tennis, they needed less space than for the real sport, before they moved onto the newest version of a racing game. Round after round, they pushed their cars to the limit to win the cup at the end of the set of four. They switched to a brawl style game where they could fight each other for number one.

"No! Don't you run away," Eilene yelled at the TV screen. She jammed her thumb into the remote harder than before as if it would help her attack.

Dwayne pressed A, and his character jumped away from the attack onto a higher platform. He laughed as Eilene resorted to physical ribbing to break his concentration. They jabbed elbows into each other's arms or shoved each other's feet and knees.

"You'd have better luck winning if you could trigger combo attacks. Plus, that finisher button has been blinking for about a minute now. You just have no strategy," a new person in the room said. The interruption startled Eilene and allowed Dwayne to get several good hits on her character. She launched off the platform, and the game timer ended.

They pivoted to see their resident goth lounging on a recliner.

"And you think you could do better?" Eilene threw her arm over the back of the couch.

Scott shrugged.

Dwayne flipped through the character screen with their remotes and chose two new characters. "What brings you here?"

"Ethan," Scott placed his hands behind his head and leaned back farther on the seat. He nearly blended in with the dark fabric on the chair.

"Does he need help?" Dwayne stood halfway. Scott shook his head, and Dwayne returned to his seat—he should've known if something pressing happened the other would've said it before debating strategy. As Ethan grew healthier and more demanding, his actions grew increasingly more frustrating and tiresome for everyone involved. "He annoyed you too much as well?"

Scott nodded, and Dwayne laughed brightly.

"This is why he gets left alone," Eilene pushed her angled bangs off her forehead. She picked up her remote again and chose a small pink character on the screen.

Dwayne started a new round. As they dueled, they fought on the couch with jabs and grapples at the other's remote. Scott tried to relax while he watched them, but he couldn't help but recall the conversation with Eilene weeks before. The one where he encouraged her to tell Dwayne about her feelings for him—used his own experience of keeping quiet to keep her from making the same mistake. He wanted to be on the couch with her laughing and play fighting, but, once again, Dwayne remained at her side like a loyal guard dog. After the end of the next round, Scott stood to leave and find another activity, but Eilene's soft voice stopped him.

"Join us?" Her hopeful gray eyes met his, and he swallowed hard. She held out a third controller. Scott's lips parted and, against his better judgement, his right-hand rose from his side and closed around the remote. His fingers brushed hers and a wave of happiness rushed through his chest as she let go; it made him feel like he breathed for the first time in years.

A video call from Scarlet interrupted them about an hour later.

Dwayne answered the phone with one hand while he continued controlling his character on screen with the other. "I'm busy, Mulan," he said in Mandarin.

Scarlet slipped into her native tongue without question. "Playing video games?"

Many in Elementōrum Patriam spoke multiple languages, but only Luana among the Council refused to learn a language besides English.

Eilene grabbed his phone and spun it around, so it showed her leaning against Scott. "He's here with us." She tucked a lock of hair behind her ear. "Aren't we cute hanging out together?"

Scarlet rubbed her nose and bit her bottom lip. She held back her comment on the red flush coloring Scott's cheeks. "As cute as both of you are, really," she smiled at the uncomfortable look Scott adopted and the glare he sent her way. "I need to ask Dwayne a medical question about Ethan."

"What do you want to know?" Dwayne tried to grab the phone.

"Series and I wanted to start the physiotherapy with Ethan to give you some relief—but he says it's painful."

Dwayne hit pause on the controller. "I'll come check it out—make sure there's nothing serious going on that we can't see on the outside." He ended the video call and pushed off the couch.

"I'll come with," Eilene said.

"Nah, stay. I shouldn't be long." He nodded to Scott. "See if you can't get that one to talk more—or you could kick his ass at a game."

Dwayne didn't wait around to hear the rest of their conversation as he hurried through the winding halls to the infirmary. He pushed open the door to Ethan's room and paused when he saw him sitting on the bed clutching his lower back, talking with Scarlet and Series.

"But if you knew about the nine elements—you said they were mentioned before—why didn't you explore it? Is that not a part of the Council's job?"

"Well," Series hopped onto the counter, "it's not like it said, 'Hey, there's nine elements.' That would be too simple." She rolled her eyes. "You know there were nine victors the same way we do. We didn't know why the original Council doubled elements, but that was the assumption for a long time."

"And we don't know the reason why we went from a Council of nine to seven. Obviously, we do now since Eilene found that book." Scarlet waved Dwayne over. "I'm sure we'll tell Elementōrum soon. Renew the Council of nine."

"Hurts in your spine?" Dwayne's question made Ethan jump, and he grinned. He reached out his hand when Ethan nodded, and it glowed green. "Lunbar injury affected nerves L1 through L5. Pain clear into hips, thighs, buttocks, and down the legs. Simple fix."

"That doesn't sound simple." Ethan rubbed his lower back.

"You're the one who failed all their Life tests." Dwayne removed a syringe from a chilled box in the corner.

"Fair enough." Ethan followed his instructions to lay down on the bed on his stomach. "The Academy infirmary wasn't too fond of me after the ammonia-bleach incident."

"That was you?" Scarlet laughed. "You nearly killed everyone in the entire room."

"I see my horrible legend precedes me." Ethan cringed as Dwayne inserted the needle near his spinal column.

"You should be good in about twenty-five minutes, Namune." He nodded to Ethan. To Scarlet and Series, he said, "Let me know if you need anything else with the physio. I really appreciate you taking that over for me."

"No problem. Enjoy your afternoon," Scarlet pushed him toward the door.

"Namune?" Ethan asked once Dwayne left.

"You got a nickname." Series smiled. "Congrats, you're one of us now."

August 26, 2316

"I'd like to make a request," Luana announced during dinner. She set a stack of papers on the table between Eilene and Scarlet.

"I'm not doing your paperwork." Eilene lifted the fork to her mouth and pushed the stack a little closer to Scarlet with her free hand.

Luana growled. Hans gestured for her to stay calm.

"I'm requesting you and Scarlet both write the directive in educating the elementalists about our lost history. It's up to you how the teachers will be given information to present it to current students, as well as how it will be delivered to those who already graduated from the Academy."

"You're trusting us with this?" Scarlet picked up the first few pages and flipped through in awe.

"Hans suggested the both of you are the best choices for this task, and I had to agree. On the premise that Miss Water Wheel found the information in London."

"Who are you calling 'water wheel'?" Eilene's hand balled into a fist, but before she had a chance to stand, Scott's hand grabbed her arm and held her in place. The entire room stopped—he never reacted like that. Scott cleared his throat and removed his hand. Eilene remained in her seat and avoided looking at him.

"Dickens knows what she's doing," Dwayne confirmed with a full mouth.

"Eilene and I will be more than happy to take care of it. Do you have a deadline in mind?" Scarlet smiled.

"It's a bit rushed. If possible, I'd like to have the first few lessons distributed by September third. I arranged for our public press conference with the seven of us on September second."

"We can do it."

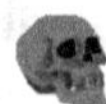

September 2, 2316

The Council handled the press conference in the morning and prepared themselves for the start of the annual Culture Festival in the afternoon. Ethan would miss the festival, but he wasn't an official member of the Council and everyone he knew from before thought he died. He couldn't participate no matter how much he begged. Dwayne hooked up the room with a television to have something mildly entertaining while they attended.

At lunch Series pulled her phone from her pocket and groaned. She turned the screen to face the others. The temperature showed over one hundred degrees Fahrenheit. "There's no way I want to wear dark red in this weather."

"We're only required to be there for the first fifteen minutes. We need to start the ceremony then we're free to come back here. You know that," Luana snapped. Her stress grew to ultra-high levels during the days preceding their political appearances. Luana's element reacted accordingly, and Hans kept a closer eye on her to ensure she wouldn't spontaneously combust into flames and reveal her face. They still needed to update their robes to be fire-resistant.

The Culture Festival, among the most popular celebrations in Elementōrum Patriam, moved as a caravan and spent seventeen days traveling between cities. The fair had a myriad of food carts and handmade goods. The festival always started at the Academy. The day focused on eating, and night showcased large spectacles of dance and music. All the elementalists came together to share their world heritage without separation. Every country was represented. Only the Elementalist Olympics rivaled it. Since most of the elements were listed as banned from the regular Olympics, they hosted their own to celebrate their people's talents in sports and other skills.

The Council only had to appear long enough to open the festival; common tradition dictated for them to disperse among the crowds and partake in the merrymaking. They never stayed for the night events as they couldn't participate in any dances or musical performances since it would reveal information about their identity. Series longed to participate in the dances of her Hopi people. Because of these desires, the Council introduced their own tradition to continue the celebration in their home.

Luana stood and placed her empty dishes in the dumbwaiter, taking them to the kitchens. She recognized the excited expressions on her fellows' faces. They craved authentic dishes passed from generation to generation of elementalists from foreign countries. A few carts boasted elementalist authentic cuisine from the settling of the country.

Hans' skin crawled as he thought about the carts that would host kolbasa and pirozhkis. Eilene went on the hunt for tomato-based stroganoff. Scarlet whispered under her breath about finding jiaozi since the Academy kitchens could never make it quite right. The previous year, the Chinese food carts failed to make any, and she wanted them to redeem themselves.

They walked the empty halls in a formation like migrating birds. Outside the Academy on the marble steps leading to the lower Academy, a crowd stood. They cheered when the seven stepped onto the small platform. One microphone waited behind a large blue ribbon. An Elementalist Sign Language Translator stood off to the side in front of their own camera to broadcast the speech to their d/Deaf people. The waiting crowd filled with Academy staff and students, and they quieted when Luana took her place in front of the microphone.

"It's my pleasure to speak with you a second time. Today, we celebrate an auspicious occasion. Not only are we bringing together the world on our continent as one body, but we brought great news to you this morning regarding our history. We will now open the three-thousand and seven-hundred and thirty-first Culture Festival. All of us on the Council are excited to walk amongst you and partake in the wonderful food and celebrations." Luana stepped down from the platform to cheers. She walked to the large ribbon, and one of the attendants held a microphone close to her face. "As this is the year of Life, we will have our Life elementalist open the ceremony."

Another elementalist handed her the large scissors. Dwayne walked forward from his position and bowed at the waist in front of the leader. He stretched out his arms with his palms up and waited for Luana to pass him the scissors. When he straightened, she waited in a similar position. Once they both stood upright, Dwayne cut the ribbon to a raucous of cheers and applause. Music started and the people immediately milled to their chosen carts.

Eilene grabbed Scott to her left and pulled him along behind her into the crowd. Dwayne joined them. She stopped at one of the food carts from Spain and dropped several coins into the tip box before she asked for a serving of Patatas Bravas. The two men didn't order anything, but Dwayne stole several potatoes from her plate as they wandered to the other sections. Eilene offered some to their other companion, and Scott did his best to deny, but she persisted. He relented after a few jabs at his character. Dwayne couldn't see either of their faces under the hoods, but he had a feeling Scott was embarrassed.

"Now this is where we want to be." Dwayne spread his arms and gestured to the carts of food and merchandise filled with Botswana originality. Eilene laughed at the happiness creeping into his voice. Dwayne ordered several dishes and gestured for them to commandeer one of the empty temporary tables. He explained each dish as he set them down to share. "Seswaa, stewed beef that's heavily salted. Don't eat if you have a heart condition or high blood pressure. Serobe, probably better if you don't know what it's made from. Matemekwane, they're dumplings—and Magwinya, otherwise known as fat cakes."

"The way to convince me to eat Serobe is not by telling me I don't want to know what's in it. That dish is entirely yours."

"Come on, Dickens. It's amazing." Dwayne lowered his voice.

"No, thanks." Eilene was determined to not try any Serobe until she had a chance to look up the ingredients. Scott muffled his laughter with difficulty. She nudged him with her arm and leaned into him. "What food do you want us to try?"

"Nothing in particular. American cuisine isn't in short supply." He shrugged and elicited a sigh from her.

"I forget you're from America. Anyone else have any ideas for what we want next?"

"French crepes sound good right now."

"French food next."

CHAPTER SEVEN
Memorial

Unknown Date

Pangea

Messina stepped across the brittle ground and stared up at the piece of land they communally placed in the sky. He twisted to face his companions and smiled at the collection of people from across the world. They wouldn't be there, creating their own country for the *Homo elementa*, if the nine didn't put in effort. Vasha swept her brown hair behind her ear. Messina's tebenna, a single piece of cloth hung as a cloak, shifted under the wind's scrutiny.

"Do we have a name for our country?" Vasha asked.

"Elementōrum Patriam," Ricci spoke from the back of the group. She joined Messina at the cliff's edge; her dark brown hair followed the wind and whipped her dark skin. They made a pair dressed in matching colors. Ricci accessorized her chiton with a belt. Messina tugged her tebenna into place as the wind tried to lift it away.

"A fitting name," Ubuntu agreed. Around his shoulders, he wore a leopard

87

skin mbata as a sign of his high status. Around his upper arms and just below his knees, the amashoba, the tuft of a cow's tail, gave him a broader appearance. The ibheshu and slene, two pieces creating a cover for his genitalia, swayed against his legs in the breeze.

"Elementōrum Patriam, with the elementalist people." Yahav's simlāh, a cloak, highlighted the bronze undertone to his skin.

The body of land lifted higher and higher. Water rushed around them and filled the new crevice. The power of the elements combined into one force.

For a while they worked in harmony with the humans—they sent Life elementalists to heal the sick, and Water and Storm elementalists provided for the crops and supply water for drinking. Doubt fed into the humans' hearts, and the elementalists found themselves at war with the other race.

Elementōrum Patriam would be their own place. They would leave behind the nine cities they founded on Pangea and create new ones. They'd create a society that accepted every culture and every person who had their abilities.

Vasha stepped to the tip of the cliff where she could feel the rumbling of the water under her feet against the rock. She played with the Boulder Opal around her neck and felt the rush of power in every nerve and cell of her body. She remembered how the nine united and the brightness of their glowing eyes as the first Council tore the land apart. Vasha wanted to feel it again. War sung in her veins since she saw Moscow burn to the ground.

"We will end our wars with the humans today. Our people will be moved to our new country, and there we will nurture our mutation in kindness," Messina spread his arms and stood on the precipice of the sheer break. "The earth gifted us the chance to control its Storms, to hold in our hands the balance of Life and Death—we can view the Supernatural universe as it is and stop time. We can change the Fortune of those around us, to make Fire, Air, Water, and Earth justly ours. It is time for the elementalists to rise."

"And we will be the Council to govern them." Wabaunsee smiled into the rising fog and pulled the thick furs of his native nation closer to his skin.

The earth rumbled under their feet. Water met the bottom of the basin in a sudden rush. Victor held them steady against the pressure.

Ricci looked up in awe. "A waterfall, in our country."

"You'll carry us up, won't you, Victor?" Messina asked.

"Of course." The Ethiopian Opal around Victor's neck flashed with power, and he reached out to grab Messina's and Ricci's hands in his.

When they all stood on the open edge near the new waterfall, they reexamined the spread of untainted land ahead of them. They could see the tips of mountains crisping the horizon. The air was thin at the new elevation, but they didn't feel it. Elementalists could out survive the humans on almost every level.

Vasha turned back to see the view off the side of their country. "Do you think we'll really be safe here?"

"Yes," Messina's eyebrows furrowed together.

"I don't believe you."

The humans destroyed and ransacked their precious cities—they'd come to their new country, too. Moscow, Hong Kong, Pompeii, Kaerlud, Cochabamba. All gone. She took a step back against the edge, and her balance faltered. Vasha tumbled through the air. The Council screamed, and Victor jumped after her; a red glow stopped him mid-flight. The opal around her neck drifted away from her chest glowed a bright red. In a swirling mass, the nine elements surrounded her like a comet's tail. Her body twisted in the air; her eyes were the same bright color as the opal.

Vasha's body slowed its descent and hung in the air. Her mouth opened in a silent scream—Pangea quaked. The glow intensified, and she controlled the elements as one. The Earth suffered under her awakened power, and the land ripped apart. From their position in the sky, they watched the great masses of land shift and open crevices. The ocean poured into the gaps. The animals of the sea churned with the water, and several new coastal cities split and fell. Seven continents in place of the one original. Eight, with their creation in the sky. A new world for humans and elementalists. A new start.

Vasha's body vanished into the crashing waves below, and they knew she wouldn't return.

Victor searched for her, but he could only retrieve the necklace from the surface of the water, flung by the waves. He returned to the other seven with it clutched between his fingers.

Ricci pulled her own necklace free. "We should hide this power away until the time is right."

The others murmured their agreement.

September 3, 2316

The Council Chambers, The Academy, Elementōrum Patriam

"Cereal?" Dwayne stared at Luana's breakfast with disappointment.

She chased the soggy, colorful dregs of Trix around the bowl with her spoon. A half-empty sugar cup, usually used for tea and coffee, sat in front of her. "It's a very cultural food for those of us born in good ol' 'Murica." Her voice dragged with sleep and several short nods brought her dangerously close to drowning in milk.

"You can try some sorghum." He offered her the bowl from the dumbwaiter.

"Corn meal hardly sounds good when it's made into corn bread. Why would I want to eat it for breakfast?"

"How do you not like corn bread?" Series passed the pair on her way to the dumbwaiter.

"Am I not allowed to like different food?" Luana asked.

Scott and Hans filed into the room, still in their pajama pants. They waited together in silence but took seats on opposite sides of the table when the food arrived. Hans took his customary place next to Luana and nudged her to see if she wanted any kasha. Scott usually sat near Series but forwent the quieter space to sit nearer Dwayne, anticipating Eilene would sit between them, with his American classic: bacon and eggs. Scarlet arrived in the room at the same time as her rice porridge and baozi—already dressed for the workday.

Eilene, the last to wake for the day, still wore her loose nightgown. She only collected a steaming mug of hot chocolate from the dumbwaiter before she joined them at the table—exactly in the spot Scott predicted.

"That's hardly a breakfast," Series criticized over a bite of French Toast.

"I don't like breakfast." She used Dwayne's spoon to steal a taste of his food. "I love sorghum."

"Mine!" He jokingly shielded his bowl from her and took several hurried bites.

"I would try to steal some of Scott's eggs, but they're harder to nab." She winked at him. He offered her a piece of bacon.

"Sorry, I don't like bacon," Eilene declined with a soft touch to the back of his hand. Dwayne and Scarlet didn't drop their utensils in surprise at her statement, but the others did with a rather loud clatter. Several pieces dropped all the way to the floor. A grin crept onto Eilene's face as the others processed her statement. Several moments passed before she muttered, "There's nothing to be shocked about."

Dwayne provided a topic change before the others could find it in themselves to interrogate her further. "Molelo, Namune is healthy enough to leave the infirmary today. I plan on releasing him which means he'll need a room, and we need to set up an initiation run."

"I'm glad he's being released, but it does create more work for us." Frustration bled into Luana's eyes.

"What run are we going to give him?" Series couldn't hide her excitement as she finished the last few bites of her breakfast.

"Scarlet, I'd like you to pick out one of the runs for Ethan." Their leader leaned into the center of the table to meet the woman's eyes. She pushed another bite past her lips and chewed thoughtfully before she answered.

"I can, but Eilene and I planned to work on the lesson plans today. We want to distribute them alongside the history books."

"I forgot you are on that team." Luana frowned.

"I'll do it." Hans shoved his plate away.

"Thank you." Luana pushed the soggy cereal around with her spoon. She stuck out her tongue and crinkled her nose. She pushed her bowl away, too.

Scarlet took the opportunity to wiggle her eyebrows at the Russian. He blatantly ignored her attempts to catch his attention.

They fell into a comfortable silence as they finished their meals. Series and Dwayne caught a few more Zs in their seats until the arrival of the dumbwaiter. The bell snapped them into action. Scott ran water in the sink to wash the dishes.

Eilene passed her cup to Scott and gently bumped his hip with hers. She leaned in to whisper, but missed the flush of pink across his nose. "If you survive your tasks with Luana today, I'll see you at lunch."

Eilene followed Scarlet through the halls to the offices where they could work on the lesson plans. She felt like skipping. Scott was finally warming up to her.

Luana set her dishes on the counter. "Series, will you help me review laws and bill proposals today?"

"Will we be going over any of the proposals from the Uns today? Last I saw, the paperwork started to pile up." Series used her fork to scrape the remnants of syrup into her mouth before she also set her plate on the counter.

"Our research trip didn't help either." Luana pursed her lips. "It'll be the first matter of business today. The Uns are so hard to deal with."

Dwayne stood. "I'm going to make sure Ethan is ready to leave."

"Once you're done, join us in the law room. Same with you Scott, and Hans. Your tasks shouldn't take long."

"This documentary on elementalists is strange. I can't decide whether they're trying to explain the biology behind our mutation or paint us all as mass murderers," Ethan said when Dwayne entered the room. He stared at the TV projected on the wall, and Dwayne took a momentary glance to register which one Ethan chose.

"It is human made. That's to be expected." He pulled a pair of gloves from the box on the wall and snapped them into place. "There's over a thousand movie options on there, you could watch something else."

"Not all of those movies are good—you know that, right?"

"I'd be nice if you want to leave today. Otherwise, I'll leave you here on your own for another week."

"I'm able to be released today?" He sat up and tried not to pull at the IVs and monitoring cords still attached to his arms.

"If your vitals are as stable as yesterday. We needed twenty-four hours of healthy vitals before I'd be willing to release you. If your behavior is up to par, I'll show you to your temporary room."

"Temporary?"

"Considering the circumstances. There are also several factors leading to our decision, but we'll explain them later. Depending on other decisions as well. If you choose to stay here."

"If I choose to not stay here?"

"Molelo will make that call. We have the technology to wipe your memories of all the time you spent here, but no one will believe you came back from the dead. It's in your best interest to stay, but nobody will force you." Dwayne opened his medical screen and sorted through information.

"Luana calls all the shots around here. Is she the oldest?"

"She isn't, but she has time seniority. The previous Council chose Molelo to join them when she was eight. We treat her as the leader because of how long she's worked as a governmental body. She's only the leader over Fire since we're all over our own entity, but she chooses what we work on day by day—unless we make a good argument. She knows what she's doing for the most part, and we're by her side if she doesn't."

"You've thought the hierarchy through."

"All those nights where you lie awake questioning your existence."

"And you remember every terrible thing you've ever said." Ethan closed his eyes when Dwayne pulled one of the IV drips from the catheter. "Do you ever fight over issues?"

"Yeah. Solo usually steps in to mediate since Molelo is emotionally charged about her opinions. She was raised here, and she sees things a little different from the rest of us. We spent more time outside the system."

He placed gauze over the place where the PICC line attached to Ethan's arm before he pulled the canula out. Ethan winced but tried not to move, so Dwayne could apply self-adhesive tape. The Life elementalist checked his phone before detaching the rest of the cords holding Ethan to the bed.

He collected a paper bag from the hallway and handed it to the patient. "You'll find a few different sets of clothes in there. Put on what fits in the bathroom, and I'll show you to your room."

"Are these yours?"

"Mulan went on a shopping expedition a couple days ago. There's more in your room, but we have no idea if they'll fit."

"Thanks." Ethan stood from the bed and hurried to the bathroom; the robe he wore opened in the back and let in an uncomfortable breeze. Ethan called through the door. "They've made you my guard dog?"

"Hurry up and change."

Ethan found a pair of pants, but they were too large at the waistband and refused to stay up. He pulled one of the T-shirts over his head and found it fit nicely around him, if not a little tight around his shoulders. He held the waistband with one hand—no belt in the bag.

"Ready, Namune?" Dwayne didn't turn around when he exited the bathroom.

"You don't happen to have an extra belt, do you?"

"I don't, but you can use this." Dwayne tossed one of the bed straps from a drawer to him. "Just give it back to me once you get a real belt."

"No problem."

Dwayne led him out of the hospital room, and Ethan took a deep breath when he saw the plain gray hallways. The color stimulation amazed him after weeks of bare white. He followed obediently behind Dwayne and struggled to keep his path from wandering when he saw lights on behind partially open doors. Dwayne stopped down a particularly dark corridor and triggered a door to slide open.

"This is your room. The outer switch is here," he indicated the spot. "You get to figure out where the inner mechanism is. I'll call for you when the trial is ready."

He took two steps away before he heard Ethan groan. They set the Council rooms to remain stark white so as not to waste power when unoccupied. A grin crept onto his face.

"Oi, Namune."

"Yeah?" Ethan turned back.

"Ask and you will receive."

"Huh?"

Dwayne vanished down the hall and left Ethan outside another prison. Ethan took a deep breath and reluctantly stepped into the room. The words from the Council member rang in his head, but as the door slid closed behind him, he couldn't figure out what it meant.

Scarlet dictated to Eilene. The keyboard, embedded in the table, registered her touch as her hands flew across the non-existent keys. The screen in front

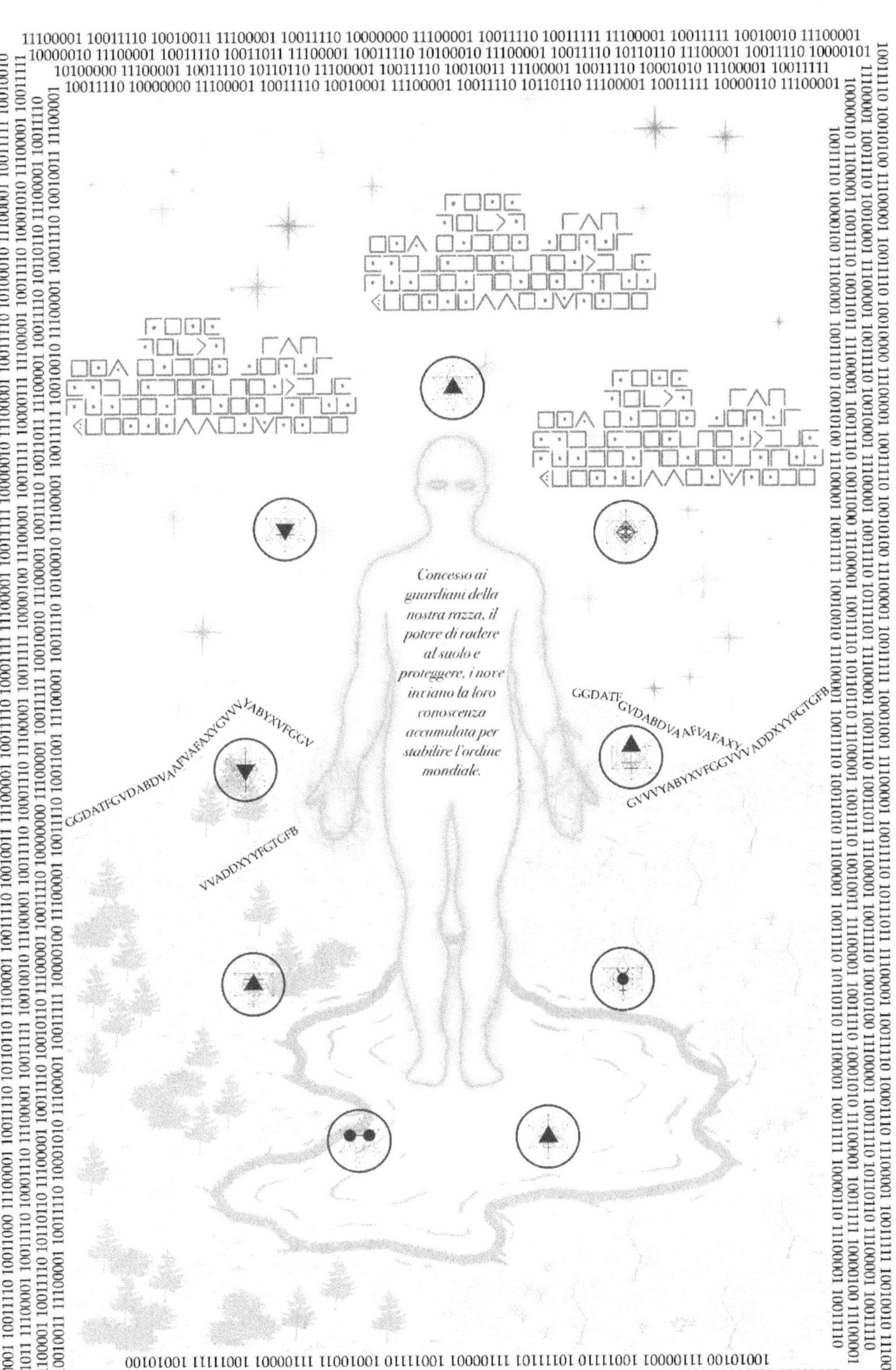

Concesso ai guardiani della nostra razza, il potere di radere al suolo e proteggere, i nove inviano la loro conoscenza accumulata per stabilire l'ordine mondiale.
GGDATFGVDABDVA AFVAFAXYGVN YABYXVFGGV
VVADDXYYFGTGFB
GGDATF GVDABDVA AFVAFAXY
GVVVYABYXVFGGVVVADDXYYFGTGFB

of her resembled a single pane of glass, the same as their phones.

"At least I finally understand why there were nine victors when the original Council came together. I couldn't figure out why they would double up on a particular element," Scarlet yawned. She mused through the pages of maps and sketches of the early cities before she came to a page which made her stop. "What's this diagram referring to?"

Eilene inspected page ninety-five. "It's obvious the text in the center of that human-like figure is Italian. None of us know it—but it'd be easy enough to send through a translator app. I do love how awkward the binary code border is. How in the world are we ever going to figure out what these other codes are." She pointed to the clouds and mountains. "I mean, these could be tied to any language. We'll need a whole team running checking to see which one they line up with."

Scarlet ran her fingers across the page. "We'll need to ask Luana to bring in some professional translators and code breakers to work on decoding the message. You see the person in the middle there, their eyes are empty and have that fuzzy outline. I want to assume the artist wanted to draw them glowing. You can also see basic representations of the nine elements around here. I think it has something to do with the Council, but I could be wrong." She closed the book. "I'll talk to Luana about the translators."

"I guess we should move onto lesson two while we're ahead." Eilene stretched her arms over her head and the joints in her shoulders popped.

"And steal Scott this afternoon."

"Perfect plan."

A knock on the door interrupted them and Hans peeked his head into the room. "The run is set-up. Time to go."

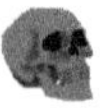

Ask and you will receive. Dwayne's words echoed in Ethan's head as he gauged the room.

He licked his lips and categorized the obvious things. The stark white bed directly in front of him, settled against the left wall parallel to the exit. A nightstand stood on the opposite side of the bed, but no other furniture. Ethan took a seat at the end and closed his eyes.

"What on earth does 'ask and you will receive' mean?" He mumbled under his breath. When he opened his eyes again, the walls echoed the phrase Dwayne gave him earlier with plain, serif, black text. He blinked several times, and the words disappeared.

Ethan wondered if the white walls affected him. *If there is a button to open the door, maybe there's other buttons as well.* He assumed they reserved the wall for the door, meaning he could explore three other walls. Ethan faced the wall to the right of the entryway. He wandered his hands up and down the wall as high and low as he could reach. The first button he found launched four dresser drawers into his body and sent him sprawling across the ground. He rubbed his ribs in displeasure and glared at the clothes.

In the top drawer, he found a few pairs of underwear. Ethan quickly jumped out of his pants and found a more comfortable pair of dark gray cargo shorts in one of the lower drawers. He threw the larger jeans into the dresser before he closed it and moved onto the next discovery. He had a private bathroom in the same white color, everything in a non-hidden place with no issues finding the sink, toilet, or shower.

From the bathroom, he moved to the wall opposite the entryway, he found the closet and changed his shirt to a size larger. He took a couple of the smaller shirts and placed them on the floor directly under the buttons—except, he couldn't remember where the dresser hid in comparison to the bathroom. He glued himself to the wall in hopes he wouldn't have another fight with the dresser drawers, but he picked the wrong side and sent them painfully into his spine.

Ethan collapsed on his bed with an annoyed huff.

"It'd be so much easier to know where everything is without taking the chance of being attacked by sadistic furniture." His voice was muffled, but the room responded all the same. When he turned his head to face one of the walls, a single word faded away. *Ask.* "Can you..." he drifted off. "Please mark the buttons with their functions?"

His voice cracked at the end as he thought about whether he should phrase it as a question—even if the instructions said "ask"—since the room remained an inanimate object. The room humored him and placed large, black chalk styled letters above each button. He experimented with several fonts before settling on a simple sans-serif font above each button.

He laid on the bed and wondered if the rest of the room could change on a whim, too. Ethan took a deep breath before requesting blue walls, a cedar floor, and green covers. Without delay, the changes occurred. With excitement, he said, "Mississippi sky and Nevada mountains?" The room catered to his every whim.

A knock at the door made him jump, and he hurried to answer it. When he pushed the button to leave the room, he could barely see across the dark hallway.

"Hello?" Ethan stepped out of his room. The door shut behind him and plunged him into darkness until a small light appeared at the end of the hallway. Without hesitation, he walked toward the light. When he reached it, another flickered farther down the hall.

He followed the lights. They appeared one after another and vanished behind him. Excitement bubbled in his chest at what might be at the end.

As he approached the end of a long corridor, a door stood slightly ajar. Anticipation railed in his stomach. His hand landed on the metal paneling and pushed. On the other side, nothing but a slim beam of metal stretched over a pit without a seeable bottom till it met a platform on the other side. The height didn't scare him, but the beam had no anchors to the small platforms. The far end of the beam barely rested against the ledge on the other side near a door. The bright blue sky overhead lit the path it wanted him to take. Ethan didn't know if the beam would shift under pressure if he tried to cross it like indicated. He tried to turn back, but the door swung closed. Ethan couldn't budge the handle. He took a deep breath and pushed his tongue into the hollow of his cheek until it bubbled out.

He took several moments to consider the position of the beam before he dropped on all fours and balanced his weight in a steady crawl. Despite his best attempts to keep the beam steady, three-quarters of the way across an ominous creak issued from the metal as it fell away from the second platform. Startled, he used his legs to stand and jump in one motion. Ethan didn't make it far enough to land on the platform, and his already sore chest took another beating as he grappled with the platform. His fingers gripped the edge, and he used the motion to help his feet find purchase against the stone wall. With firm footing, he hoisted his arm into a better hold on the platform. Ethan's hand collided with a rope, and he grabbed it immediately. The fibers burned against his skin, but the grip allowed him to bring up his other hand and pull himself to safety.

Panting with exertion, Ethan laid on a platform for a long minute. When a breeze ruffled his hair, it reminded him of the precarious platform with no visible support. He scrambled to his feet and stepped through the next opening. The door clanged as it sealed behind him. The floor vibrated under his feet as the room shifted around him. Squinting through the dark, he saw the walls expand into an octagon, and light flooded the room. The room used a forest-like appearance with waterfalls and dense foliage. He stood on a small square pedestal several feet above the floor. Each wall had a large door made of jungle wood with the coordinating elemental symbol burned into the material. Above each door, a crystal glowed with the color for each element. Orange for Fire; blue for Water; green for Life; white for Air; red for Earth; yellow for Storm; gold for Fortune. One crystal, a dark purple, had no light. Seeing the empty door, he wondered, not for the first time, how the Council claimed ignorance to the existence of Death and Supernatural elementalists. For any other element, two empty doors would stand where Ethan should.

"Ethan Silverspoon," a voice greeted him, sounding suspiciously like Luana.

"Hold up," he put up a hand to stop them. "This isn't some elaborate hoax to try and kill me again? I thought we finished this."

A loud pitch of audio feedback screeched across the room as someone else struggled to take control of the microphone. A moment later Series appeared on the line. "No killing, a proposition."

Another squeak as control turned back to the Council head. "We want to ask you if you are willing to serve for the rest of your life as a member of the Council which protects the elementalist people? Are you willing to negotiate with those who oppose us? To keep peace between humans and ours? Prepared to set clear lines between our laws and those which govern the Uns? Are you willing to be the eighth member of the Council who will help us find the ninth?"

Ethan's face crinkled in thought, and his shoulders rose with his deep breath. His decision would dictate his future, whether he remembered his time with the Council and accepted the responsibilities or forgot and returned to the land of the living. His posture straightened, and he focused on the orange light.

"I will. I am willing to join the Council."

"Good job, Namune," Dwayne complimented.

The room shifted again to add a ninth wall and door. Ethan's platform lowered to the floor as the doors under each crystal opened. The Council walked toward him.

"Glad to have you with us." Scarlet grinned.

Ethan nodded hesitantly.

Series grinned and clasped her hands behind her back before saying, "Welcome to the Council."

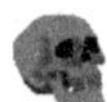

October 13, 2316

Salt Lake City, Salt Lake County, Utah, United States of America

She sat in a bus terminal in downtown Salt Lake. Despite the warm days in late October, the nights were cold. Snow became a regular friend. She wore a black jacket with the hood up. The woman pulled out her phone and unlocked it with her fingerprint and scrolled through an open playlist, changing the song in her headset.

She pushed the hood of her jacket down and pulled her long blonde hair free and tied it into a ponytail. She pushed a few annoying strands out of her right eye before she looked up and down the street, wondering if the bus planned on coming to the stop at all.

She drummed her fingers against her leg to the beat of the music as an older woman, somewhere in her fifties, took a seat next to her on the bench. The young woman clicked a button on her phone, and the screen lit up again with the time imprinted at the top.

Ten minutes late.

She didn't want to draw attention to herself, but because of frustrating public transit, she would be late for work. Not a rare occurrence with the buses lately; they regularly put her job on the line. She hit her head against the glass of the terminal and let out a low *huff* of air.

"You seem to be anxious about the bus arriving, dear." The other woman smiled.

She removed a headphone. "The bus is making me late to my job *again*."

"You remind me of myself in my younger days."

She didn't have a response.

"What I want to say is: your job is important, but sometimes there are more important things in life. I wish you luck with getting there on time. My name is Eren." She put out a hand, and the younger woman stared at her. Strangers didn't typically impart wisdom to her in bus terminals.

Slowly, she raised her own hand to meet Eren's. "Kristen."

October 18, 2316

The Council Chambers, The Academy, Elementōrum Patriam

"I am going to die." Ethan's head hit the table in the library.

Scott's eyes drifted momentarily from his perusal of an English-to-Spanish dictionary.

"Are you having comprehension problems with the text?" Eilene climbed the ladder on one of the aisles and continued to reorganize the shelves while putting away texts they already studied. Once the books rested neatly on the shelf, she descended the ladder and lifted a new stack.

"It's not comprehension necessarily—I hate being told to read something. As soon as it's treated like a necessary assignment, it makes it ten times harder to read the book. I like choosing my own material and considering suggestions or recommendations from friends or online. I do like reading even if I don't do it often."

"Ah, a common problem." Eilene nodded. "I know several people who claim they don't like reading because of reading assignments. It is a matter of finding the right book."

"This isn't so much a matter of finding the right book, though—I just need to buckle down and read without complaining because this is government stuff. It's just boring."

"A harsh truth of our day-to-day activities. I don't think any of us wanted to be politicians when the offer came through." Eilene let out a short yawn. "Granted, we are more of a figurehead than a ruling party. Kind of like a Constitutional Monarchy. Do you want me to summarize the material for you? I've read them all a few times over."

"That would be appreciated, actually. I can help you reorganize the shelves while we work." Ethan hopped out of his chair and lifted a stack of books to

Eilene high on the ladder.

"The first book Luana assigns us to read is by far the most boring."

Scott snorted in the back of the library, and Eilene rode the ladder to the end of the aisle to peer curiously at him. He cleared his throat and refocused on the book in his hands. Ethan smothered a laugh with a short coughing fit.

"The book gives an overview of the role Council members take upon themselves. It also discusses the events the Council took part in over the course of world history. Of course, the only names of Council members anyone knows are the original nine.

"Those nine members played key roles in founding Elementōrum Patriam. Vasha tore Pangea apart after the Council lifted our country into the sky. Nine of the cities are named after them to honor their sacrifice. The early wars with humans were brutal, one-sided massacres if you managed to have the elementalists on your side. Sometimes, we split into factions opposing each other, and the wars were bloody. There's a long history of them included, but most of the issues are long resolved.

"In turn, deities started to crop up around the world for various peoples. Some of them tried to adopt the elementalists as their gods, but we are not deities. We come from the same genealogical branch as humans, but we have a few extra special abilities." Eilene twisted a ribbon of water through the air as proof before it filled Scott's empty glass. He gave her a short nod of thanks and took a sip. "Around two-thousand BCE, after the deification of our powers got out of control, the Council members adopted the red robes to help separate themselves and paint us as the bad guys. The Council is long viewed as an opposing and violent force who could end the world as we know it.

"The tricky thing about religion is we didn't want to be identified with only one single expectation or aligned interest. Freedom of religion and the ability to worship that religion without argument is something we put a lot of focus on. We don't believe it should be forced on anyone, it's a matter of personal belief. If we tied ourselves down as gods, we would be expected to act as deities do. It would force our people to follow a false belief system.

"For us, the robes are symbolic of blood we spilt while building our country. It is a reminder of the sacrifice of the elementalists who came before us. It's a completely different view from our people. For them, the robes are a symbol of fear and expected respect—not something solemn. It's important to keep those differences in mind as we work to move forward with laws which will affect our country.

"Once the book covered a fair amount of history, it talks about how the Council moved to a seven-member system, but there are no more names for the elementalists." Eilene concluded her monologue on the book and reached for the next stack Ethan offered. They managed to rearrange four full rows of shelves while she spoke. Her words easily captivated her listeners, and even Scott set aside his reading. "Ethan, do you have any questions about the material?"

"Not many. You make it more straightforward than the book." He smiled, and Eilene laughed. "What specific duties do we have as Council members?"

"There's several books which cover the answer to that question. It all depends on where you want to start." Eilene stroked the soft spine of a velvet-covered book, the title embossed in gold, before she slid it home on the shelf. "The ones I most recommend are *Duties of the Council, Laws of Elementōrum Patriam, The Importance of Identifying Rogue's, Why the Uns are Uns, A Country Divided, The New Glory,* among other titles. Each one has its own insights and individualized areas of research. Each one of them approved directly by a Council member, not of the present Council. Is there one which stands out to you?"

"I've always wondered about the Uns. It sounds the most interesting." Ethan pulled the noisy ladder around to join Eilene on the higher shelves.

She dived into the next bout of exposition. Scott stood from his own seat in the library and helped them sort—content to listen to her weave images and stories in their heads.

CHAPTER EIGHT
Calamity

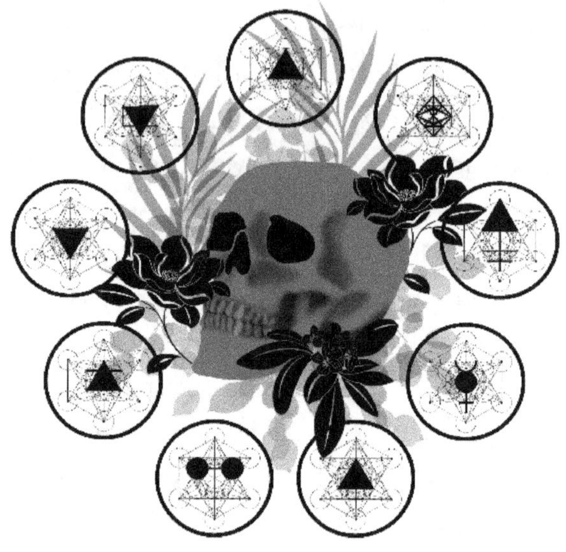

October 19, 2316

Why, Pima County, Arizona, United States of America

A man stood on the porch with his hand on the knob of the green door. His gaze drifted to the cream trim as his thoughts turned sour. He didn't want to go in. Without his wife, he found it tough to raise his daughter. Charlotte Slattery, a five-year-old ball of trouble with the cutest face. Tyr couldn't resist. He knew the minute he stepped into his house he would play for the next three hours whether he had the energy or not. He rested his forehead on door and recoiled quickly from the sunbaked metal. Tyr took a steadying breath and pushed the door open.

Charlotte popped over the couch along with her nanny, Karin.

"Daddy!" Charlotte cried out. She threw herself into her father's stomach.

"Hello cutie." Tyr pressed a kiss to her forehead before he pulled her into a warm hug.

"Charlotte was better today, not as much trouble." The nanny's dark red hair shone in the sunlight from the front window.

"That's a good girl. What would you say if I say we can go out for ice-cream as a celebration?"

"Yes!" Charlotte cheered. Her long brunette hair flipped into her father's smiling mouth as she spun in circles. She threw her arms out and clipped her father's chin with one of her fingers. Tyr spat out her hair and pulled her back against his body to try and contain her energy. "Daddy, you're not supposed to eat my hair."

"Then can I eat your tummy?" He pulled up her shirt and blew a raspberry on her stomach. The child squealed and wiggled away from her father. Her blue eyes sparkled in the filtered sunlight and reminded him of his late wife.

"I'll be going home, then. See you tomorrow at six." Karin picked up her purse and keys.

"Can, tomorrow, you paint my nails?" Charlotte asked.

"Of course, I'll bring all of my colors." Karin winked and closed the front door behind her.

"Ice-cream?" Tyr said.

Charlotte ran to find her shoes, so they could leave.

October 21, 2316

Lagoon, Farmington, Davis County, Utah, United States of America

One long and tiring trip from Arizona later, with a five-year-old in the back seat, they arrived in Utah for a three-day vacation. One day spent in the hot, mountainous desert sun walking around an amusement park, two spent driving. Tyr held his daughter's hand tightly as they walked through the park. Older couples watched their grandchildren on the smaller attractions. Circling rockets and spinning teacups surrounded them as they looked for the next ride. A nearby cotton candy vendor waved his clever and large creations of spun floss, but Tyr gently steered Charlotte away—she didn't need any more sugar after their disastrous snow cone experience.

Charlotte skipped at her father's side and watched teenagers and young adults grab each other to wait in hour long lines for the newest and best roller coasters. Some of the larger rides intrigued Tyr, but he didn't trust himself to take Charlotte on them yet.

"I want to ride the animal train." She pointed at the small locomotive chugging its way around the large pond. Tyr looked over the crowd and winced at the long line.

"Okay, we'll ride the train and then head back to the hotel for the night."

Charlotte hummed and pulled her father to the line. While they waited, Tyr hoisted her up onto his shoulders where she could see the park. When their section of the line prepared to board, he lowered her back to the ground. Charlotte slipped from her father's grasp and ran for the front car. Tyr hurried after her, uneasy about the separation in case anyone harbored less than desirable intentions.

The train conductor smiled warmly at them and kept their trained eye on the loading process for each car.

"Which animal are you most excited to see?" Tyr put an arm around Charlotte while he buckled them both to the bench. As one of the nearby rides shuddered to a stop, ripples echoed across the pond's surface.

"The buffalo!"

"They're very big."

"But their fur looks really soft."

"You know not to pet the buffalo, right?" Tyr worried his daughter didn't understand animals instinctually acted like... animals.

"Karin says we never go near wild animals because they don't know us. They think we are strangers and when we see strangers, we stay away."

"Very smart," he brushed her hair softly behind her ear. The ride jolted to a start and distracted Charlotte for a moment. She tried to stand up, but the belt kept her in place. She settled for pointing across the car.

"Daddy, there's a duck!"

October 25, 2316
Why, Pima County, Arizona, United States of America

Tyr lifted Charlotte on top of her worn mattress. The little girl threw her arms in the air and let her father undress her for the night. He picked up the green frog pajamas she chose and helped her climb into them. Tyr directed her to the bathroom, and she bounced on the bed a few times before dropping to the floor.

"Is daddy getting in his pajamas now?" Charlotte dragged a small, yellow stool from the kitchen toward the bathroom.

"Yep, I'm going to wear green like you."

"You're not supposed to copy me until I'm a celebrity." She struggled to grip the edges of the toothpaste drawer.

"Should I wear blue then?" The closed bedroom door muffled his question.

"No, green!" Her shout sent toothpaste foam all over the mirror and counter.

When they finished their nightly routine, and Tyr wiped the bathroom clean, he tucked Charlotte under the covers in her bed. She kicked her legs while she impatiently waited for her dad to pick a bedtime story. Tyr brought several options. He took a seat on the edge and held out the books to his daughter. She chose one with a colorful animal on the front.

Half-way through the story, Charlotte fell asleep. Ever the cautious parent, Tyr finished the book before he left the room. He moved the books to her nightstand and pressed a soft kiss to her forehead. He turned out the light and closed the door with a quiet click.

Unable to fall asleep in his own bed, he returned to Charlotte's room. She lay on her side and slept peacefully under the light of the moon filtering through the curtains. Tyr climbed into the bed at her side and, with his daughter in his arms, he slept.

November 3, 2316

On the floor in the other room, Charlotte played with several of her toys. Karin watched her from her position in the kitchen, working on a few batches of cookies. After deliberation, she decided on sugar cookies. While not terribly popular, they were easy to make. Karin glanced up from cutting her circle and smiled. The afternoon sunlight filtered through the front window and gave

Charlotte an angelic appearance. In one hand, she held a GI Joe, and in the other, a Barbie. Barbie towered over the smaller soldier, but Charlotte didn't bat an eye. Her pretend conversation for the dolls warmed Karin's heart as she rolled out the dough.

"If I don't kill the enemy out there, then you may die." The Barbie danced across the floor. "How brave for protecting me. I feel like I'm your princess."

Karin slid the cookie sheet inside the oven.

"Baby, you're not a princess. You're my queen."

The nanny snorted and covered her mouth with her hand to try to hide the noise.

Charlotte looked up. "Karin, why do grown-ups call each other 'baby'?"

"It's a nickname. Babies are precious. It's a way of saying you want to take care of the other person. I'm not sure where it came from."

"Does daddy call you 'baby'?"

"No."

"Do you want him to?" She stood up and carried both dolls into the kitchen. It took her several moments to struggle onto the stool at the counter while still holding her toys.

"I'll be happy with any nickname your father wants to give me."

"There are lots of nicknames?" Charlotte snuck her hand over the counter and pulled a small amount of dough off to eat raw.

"A whole bunch."

"Daddy calls me 'baby', sometimes."

"Parents do that with their children." Karin passed her a larger chunk of the dough.

"Can you bake cookies with your hands?"

"Human hands aren't warm enough to bake them."

"How hot does it have to be?"

"Three-hundred and fifty degrees for these cookies."

Charlotte hummed and rolled the dough in her hands. She closed it between her palms and a bright flash of light later, the little girl held out a baked cookie. "Like this?"

"You're good at magic. What did you do with the dough I gave you?"

"It's right here. I baked it with my hands."

"There's no way you did. You did a magic trick. You switched your dough with a baked cookie."

"I didn't, I baked it in my hands. I can do it again."

Annoyed, Karin grabbed the cookie, expecting it to be cool, and nearly dropped it when it burned her fingers. "How?"

"With matches." Charlotte held out her hands and red flame burst around her skin. Karin failed to hold in her scream at the sight.

"Matches?" she repeated dumbly.

"When daddy asks me to light the candles, I do it like this. He always says I'm good at using matches. It's matches."

"That's not matches, Charlotte. You shouldn't be doing that."

"But daddy lets me."

"Well, I'm banning it until I speak with your father. You can't light candles that way. It's wrong."

"It's good."

"Charlotte," she warned softly.

"No!" The child reached for the cookie she flash-baked, but Karin slapped her hand away.

"You don't get cookies if you keep doing that."

"Give me my cookie. I baked it," Charlotte demanded. She kicked the counter repeatedly with her legs.

"You're going to time out. Go to your room."

"No!"

"Charlotte!"

"No!"

Karin grabbed Charlotte around the waist. She planned on putting her into a forceful timeout, but she didn't count on the child defending herself. Charlotte screamed. Fire, uncontrolled, swept from her in waves. It curled around the wood paneling of the cupboards. The dolls on the marble counter melted. The flames clung to the drapery around the window. Karin's skin blistered and burned.

She dropped Charlotte, and the girl ran fearlessly from the flames without a single touch. Charlotte watched from the doorway with wide eyes as Karin writhed in pain under the heat with no escape. She couldn't push herself to stand. The room went up in flames on the next wave.

The child, flames following her every step, ran up the stairs and into her father's bedroom. Charlotte hid under her father's bed. She held her hands over her ears, but it didn't drown out Karin's screams.

The bed above Charlotte caught fire and burned to ash around her. The floor weakened next, and she fell through to the first floor. Charlotte scrambled into the corner of the room to hide. The wail of sirens joined Karin's cacophony. Tears ran down Charlotte's cheeks.

Water battered the house as firefighters tried to extinguish the flames, but it wasn't enough against Charlotte's rage fueling them.

Firefighters broke down the front door to reach the people inside, informed by neighbors who recognized Karin's car out front. Karin's screams were gone. The door to the room Charlotte hid in was torn off its hinges. Her eyes locked with the firefighters. They backed away and shouted something unintelligible to the others.

Charlotte remained in her corner, crying, as the house burned around her.

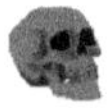

The Council Chambers, The Academy, Elementōrum Patriam

Luana stood in front of one of the walls of gray filing cabinets with a stack of papers cradled in her arms.

Hans silently continued to file his own pages. The crash of 2180 imprinted on humanity as one of the biggest informational losses. None of the information stored online had a reliable backup; as a result, the elementalists and the world lost a massive amount of invaluable data. Paper records returned to fashion. Old versions of documents appropriately shredded and recycled.

The printer roared to life in the corner and shuddered out another few hundred pages before it beeped contentedly and shut off. Luana pursed her lips and flicked her ponytail behind her with enough force to flip it back into her own face. She sputtered, and Hans let out a quiet guffaw.

None of them enjoyed filing, but no ordinary elementalists could be allowed inside Council chambers. Their chambers remained their only sanctuary from the outside world.

"I propose a competition." Hans opened one of the drawers with a loud click. He shuffled several pages and stuffed them into one of the unfortunate, overflowing manila folders. The drawer slid shut again. Luana focused entirely on him. "We could see who can file faster."

"What does the winner get?"

"Bragging rights."

She laughed and looked at her own set of papers. "The 'no real prize' deal."

"I can tell you're scared. It's understandable." He took hold of the handle of another drawer, but a light kick to his shin stopped him.

"I'll accept your wager."

Hans strode across the room and pulled the fresh stack from the printer. He roughly split it in half and added to both of their piles. "I'll give you the honors."

Both tackled the project differently but stayed evenly matched for twenty minutes. Sweat dripped down their faces, but they hardly noticed long enough to wipe it away. On the last set, Luana finished milliseconds before Hans and she stood, narrowly missing hitting her head on his open drawer. It shut behind her, and she found herself pinned to the cabinets in a kabedon stance, one of Hans' arms to the side of her head and his large stature bodily keeping her to the shelf.

"I won," her voice cracked around the words.

"Bragging rights are yours." He smiled and leaned in.

The door opened with a flourish and hit the table behind it. Hans slid away gracefully instead of jumping back like his nerves screamed at him to do.

"Sorry to interrupt," Series' eyes flitted between them, "but there's an emergency. A five-year-old in America awoke her elementalist abilities. There's one confirmed death. We've been called in."

"Fill me in on the way upstairs." Luana pulled her phone from her pocket and hit the emergency app installed on the home screen. With one swipe of her thumb, sirens blared through the academy and alerted the Council, and appropriate parties, that they would leave the country immediately.

Gathered in the main entryway, The Council swung on their robes and left the chambers in a flourish of red. As they stalked through the halls, elementalists leaped out of their way. Ethan tripped a handful of times on his robes, but they made it to the transportation pods in record time. The mechanical team sent them off with a salute.

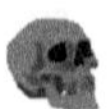

A projection of Luana sat in the middle of the second pod and Ethan found it terrifying how the image moved to accommodate his slightest movements. He could never escape her gaze, and he wondered if she could see all four at once.

"Series gave me the basic rundown of the situation." She rubbed her eye with an irritated expression. "A five-year-old in Why, Arizona awoke her elementalist abilities as a Fire elementalist, confirmed. The firemen are standing by with a water hose, if necessary, but we requested they hold off on spraying her."

"Can she take that much water pressure blasting her?" Scarlet's voice filtered across the call.

"Yes, because it's just water. Water isn't stronger than fire—basic elemental facts. She killed someone, most likely a parent in the home with her. The house is in ruins and every flame except for the child is put out. Our mission is to recover her without further deaths or damage to the surrounding area. She, or a potential second parent, may resist removal, and we need to be prepared for removal by force. If necessary, I will give the signal, and Hans will subdue the child."

"Understood." Eilene leaned against Dwayne's shoulder and missed the twinge of annoyance from Scott across the pod.

"Dwayne, Scarlet, and Eilene, I expect the three of you to be on cleanup duty. You'll need to repair the surrounding area where possible and work with local law enforcement to settle any disputes about damage claims. Series, you stay at the pod and arrange for a psychologist and therapist to be ready for when we arrive back home. The child will no doubt be scarred by the events today, and her mental health is our priority. Ethan, stick close to Scott, and he'll show you the basics of standing as a sentry between us and the humans. If anything happens, you'll need to step in."

"Clear as day," Dwayne confirmed. "We'll handle it according to your specifications."

"I want to be in and out within thirty minutes." The projection cut off and left them in silence.

"I assume not all removals are easy?" Ethan shifted to sit on his foot, a comfortable position for watching their descent from the window.

"Not by a long shot." Eilene shook her head. "I heard from the others yours was an interesting disaster."

"Disaster for sure, but I left easily."

"Yeah, your removal was easy, but do you know how many humans we had to resuscitate that night? Not to mention all the countless elementalists we found mixed in with that bunch. It was a long night." Scott closed his eyes and rested his head against the side of the pod.

"You were there?"

He made a non-committal noise. "I was still newish. I didn't recognize you until we looked up your file when you joined the Council."

"I remember reviving people that night. I was still new to the Council myself," Dwayne chuckled. "Dickens didn't join us till the next year." He smiled at her. "You would've been a great asset. Not that Ruben wasn't great."

Scott nodded.

"Does the entire Council always show up to remove kids from Earth's surface?" Ethan thought back to all his previous encounters with the Council, including all seven.

"No, we actually have a large-scale operations removal team. There's at least one member for every language in the world, and we try to have the elements as diverse as possible. It's only the highly dangerous situations or the ones where we sense a particularly powerful elementalist that we get called in. I think almost all the current Council members were pulled by previous Council members. Most of the time we try to send only one or two members—but a death changes the situation entirely. Collateral damage, a couple Council members can sort it out in no time—a death, well," Eilene shrugged, "We changed the lives of some humans without meaning to. We'll need to pay the repercussions. It'll never be enough to make them happy. We can't bring dead people back to life."

"Why can't the normal removal team do the dangerous ones?" Ethan rolled his shoulders against the glass and glanced around the five-seater compartment. He had no room to stretch out his legs when with other tall people.

"They lack the same finesse and control that a Council member has. Even if we're younger, we are the strongest representatives in the country. If we sent in someone less capable than Hans to subdue the child, say we can't get her out without using our abilities, there's a chance she'd be killed by a less stable hand." Dwayne put an arm around Eilene and pulled her further into him subconsciously. "We don't want to kill our own people."

"Which is why we're forbidden to spar with one another without two instructors present," Eilene yawned. "There's a fifty-one percent chance we'd end up killing each other in a head-to-head spar without someone to intervene. With someone there, presumably more powerful, they can break up the fight before it turns deadly. As Council members, we rarely spar with each other. Instead, we use specially designed technology which can take the brunt of our power without being destroyed."

"Most of the time," Scott amended her statement quietly; a scowl settled on his lips.

"Ignoring the rules on sparring," Dwayne said, "we have a child to extract."

"Do you think their parents will resist?" Ethan stretched his arms above his head.

"It's happened before. We must take them per a governmental contract. If we don't, we take liability for all damages and deaths they cause." Eilene flipped her hair into a bun.

"It's a legal obligation." The Death elementalist nodded in understanding. "We're going to Arizona?"

"Yes, Why," Eilene paused and pursed her lips, "I wasn't questioning you, by the way."

Dwayne rolled his shoulders and looked at the approaching desert landscape. "It's fascinating how the desert here is different from Kalahari."

"You would think they would be the same." Eilene's eyes roamed over the sage brush covered mountains and rising rock spires. "This one resembles the landscape in the City of Barren more than anything else."

"Elementōrum Patriam is part of the east coast, not the west." Ethan pitched in. "I feel like I'm back home in Wyoming—or Nevada. This whole area is just the same stuff. Fire fodder."

They spent the rest of their ride in relative silence and exchanged snacks and drinks. A short way out of landing in Why, they put on their robes. Ethan struggled with his, especially when getting the black mesh face piece into place, but Eilene helped him fit it snuggly to conceal any defining features. Once the pods stopped outside the line of emergency vehicles, the doors opened, and the eight Council members stepped out.

The crowd of humans parted around them as they moved toward the safety barriers and through the throngs of emergency personnel. Whispers followed their every step. Ethan did his best to face straight ahead like the others instead of looking around. What remained of the house smoldered under plumes of dark smoke. A body lay on a gurney under a black covering. They didn't see the child in the immediate vicinity.

Luana approached the fire chief who had a sheepish frown. "I'm sorry, we had to blast her with the hose. The fire was spreading to other structures." He pointed to the burns on the upper floors of the other houses.

Luana made a gesture, and Dwayne, Scarlet, and Eilene moved away immediately to assess the damage and see what could be repaired or what would need to be paid for. Ethan and Scott moved forward to flank Luana. Hans stood at her side.

"Where is the child?" Luana asked.

"Still inside the home. We couldn't safely remove her."

Hans took off toward the remains. With their new fire-resistant cloak material, he didn't hesitate to step over a burning section of the wall to get to the crying child. He had no fear of the flames as an Earth elementalist. He emerged with her a moment later, cradled to his chest and smothering her flames with an encasing of dirt. He lowered her to the charred front lawn. When he pulled away his ability, her flames leaped out again in a swell. The firemen raised their hose, but Luana swept the flames away with a simple wave of her hand. She approached slowly where the girl lay.

It would be in their best interest to make sure she came with them willingly. Even from a distance, Ethan could see the girl had several broken bones from the blast of the hose. Flames leaped off her body in dizzying patterns.

Luana kneeled on the ground in front of her.

"What's your name?"

"Charlotte Slattery."

"I see you can control fire."

"My daddy calls it 'matches.'"

"Your dad knows you can control fire?"

"He always says I'm good at using matches when we light candles."

"I see." Luana crossed her legs and took a firm seat on the dry grass. "You're very pretty. How old are you?"

"Five." Charlotte wiggled her toes in the charcoal. "The firemen sprayed me with the hose. I don't know how to stop my matches."

"It's really easy. Do you want me to show you?"

"You know how to do matches, too?"

Luana nodded and put out her hand. It lit up in bright red flame and the girl marveled at it. "It's a special ability we share. When you're scared of the flames, they get stronger, and you can't control them. If you're not scared, you can do it at will."

Charlotte touched her flaming palm to Luana's and shifted as much as her broken bones would allow. "I don't want to be scared of my matches."

"There's no reason to be."

The flames around the child ebbed in the near silence.

"Do you want to learn how to control them? You can come back to my home with me, and we'll show you how."

"I'm not supposed to go anywhere with strangers. Daddy and Karin told me that."

"Who's Karin?"

Tears spilled down the child's cheeks, and her flames flared up again. The firemen held up their hose, but at the approach of Scott and Ethan, they lowered it again. "Karin is my nanny. I heard her screaming when my matches got out of control. She was rolling around on the floor. Daddy always praised me for using matches, but she tried to take them away."

The Council's gazes flitted to the body bag on site.

"That would be distressful." Luana placed a hand on top of Charlotte's head. "I have a secret for you."

"What is it?"

"If you come with us, I know you can show the whole world what you can do. Karin is right to say you can't follow strangers, but we aren't strangers when we have the same ability."

"We're not strangers?"

"Nope! I know your name is Charlotte, and you're five years old. I also know you can control Fire. We're practically best friends already."

The child giggled, and the flames disappeared.

"Look at that. They're gone. Do you want to come with me and show everyone what you can do?"

Charlotte took Luana's hand.

"Life!" Luana called over her shoulder.

Dwayne obediently walked to their side and reached out a hand. A green light emitted between them.

A sharp voice cut through them.

"Step away from my daughter!"

Tyr sat in his office at work and pretended to concentrate on problems he needed to address. He had a headache, and the blue light caused burnout in his tired eyes. He only had a small amount of work to complete for the day, and it didn't look like he would get more. Tyr leaned forward on his desk and pressed the palms of his hands into his eyes. After a low, distressed groan, he turned back to his computer. Instead of jumping into his work, he turned to Google to look for new romantic spots where he could take Karin on a second date.

Charlotte used to be the only source of worry in his life, but Karin moved into a free space in his mind. Her appearance consumed him. Once he found a few potential options to check out, he did his best to focus on his work.

He worked for an hour before the ringing of his cell phone interrupted him. He scrambled to silence it as electronics should be on vibrate at minimum during the workday. Tyr stood and speed walked to the break room where he could take the call without interrupting his coworkers.

"Hello?"

"Tyr? This is Sarah, your neighbor."

He recognized the name.

"Your house is on fire. There's a body—the fire crews are having a hard time putting it out."

The phone dropped from his hand to the floor.

There's a body. The words echoed around his head and swirled into a terrified spiral of the worst possibilities.

"Tyr? Tyr? Are you still there?"

He scooped up his phone and tore through the office to his desk. "I'm on my way, Sarah."

"Tyr, where are you going?" His boss yelled after him.

"My house is on fire. I'm going home." He raced down the stairs to the underground parking and tore out of his assigned stall in his hover car.

On the drive home, he managed to stick to a speed that wouldn't get him flagged for speeding by any passing cops. At his street, he couldn't pull into it because of the emergency vehicles, and he parked illegally on the corner. As he shoved open the door, Tyr noticed two transportation pods on the street, and his heart stuttered in his chest.

I won't allow it.

Frantic running down the street. An illegal jump over the barricade. A cop yelling after him. The elementalists on his charred lawn. In agonizing slow motion, between each pound of his shoes on the concrete, the child placed her hand in the elementalist's. They called for someone else who approached. They knelt and a green glow emitted between their hand and Charlotte's body. The words clawed their way out of his throat before he could think about doing anything else.

"Step away from my daughter!" Heavy breaths escaped his lungs as he drew near to the edge of the street. The emergency personnel stopped their own chase—their eyes flitted back and forth as if watching a tennis match.

"She is one of us." The woman, he assumed from her voice, wrapped her hand tightly around Charlotte's.

"She is my daughter." Tyr took a step closer to them and watched the little girl shrink away. "You can't take her from me."

"We are required to by law—we apologize for any strain this may cause your family and will provide adequate compensation to repair your home," the woman said.

"You think you can buy my daughter?" Tyr's voice cracked over the words. "No monetary value could cover the cost of you taking her away from me."

"It is hard to lose a child, but she is an elementalist. This is for your safety. There is no other way."

"Daddy, I want to go with them," Charlotte said. The Life elementalist, Tyr assumed, helped her sit up. She stood on shaky legs and ran toward her father. The elementalists didn't stop her. "They can show me how to control my matches."

"What are your matches?" Tyr bent down to gather her in his arms.

"When you ask me to light candles, the matches come from my hands."

One of the elementalists took a step closer. Their hands covered in a thick layer of earth.

"What do you mean by matches? Matches are in a box," Tyr said.

Charlotte shook her head. She stepped back. Held out her hands. The elementalist took another step forward. "Matches." Her palms erupted into flames. The flames spread across her arms and down her spine. She panicked, reached out for her father. He fell away from her, scrambling to get back. Charlotte burst into tears. "Daddy doesn't want me."

"No!" Tyr shouted. "No, Charlotte. Of course, I want you. You're my baby girl. My sunshine. My everything."

She tried to run for him again, but the Earth elementalist stopped her. They encased her inside a shell of dirt until the flames extinguished. However, they didn't put her down again.

"Charlotte," Tyr asked hesitantly; he didn't want the elementalists to harm her. "What happened?"

"I don't know." Tears tracked messy patterns across her skin. "Karin told me not to use my matches, and I got mad. You always said I was good at using matches. Everything got really hot. Karin was screaming for a really long time. Then everything was ash."

Tyr's eyes trailed across the burned lawn to the body bag just outside of the ambulance. *Karin.*

"If I... d-don't go with... them to learn... to control... my m-m-matches... then d-daddy will scream... too," hiccoughs broke her words.

"No," Tyr reached out for his daughter. "No, that's not true. Daddy won't. He can help you with your matches. Daddy can't live without you, Charlotte. You can stay with Daddy."

"Not allowed, sir," a police officer broke in. "I'm afraid your daughter will have to leave with the elementalists today."

"You can't let them do this to me," he pled.

"This is yours." Another elementalist walked forward, female, and held out a bank card to him. "There should be enough to pay for the damages to your home as well as extra for displacing you and your daughter."

Tyr bit his tongue. He knew no matter what he said, it wouldn't stop the outcome of the situation. They paid him off for his only child with a laughably low amount of money.

The Earth elementalist lowered Charlotte to the ground. The dirt dropped from her small frame. One of the elementalists wrapped a fire-retardant blanket around Charlotte's shoulders before they hoisted the child into the air again.

"You'll be safe with us," the Council member said.

"Charlotte, I love you," Tyr called after them, his voice nearly inaudible over the sound of the emergency vehicles. "I will come for you." He struggled to his feet, and one of the officers watched him closely to ensure he wouldn't chase after the elementalists.

Charlotte stared over the shoulder of the Council member until the moment the pod door shut. Tyr raised a hand and clutched at his shirt; he pulled at the fabric above his heart. A broken cry tore from his chest, and the hand of the police officer didn't ease the pain.

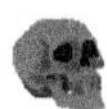

Transportation Pod #1

They placed Charlotte in the second transportation pod with Eilene, Scott, Dwayne, and Ethan. While they didn't have elementalists who could easily combat fire, they didn't have much worry of her bursting into flames. Eilene was also much better with children than Luana. Hans encouraged the women to take a nap on their return trip to Elementōrum. Only Scarlet and Series took him up on the offer. Luana's weight pressed into his left shoulder, but her eyes stayed fixed on the window. In the dim, evening haze of light, Hans recalled her build when they first met. Even though he didn't know her by more than the red robe, she didn't change. Small and slender.

He cleared his throat. Scarlet shifted at the sound and captured their attention. Hans let out a long breath and closed his eyes. The first time he met Luana, he didn't know his own fate. Hans' family returned home from a vacation in Russia to visit his human grandparents, only to find their daughter sitting in the kitchen of their home. Odessa wasn't on break from the Academy, and she revealed how she ran from the Council after she received the invitation to her death sentence. Hans' father, outraged to find she returned and put their family in danger of harboring a criminal, threw her out onto the street. The Council caught up to her as expected, and Luana beheaded her on their front lawn. Despite being nine years old at the time, he hadn't forgotten.

Hans nudged her. "It was you, wasn't it?"

"It was me what?"

"You're the one who killed Odessa, my older sister."

Luana's head slipped away from his shoulder, and she tugged at her fingers. The Council invited her to join at eight years old. She took over as their informal leader because she had tenure ruling Elementōrum Patriam, with Hans as second to her. He knew what her flames looked like.

"Yeah," the affirmative barely audible. "How did you know?"

He opened his eyes.

"You're short. You were smaller back then." Hans chuckled darkly with a deep frown at the glare Luana sent his way. "I know your age, and I know about when you joined the Council. You would've been new to the government, but the person who killed her wielded fire—your fire. It's not hard to imagine you, or any of us, killing someone."

"You're too smart, Hans." She returned her head to his shoulder. "I'm sorry for killing her."

"She was a Rogue. You did your job. It's wrong for you to feel sorry when Odessa would've been a threat." He threw an arm around her shoulder and pulled her close.

Luana nodded, and Hans turned away. Since the Council swore their identities to secrecy, the government reported new Council members as Rogues and recorded a fake death. When Hans' father learned the Council identified his youngest child as a Rogue, he believed he failed to continue the line of elementalists; he couldn't handle the news.

On the day Hans accepted the role as a Council member—the Council told him his father committed suicide. His father, for all he knew, had two dead children and one Un. Hans knew his mother still lived, but he couldn't meet her anymore—he provided her no comfort.

It was Luana's flame that led him through the trial. The duty usually fell to her. They occasionally deviated with other forms of light; he remembered the Water elementalist leading Scott through his trial with a light trapped inside a water droplet.

The trial was designed to read memories and build trials around fears—but the Council had access to which ones it would choose. At the time, Hans thought they wanted to kill him because of his strength. When he faced the empty desert and electrified invisi-fences that burned his brother, he naturally backed away out of fear. It took a long while before he could separate reality from his perception. Luana's flame gave him comfort as he stood in a catacomb-like room with nine tombs. He promised he would kill others like his sister only two months after her death; he hated it still.

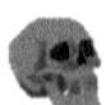

The Academy, Elementōrum Patriam

Charlotte didn't speak for the entire ride into the sky where Elementōrum Patriam waited. The pod lowered itself in its soft spiral until it reached the unloading platform of the docking garage. The Council stepped out of the pod and flanked the small child. Whispers followed their procession into the main entry where a line of Academy professionals greeted them.

"Fire," Luana called.

A woman with graying hair pulled into a tight ponytail stepped forward immediately. She turned with military precision and walked toward them.

"Charlotte, this is Madame Dyan. She is one of the many teachers at our school. She'll help you to control your power," Luana said. "Madame Dyan, this is Charlotte Slattery. She is a confirmed Fire elementalist. We pulled her from a loving home with a doting father. Please take good care of her."

"Of course, your grace." Dyan bowed respectfully to the Council members. Her thick French accent washed over them. "Lady Charlotte, would you like to meet the other teachers who will help you grow?"

Charlotte turned back to the Council. "You're leaving me?"

"I'm afraid we have to, but Madame Dyan is exceptionally kind. She'll be a much better teacher than me. I look forward to hearing the report of your progress. Please make sure you work extra hard!" Luana encouraged.

"Madame Dyan, can I see your fire?"

"Of course, little one." The woman held out her hand the flames danced in colors across the rainbow. Charlotte clapped and grasped the woman's hand.

"Please show me how to make a rainbow."

The Council slipped away while the officials distracted her. The other officials of the academy bowed as they passed. They treated the return to their chamber with less urgency than their exit, but they made sure to walk upright and calm.

Once inside the main hallway, as they doffed their robes, Dwayne suggested playing video games for their evening relaxation activity.

"We get back from rescuing a child from an extremely tense situation where she has committed accidental manslaughter, and you offer virtual tennis as a solution?" Series gently hung her robe on its respective hook and watched him out of the corner of her eye.

"I have to agree with Dwayne—it would be more fun," Scarlet said as she spread out her robe to avoid creases. "I'd hate to give any more thought to politics after the day we had."

"I think it's a great idea," Luana admitted. Her shoulders slumped forward, and her face rested, devoid of any distinct emotions. "I can't possibly think straight after today. Emergency pulls are the worst."

"I'm up for a game of ping-pong—I don't think I can bring myself to make the full swings tennis requires," Ethan said and stretched his arms over his head.

"Fair assessment." Eilene leaned against Scott and let out a slow breath. "I think I may nap lightly while you guys play."

"Perfect plans." Scarlet smiled and headed down the hall.

CHAPTER NINE
MIA

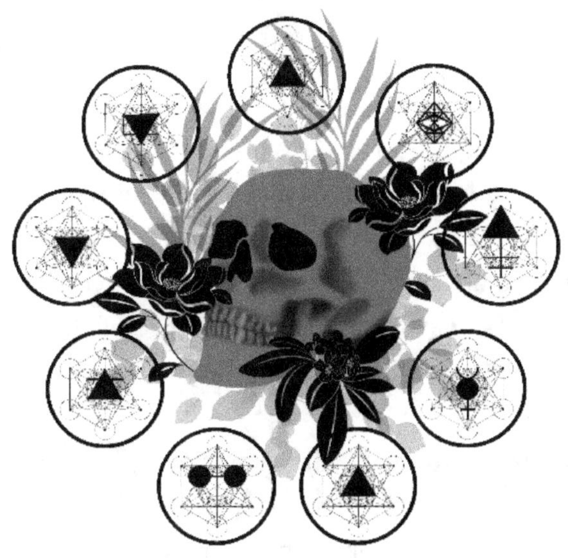

They took my daughter. Tyr reclined on the bed in a cheap motel he found in town. He convinced himself of bedbugs in the sheets, but he couldn't find it in himself to complain to management. *They will pay.* He clenched his teeth, unable to pay attention to the true crime show on the television. It could only get one channel, and he considered most of the shows on the network trash. Tyr couldn't return to work until he finished dealing with the grief of the situation—he didn't know if it had a significant ending point. *She is the spot of brightness in my world—it's their fault she's not here.*

Tyr turned off the TV. He rolled over on the bed and stared out the dingy, half curtained window. He saw a few people make their way past in swimsuits. He needed a plan to get his daughter back from a country twenty-five thousand feet in the air.

If they never existed, my life would be normal. I would still have my daughter. The elementalists are a plague—leaving only destruction in their

125

wake. It is my duty to stand against them and take back what is rightfully mine.
Tyr sat up. He needed to research and find help. If he wanted to be successful in affecting the governmental policies impacting the elementalists and the humans, he needed other parents like him.

November 15, 2316

Tyr browsed through the open tabs on his computer screen. He spent the last several hours studying phenomena in the news regarding children. He assumed at least some of them would end up as elementalist children; the Council kept elementalist records sealed. Small snippets slipped through, but the information never gave them a clear picture of the elementalists as a people. On public record, Tyr only found the yearly census numbers for their population.

He turned his attention to the newsworthy topics of children who performed miracles. He thought he might be able to trace their journey through life until an empty drop off point indicating a death, or transfer to Elementōrum Patriam.

MIRACLE BOY SHOCKS DOCTORS

July 5, 2302

LEWISTOWN, MO (TMP) — After the tragic events in Harlowton, Montana earlier this week, the result of the capture and killing of a Rogue elementalist a month before, search crews found a child still alive after a mysterious massacre.

Investigators found the town desolate after several employees from different establishments failed to show up consistently to work. A concerned family member, who hadn't heard from their sister in a couple weeks, became the first to reach out to law enforcement outside Harlowton when they couldn't get ahold of the police station in the city.

When search crews found bodies in the first few

houses searched, it warranted larger action from the community. They put together a search team and found an incidental massacre. They expected to find no one alive, but to their surprise, one minor lived through the death of the entire city.

Equipped with gas masks, crews found rotten and spoiled food in the house he lived in. He appeared sickly as though he hadn't eaten for several days, and emergency personnel transported him immediately to a hospital in Lewistown.

A toxicology report revealed the child as clean for the same substance which killed his biological parents. Lewistown officials call it a miracle; they found five-year-old Ethan Silverspoon safe. Doctors at the hospital stated any more starvation or dehydration may have killed the child.

Doctor Skastone stated: "Ethan will be a miracle people talk about in Lewistown for years to come. His survival is a happy surprise, and we look forward to reuniting him with family members. I'm sure they're grateful to still have him in their lives."

Child Protective Services announced his grandparents, currently residing in Nevada, would collect their grandson and take him home with them. They are ecstatic to have their grandchild in their possession.

Tyr frowned and closed the tab. He didn't gain anything from the article. The next one didn't have a promising title, but he figured it couldn't hurt to skim the few paragraphs.

Young Teen Vanishes Overnight

February 15, 2310

ELKTON, VA (TVT) — Parents of star student, Kristen Delavida Reyes from Elkton Middle School, awoke in the morning to find their daughter missing. The teen did not leave behind a note; there are no claims for ransom currently, and no signs of a visible struggle inside their home.

They never had trouble with their daughter before this incident. Her father said they are a close family, and he and his wife cannot fathom why she vanished overnight. Law enforcement is actively investigating the runaway.

Since Kristen disappeared from home, there have been several reported sightings—but her location cannot be traced. Eyewitnesses state she vanishes within a few seconds only for the next sighting to be reported several hundred miles away. Every report is investigated thoroughly, but none appear legitimate.

If you have any information on Kristen Delavida Reyes, please contact the number below.

The comments on the article focused on placing the blame on elementalists, and Tyr closed the tab with an annoyed scoff. The next tab closed by accident as well, and he used the shortcut key to restore the tab.

ORPHANAGE SPLITS FROM CLIFF AND TUMBLES INTO SEA

May 28, 2311

TACOMA, WA (WD) — Residents in Tacoma received the scare of a lifetime after a shift in tectonic plates sent an orphanage built on the cliffside tumbling into the crashing ocean waters 300 ft below.

Elementalist interference is suspected. The investigation is ongoing. A temporary memorial, which will be made permanent in the next couple of years, is set up on the edge of the cliff to signify the lives lost.

The elementalist Council arrived immediately on

the scene, after retrieving an elementalist child. The Council members created rescue teams to help the survivors. After inspection, the elementalists confirmed the collapse was not the work of a Rogue.

The Council met directly with the mayor of Tacoma to discuss the cliffside setting and the rescue of the orphans and their caretakers. The Council took at least four of the children with them. Currently, there are only ten confirmed deaths. All those living are rescued, and crews are working on recovering bodies from the wreckage and matching them with the records of those in the orphanage.

We are monitoring the situation and will update this article as more information becomes available. At this time, the names released by law enforcement are:

Michelle Johnson

Lulu Morris

Andrew Puble

Adrian Roberts

Ethan Silverspoon

The list continued, but Tyr lost his attention on the article. Instead, he stared at the familiar name. *Ethan Silverspoon.* The miracle child from Harlowton. The article said he would live with his grandparents, but several years later, he showed up in an orphanage two states away. Curious, Tyr typed the name into a new search window and found several articles detailing how he moved across the United States due to several terrible accidents. In the end, he found a death record from a few months earlier listed in the public records for the elementalists. The "ROGUE" label in large letters tagged his profile.

Tyr licked his lips and opened another new window. He typed in the girl's name from the runaway case and found her name listed on the elementalist website as a most wanted Rogue. He typed in a few other names off the list, but none of them yielded the same results as the first two names. A smile graced his lips as he realized he had a chance. He could track who might be an elementalist and get to them before the Council. He could find Kristen Delavida Reyes before the Council had a chance to kill her. A quick search found a few more names he wanted to investigate more.

With Rogue records public, he had an opportunity to find where Rogues came from and find their parents. Draw out their hatred against the elementalists. He hoped one of them might have connections to get what he wanted—his daughter returned to him. He needed solutions on how to do it.

Tyr saved the Rogue document to his computer and used the split screen function to search names online. He scrolled through the list, checking each one. Most Rogues were of elementalist descent. Kenichi Hachirō, Eilene Vos, the siblings Hans Aliyev and Odessa Aliyeva, Hasan Konstantin. Those names did him no good. However, Series Pahona—a Hopi native—her family would be in the same state he already lived in. Lí Scarlet. Tyr crossed out her name. He didn't know Mandarin to get in contact with her parents. He did the same with Dwayne Tebogo, who had no parents listed.

Scott Everton. His mother, Adelyn, was listed as deceased. His dad, however, had a "living" tag next to his name. The occupation said "biologist". No known location. No matter, he could hunt Ryan Everton down. A biologist would be right up the alley of skills he needed to bring down the elementalists. One viable option: destroying the genetic mutation. *Yes,* Tyr's smile grew wider, *he will be necessary.*

Much further down the document, past the name of the Rogue killed in Harlowton, another name stood out to him. Luana Ford. Daughter of active service Army General Mason Ford. *Military would be amazing,* Tyr thought. Someone who knew war, who could battle, who could lead. He needed Mason on his side.

What surprised Tyr most, when he did his usual Google search on the name, was a forum dedicated to uncovering members of the mysterious and hidden Council. Others, like him, found the Rogue records, and many lined up death dates of Rogues with the appearance of new Council members. They discussed pixel heights in images and compared data sets. Both Luana and

Scott showed up as possible matches for current Council members.

Tyr had information on his side.

He only needed an army behind him.

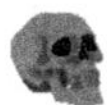

November 18, 2316

Capitol Hill Historic District, District of Columbia, United States of America

Several deep-dive internet searches led Tyr to Rare Book and Special Collections Reading Room in the Thomas Jefferson building as a part of the Library of Congress. The building boasted the largest collection of books from other countries, and he hoped to find something useful about Elementōrum Patriam among their collection.

Tyr used part of the money from the Council to fund his trip to the capitol. Before he left, he tried stopping by the Hopi reservation to speak with Series' parents, but they weren't persuaded to his cause. He decided the best option would be to focus on other parents instead of hanging around. Tyr still needed information on the weaknesses of the elementalist race. So, he made it a priority to gather information first to help persuade the likes of Ryan and Mason to join him. The more he could give Ryan regarding the biological make-up of the elementalists meant Tyr might have a stronger case in destroying the genetic mutation.

He did his duty to put out feelers in online forums to look for others with a similar mindset. He carefully used a Virtual Private Network (VPN) to bury his IP address behind further walls. Tyr didn't have much success finding others in the first few days, and he tried not to be disappointed. He had to be patient, and cautious, and think through every process. His heart didn't want him to move slowly, though. Tyr wanted his daughter back in his arms.

When he arrived in D.C., he forwent the immediate trip to the library. The plane landed later than expected, and he wouldn't have enough time to explore the archives like he wanted. Instead, he checked into his hotel, ate dinner, and planned what he would tackle the next day.

In the morning, Tyr walked to the library and entered the main building. After receiving his official keycard and badge to access all three buildings, Tyr headed to the second floor for the Rare Books collection. An associate of the library helped him find the information he needed, and he sat in the reading room, perusing old copies of books under direct supervision. Some of them were quite old, and he had to handle them with special gloves to help maintain their condition.

He moved through the pile, slowly and deliberately taking his time with each title. The associate didn't mind his pace. The librarian told him they received a lot of interest in elementalist texts since little information escaped their country.

Many of the first books Tyr explored included fictional books written by elementalist authors. He moved quickly through those narratives to the histories. The associate had a coworker return the discarded texts and bring more historical records for exploration after Tyr explained and narrowed his genre.

While he found the books about experiments on elementalists fascinating, they mostly discussed the reason behind the mutation and the extent of their powers. Tyr set aside a few of the scholarly articles detailing weaknesses in bodily function. The strange reaction they had to alcohol intrigued him. When he finally reached the histories, he found a collection of recent historical events, but nothing stood out as noteworthy.

Some factoid books included interviews with elementalists which weren't what he wanted. All the interviews portrayed the elementalists as victims or typical characters he saw on Earth's surface. Another book detailed wars between humans and elementalists, same old information he studied in school. The other librarian returned from the shelves with a new stack of books carefully organized on a cart to keep them safe during transportation.

A book with a blue velvet cover stood out. Tyr lifted a gloved hand and reached for it first. He examined the table of contents and noticed how it drastically differed from the other works. He carefully flipped the pages and read the sections of interest. A smile grew on Tyr's face. It was the exact book he needed.

He carefully closed the cover and held it up to the librarian. "Is there a place where I can copy pages?"

The librarian gently removed it from his hands. "Of course, we have a Duplication Services department which will handle any copies you need. It's in the John Adams building on the first floor. I'll write you a slip for the copies you need. It will take up to a week to get copies to you."

"Thank you." Tyr pushed a few of the scholarly articles across the table. "These as well, if you wouldn't mind."

The librarian smiled. "Of course, not. Is there anything else I can help you with today, sir?"

"You've been a great help," Tyr complimented. He took the copy slip from the worker and followed the instructions to a tunnel system under the ground floor where he could access the John Adams building without leaving the facility.

At the top of the stairs to the first floor, he saw a large fishbowl-like room with DUPLICATION SERVICES lettered in light gray across the doors just above CUSTOMER SERVICE. A few people waited in line ahead of him. Each person received a tablet to fill out their contact information, including a mailing address. Tyr stared at that box for a long while. He didn't have a house, and he wouldn't stay in D.C. long enough for the papers to be mailed to his hotel.

Tyr supposed a change of plans wouldn't foul him up too much. He could remain in D.C. until he received the paperwork, then move on to somewhere else. He could spend the down time waiting looking into more information online, tracking down Ryan and Mason, and deciding how he would approach retrieving Charlotte.

He had time to kill. The elementalists paid him a lot more than he thought he would receive.

Tyr handed in the appropriate paperwork and left the building. Just outside the doors, he stopped. An uncomfortable chill bled down his spine.

The door slammed into him hard from behind. The person exiting apologized profusely for hitting him. Tyr waved it off. He assured them it was bound to happen. He carefully moved away and sat on the ledge supporting the flower beds. He clasped his hands and leaned forward where his elbows rested on his knees. Slowly, the information he read in the library swam to the forefront of his memory.

The blue book he requested copies of mentioned nine elements, not seven. A rise and decline in population with no correlation.

Two of the elements were extinct.

Except.

He remembered the day the Council took his daughter more clearly than any other memory. He counted each red cloak. Eight. Not seven. Eight.

Tyr grit his teeth.

The rise of the lesser elements. The Council found one of them.

September 26, 2290

Greenville, Greenville County, South Carolina, United States of America

Ryan Everton hated being the responsible one in his work group. They often decided to network. At a bar. Ryan made the decision a few years previously to stop drinking alcohol. His coworkers viewed it as the perfect opportunity to always have a designated driver.

He contemplated quitting his job several times that night, and every time they dragged him to the same bar. The main problem with the simple solution: he could not afford to live for a couple of weeks without pay. Ryan needed his job.

Instead of participating in bar games with his coworkers, he attempted to keep his head down at the bar while sipping his water. He played a game on his phone to pass the time. The crack of pool balls had him looking over his shoulders to see the coworkers starting another round. He told them three rounds previously to finish their game, so he could drive them home. It might've been a Friday night, but he desperately wanted to sleep and shake off the work week.

The clock above the bar approached eleven thirty. Ryan contemplated leaving them to find their own way home. He twirled his car keys on his pointer finger and finished his glass. He stood and waved for the bartender to relay his intentions to one other responsible person.

A woman slid onto the stool next to him and adjusted her skinny jeans.

Her black leather jacket crinkled as she leaned forward to signal for a drink. She tugged off her matching fingerless gloves and set them on the counter.

"You managed to make it in this week, Adelyn?" the bartender called from the other end of the bar. She put another pint of beer on the counter for one of Ryan's coworkers.

"You know we can't stay away, Artie." She gave the woman a wide grin.

"Well, tell your friends to not take over the dart board, will you? I like your enthusiasm, but I do have other customers who come to get a little inebriated."

Adelyn laughed. "Please, your *inebriated* customers couldn't beat us sober. At least drinking gives them liquid courage."

"Too right you are." She filled several glasses with water. "I'll bring yours once I've served your friends."

"Thanks, Artie." Adelyn spun on her barstool. Her eyes met Ryan's, and he quickly pretended like he hadn't been watching her. She bit the corner of her lip. "Were you leaving?"

He pointed half-heartedly to the group at the pool table. "I'm supposed to wait for them to finish their game." He jingled his car keys as he tucked them into his palm. "Designated driver."

"Ah." She glanced over her shoulder. His coworkers started another game of pool. "It doesn't look like they really plan on finishing their game."

Ryan sunk back to the stool. "Yeah. I don't think they do."

Artie dropped off a glass of water for Adelyn.

"What brought you here to drink water?" He pointed to her glass.

"It's just something we do every Friday." Adelyn shrugged. "I volunteer with BACA—Bikers Against Child Abuse—and we have a tradition of coming to the bar on Friday and partying. We don't drink because we have to drive our bikes home safely, but it's fun."

Ryan's eyes trailed around the bar and spotted the rest of the bikers challenging his coworkers to a friendly game of pool, and darts. "How come you aren't with them?"

Adelyn leaned in a little closer. "I saw someone attractive at the bar."

Ryan inspected the patrons around the counter. He wouldn't say he found any of them particularly attractive.

She sighed. "He's wearing elbow patches and looks a lot like a professor." She tugged at the mustard yellow patches on his brown tweed suit jacket.

"Me?" Ryan asked.

She put out a hand, and he took it hesitantly. "I'm Adelyn. I work as a waitress for my day job. You?"

"I'm a biologist, agriculture specialist. I mainly focus on improving produce." He ran his tongue over his teeth. "Ryan, by the way."

"Nice to meet you, Ryan." She repeated his name with a sultry undertone. "Have you ever worked with genes that make," she whispered the last word, "elementalists?"

He shook his head. "I don't work with the genome on humans or elementalists. They're too complex—difficult to pinpoint."

Adelyn hummed.

"What's it like riding a motorcycle?" Ryan blurted.

Adelyn lifted her keys in front of his face. "Do you want to find out?"

"What about my coworkers?"

She slid the gloves back into place and tossed the keys to him. Ryan barely managed to catch them. She said, "I think they can find their own way home."

Ryan grinned and followed her out of the bar. "You aren't expecting me to drive, are you?"

December 15, 2316
Key West, Monroe County, Florida, United States of America

"Tall Caramel Macchiato!" Ryan Everton set the to-go cup on the end of the counter.

Late October filled the coffee shop with more pumpkin-based flavors and floods of tourists—the busy rushes showcased how few employees they had. The customer who collected their drink became a more recent regular of the shop. At first, Ryan labeled the man a tourist, like almost every other person in town who happened to stay close by. Once his stay bordered on long vacation and recent move to the city, Ryan figured he could plan on the customer's arrival. He had his coffee ready to go for when he walked into the shop—no questions asked.

That morning, when the man approached the counter, he stated the price and started to fill the coffee cup almost immediately. The visitor looked impressed and forked over payment. He took his eight o'clock coffee and found his usual seat near the front window where he would remain until about eight-thirty.

Ryan moved to Key West about three months after his daughter's death. The busy city made it easy for him to get lost in the crowd and shuffle. As such, no one nosed into anyone's business because, even for the locals, it was nearly impossible to tell who visited most days. The job market boomed in the area. A good thing about being busy. Ryan didn't plan on being a barista, but the job got him away from his thoughts. He liked the challenge of it.

Over the years in the city, he worked his way up the chain and became an assistant manager for the privately owned coffee shop. Ryan often took responsibility to open or close and balance books in the back. The owners put him in charge if they took a vacation.

The shop didn't stop their range of products at coffee. They sold a variety of confectionaries requiring a team of bakers in the early morning. Once the first rush finished, the cooks focused on sandwiches for lunch before they were released to go home. At night, they offered their leftover desserts and sandwiches for late night coffee drinkers and dates. Anything left at closing time, sometime around seven, would be gathered by the closing manager and donated to the local homeless shelter. It provided them with sweet treats most days and Ryan grew familiar with the workers at the shelters and the things they liked in their donations.

Occasionally, they'd serve an extra plate for him; he would sit with the kitchen staff and talk about their workday. They never asked or shared anything personal unless the person felt comfortable with it.

He liked life in Key West.

Ryan faced away from the customers to hide his yawn. He set a cup of coffee to drip while he headed into the back to collect the freshly baked food and arrange it for display. The lack of customers disappointed him. The quiet allowed him too much time to think. He became more nostalgic as years passed.

He yawned a second time as he fixed a plate of brownies and remembered how much his son liked baking with his little sister. They would make some of the most horrid messes, but he knew in hindsight, every one of them would be worth it. At home, he had a stack of bills still charging him for services rendered while Melissa suffered in the hospital from pneumonia.

Ryan received a lot of bad luck in his life.

Directly after receiving the news that his wife Adelyn died in a motorcycle accident, the elementalists collected his son, Scott. He made a lot of mistakes the night they took him. He yelled. Screamed. Attacked his son. Told Scott he wasn't his son. Ryan regretted it—especially knowing his son would be killed by the same people who took him away a few short days after Melissa. It frustrated him to know he lost everyone and would pay for it until the day he died.

If Ryan picked a time of day he hated working, it would be the night shift. Most couples came in late at night for sips of sugary and watered-down coffee with sweet cakes. Every one of them would whisper fantasies to each other about a "happily ever after". An ending that would never exist in their world, but sappy chumps still bought into it.

Despite all his troubles, Ryan had a hard time saying who he disliked more. A lot of things about the elementalists caused issues and left him a lonely man—but they couldn't be blamed for his wife's or daughter's deaths. He held partial responsibility for Melissa's, and it cut him to the core every day. If he had one goal, he wanted to bring the world to the attention of how easily the elementalists hurt those they sought to protect. They stole children away, and if deemed unsuitable, they killed them. He wanted to highlight their practices and have them change. He couldn't start a revolution, and he didn't want to try.

December 17, 2316

Tyr calculated every step cautiously. His social media presence had to be cleansed every few days to keep the trail clean. He changed his IP address frequently. He'd found a network of other people who disliked the elementalists, and it gave him an in to the community. While none of them expressed more than outward dislike of policies, practices, and their general existence. Tyr could see the seeds of destruction brewing in the back of their thoughts. In the darkest recesses of their minds. The parts they tried to keep hidden for the sake of remaining safe.

Except, Tyr knew better. He wasn't afraid to start a movement. There were others out there who would think along the same lines as him—he might even twist his desires a bit to bring in more people. There were a few he trusted. Trusted enough to keep in close contact with them. They established their own local factions.

It was a start.

Phase two currently worked behind the counter. While his arrival in Key West was more of a fluke, the happy accident of seeing RYAN EVERTON on the nametag sent a thrill through his stomach. While the elementalists didn't have an easily accessible record of every current person on their census—the Rogue records were invaluable. Tyr memorized almost every name on that list, so he could track their history. If they came from the surface, he wanted to find their families.

Ryan Everton matched the records of a death in 2310—a death registered to Scott Ryan Everton. The name was too close for it to be a coincidence. A return to the coffee shop and a few hours of digging confirmed the relationship. Therefore, Tyr stayed in Key West instead of moving on like he originally planned.

Ryan used to work in a government facility helping genetically modify produce. He had experience working with the sciences. The exact set of skills he needed to face off with the elementalists. Tyr wanted a biological weapon.

A couple of days previous, Ryan surprised him by immediately knowing his order when he walked into the shop. He grinned over the lip of his coffee cup. The unintentional part of his plan worked better than he expected. Ryan knew him.

Getting Ryan to help him would be made all the easier by the semblance of a relationship between them.

Tyr pushed away from the table where he worked with his laptop, and Ryan glanced over to see if he would need to clean the table between drinks. Instead, he left his things by the window and joined the queue to buy another drink. He graciously let a mother/daughter pair go in front of him when they walked in the door a moment after him.

"It's no trouble for us to wait," the mother tried to apologize, a bit flustered.

"And none for me at all. I'll be here for a few more hours. I'm working on a project." He pointed to the electronics.

"Alright." She accepted the position and discussed what drinks they wanted to try with her daughter. For the holidays, the café added a few new options to the menu.

Tyr inspected the drinks cautiously, but none of them really nipped at his palate.

"Same thing as this morning?" Ryan's fingers hovered over the screen uncertainly.

"If you would, thank you."

Tyr tapped his phone against the payment tower. Ryan started to turn away to help prepare drinks, but the former's voice stopped him.

"I don't mean to intrude, but I wondered if you had a child taken by the elementalists." Tyr didn't speak loudly, but a few other people looked up from their drinks anyway with uneasy expressions.

Ryan licked his lips, his mouth suddenly dry. "I did. A long time ago."

"I'm sorry to bring it up—but I just lost my daughter to them recently. I thought it might help to talk to someone with a similar experience."

He didn't respond for enough time that Tyr assumed Ryan wasn't interested. Tyr dropped his shoulders and shuffled down the glass to the pickup area.

"I get off in a couple hours," Ryan said. "We can talk then."

Tyr bit his tongue to keep the smile from bleeding onto his lips. The pain helped choke his tone. "Thank you."

"What is it you want from me other than a listening ear?" Ryan slid into the chair across from Tyr with a late lunch. He opened the wrapping and lifted the sandwich.

"I want to destroy the elementalist mutation."

Ryan's mouth hovered open. He leaned away from the meal and set it on the protective wrapping. "I'm not interested in helping with that kind of thing."

"Understandable." Tyr closed his laptop. "It really is a lofty and unachievable goal. I obviously can't do something like that." He waved his hand through the air. "Not every want in life can be fulfilled."

Ryan narrowed his eyes but determined it was safe enough to enjoy his sandwich before excusing himself and going home for the evening. "I'm sorry to hear about your loss. It is hard when they kill your child."

Tyr's lips thinned. "I'm sorry. I didn't make myself clear before. My daughter is still alive."

Ryan's eyes flickered across the stiff posture. He looked more like a man in denial—like the first few years after they informed him of Scott's death. He couldn't tell if his statement held any truth, so he chose not to say anything.

"I've found a few online forums where other parents also want to see their children—no news is good news, I think. It's just different to meeting someone in person."

"Well," Ryan shoved the last bite into his mouth. "You're S.O.L. with me. I've lost both my children. If yours is still alive, you'd be better speaking with someone who still has hope." He pushed away from the table and took a step toward the trash.

"How did you feel when they first took Scott?"

Ryan's brows crinkled together. "How did you—"

"I've been trying to track records in Elementōrum Patriam. I remember seeing your son's name on the death registry."

"And you dug a little to find out he's my son?"

Tyr nodded. "The name was too similar. I didn't think it was a coincidence."

"He was labeled a Rogue. We all know there's a law in place to kill Rogues.

He was a danger to everyone. It's better that he's dead." Ryan took another step away from the table, his knuckles white as he gripped the tray.

"If you could alter the gene that causes elementalists in the first place, would you do it?" Tyr slid his finger around the edge of the lid on his coffee.

"I don't have the knowledge required to consider such a ludicrous idea." Ryan stood frozen in the nearly empty café.

"I think you do. You used to bioengineer vegetables."

"A human genome is completely different—we still don't have a full idea of it. There is no scope we can understand to say what causes this mutation than any other mutation during the meiosis phases." He shook his head and returned his tray to the pedestal by the door. "I don't know what you're after, but you're never going to find the solution. You won't get what you want."

"I think I will." Tyr stood behind him, his steps deathly quiet, and it took everything in Ryan's power not to cringe away. The man slid a business card into the pocket of his uniform button up. "I could free you of your guilt and debt."

Tyr returned to his seat and unlocked the laptop. Ryan pushed open the door harder than necessary and tried not to run.

December 27, 2316

Ryan raised a hesitant hand to the apartment door and knocked. He heard a faint shuffling inside and nearly ran for it. However, the door opened in the next moment, and Tyr gave him a warm smile.

"Welcome, Ryan." He opened the door wide and gestured for him to come in. "Can I get you anything to drink?"

"Not currently." He hesitated over the threshold but stepped in and took a seat on the couch. He didn't lean back, and he stayed right on the edge. "What did you mean about my guilt and debt?"

Tyr did his best to keep a neutral expression. He licked his lips as he thought of the correct way to spin his intentions. "When the mutations took my daughter, they gave me a card with quite the sum of money on it. It's supposed to help ease the burden of removing her—as well as the cost to repair the house she burned down. However, I want to put it to better use. I could use that money to pay off the last of the medical debt you have."

"I assume you want something in exchange for such a generous gift." Ryan crossed his arms.

No good, the voice in Tyr's head hissed, *he's closing himself off.*

"I suppose," Tyr chewed the words carefully in his mouth. "It's nothing as big. I would happily exchange the money for some knowledge and opinions on things I'm seeing in online forums."

"Right, the forums that are leading you to want to destroy the elementalists."

"I already said that is a vain desire." Tyr waved a hand in front of his face. "Of course, plenty of people have ideas online about how to do it. Poison is the most popular idea."

"Poison?" Ryan laughed. "They'd never fall to something as simple as that."

"Oh?" Tyr sat in the chair at the desk. "I thought they had some interesting ideas. Many people know the mutations can't handle any strength of liquor or smoking. Contaminate their water supplies, and the whole people are done for."

Ryan shook his head. "It'd never work. They have strict by laws that do not allow for any dangerous substance to enter their country. Every person is searched, and the only area humans are allowed to visit is the visitors' center in the City of Joy. Even if you managed to break past their security, they're far more powerful than you or I. Not a single human would make it ten paces before they found themselves in jail."

"You know a lot about their country." Tyr tilted his head and suppressed a quirk in the corner of his mouth.

"I, too, once sought to go there—to see my son again. It was not to be. Just the same as your plans."

"If not poison, how would you do it?"

"Kill them?" Ryan's brows shot up his forehead. "I already told you. I have no intention of doing so. I never have."

"I see." Tyr turned the computer screen to face Ryan where he had a video pulled up. "I saw this reported in the news recently. A candidate running for government office—this is becoming the prevailing idea, it seems."

He pressed play on the video, and Ryan watched as an American politician pushed for more laws affecting elementalist populations living in their country. He called them "aliens" and "freeloaders" of the American system.

"They vitiate, even among us." Ryan shook his head. "Do you think politics will sway me to your ideals?"

"There's a theory online, from those who are doing some back alley digging." Tyr closed the video and opened a new screen. "There are people tracking the Council's moves—they try to figure out all they can about them. Some of them gain help from elementalists in the country who aren't quite satisfied with how their government is formed."

"What does this have to do with me?"

Tyr made the page a little bigger before revealing it to Ryan. "There are some who propose that your son is a member of the Council."

"That's a nice little trick." He felt ill. "A great appeal to emotions, but I know he's dead. I felt it when I received the news. I'd appreciate it if you didn't try and use my dead children to sway me to your beliefs."

Tyr handed him a stack of papers, and he begrudgingly took them. "At least read through the data—it didn't come from me. I'm not as skilled as the ones who proposed this." Several other names accompanied the complex chart. "Come back in a few days if you're interested in helping me. I'll erase your debt, and we'll both go on our way. There's a movement rising around the world—you're either with us or against us."

CHAPTER TEN
Desuetude

October 30, 2298

Russia Sector, City of Vasha, Elementōrum Patriam

Hans opened the front door when the bell rang. He loved to run out into the front yard and play in the street, much to his parents' dismay. The child safety door handle covers didn't stop him because he figured them out easily. A member of the retrieval team, identified by the neutral cream jumpsuits, stood on their front porch. His father moved to intercept the man. He provided a slight bow before asking how he could help them.

"Is your son Maxim home?"

"Go get your brother," Hans' father, Yerik, commanded in Russian.

Hans ran up the stairs to find his older brother and sister in the study reading together. Maxim's wiry frame laid prostrate in the windowed reading nook wearing a thin graphic t-shirt and a pair of shorts. He kicked his bare feet above Odessa's head. She sat on the floor, still in her pajamas, with her legs crossed and tugging at a curly blonde tress. In her other hand, she held the book in a streak of morning light pressed across the floor. They argued over semantics, but Hans' appearance interrupted them. Matching sets of blue eyes landed on him.

"The retrieval team is asking for Maxim," Hans relayed.

The three siblings quickly vacated the room and joined their parents at the front door.

"What's going on?" Maxim asked.

"If you'll please come with me." The man gestured for him to step outside the house. He obeyed, but he stopped as soon as he stood on the porch.

"No," he turned to the stranger, "you can't do this."

"You are an Un, Maxim. You will be transferred to your new home." The man wrapped their hand around Maxim's upper arm and pulled.

"You can't." He tried to pull away. The grip didn't relent. He looked back at his family. "Father, you can't let them do this. I'm your son."

They tugged harder. Maxim lashed out. A wave of rock encased Maxim's middle, and they lifted Hans' brother into the air.

"I'm your son!" Maxim yelled at the figures in the doorway of his house. Others on the street peered out their windows and doors to watch the events.

"You are not our son," Yerik whispered.

"Please don't do this." His words echoed between the houses in Russian.

The retrieval team member lifted him into a large jail pod waiting in the middle of the street. Three other people, already on board, sat with their heads bowed.

"*Mama!*" Maxim pressed his face against the open window. He cursed violently. "*Otets!*"

The truck pulled out of the street and drove northwest to the City of the Uns.

December 2, 2298
Border between City of Vasha and City of the Uns, Elementōrum Patriam

"Maxim?" Hans called through the fence separating the Uns from the rest of Elementōrum Patriam. His fingers pressed into the screen of the invisi-fence and the shadow imprint of diamonds cast across the palm of his hand.

Maxim aged impossibly in the first few months. He didn't look eleven. He stood on the edge of the street in Uns and stared at the snow falling in Diana behind Hans. No snow reached their desert. Another punishment from the Council's laws.

"Hans." Maxim stepped closer to the fence. While his blue eyes focused on the child, his stiff posture startled Hans. He leaned away from the fence—from Hans.

Hans' fingers pressed harder against the cold material and turned red at the tips. Maxim lifted his left hand and reached out to touch his brother's fingers, but he stopped before he touched the wall. Hans could see the outline of the same diamonds shadowed on him burned into his brother's palm. He trailed the scars to their end on his upper arm. Hans' brow furrowed, and he locked eyes with Maxim. Maxim dropped his hand.

"Are you going to come back home?"

"You know I can't." Maxim broke their staring contest and tipped his head back. He carded his scarred hand through his dark hair. His eyes trailed the path of a snowflake until it connected with the ground. "I want you to promise me something, Hans."

He nodded.

"Whatever happens, don't become like your big brother, okay?" He took a deep breath. "If you must come to the Uns, don't take their deal. It's better to be homeless. I want you to be an elementalist, though. I want you to have a better life. You need to be a leader and make things better for everyone. *Don't follow blindly.*"

"What do you mean?"

"Promise me." Maxim placed his unscarred hand against the fence. Hans watched the flesh bubble and burn.

He choked on tears. "I promise."

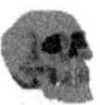

January 5, 2317
City of the Uns, Elementōrum Patriam

Maxim Aliyev laid low next to a supply warehouse. Inside: the newest shipment from the Ls, a nickname they gave the elementalists. The Uns fended for themselves behind the electric invisi-fence on Elementōrum Patriam. They had to make their own name. The Ls provided very little for the lower ranking Uns. It was why many Uns turned to a life of crime, including Maxim.

He watched a tumbleweed jump its way down the street of the barren wasteland and collide with the desert sage. Dirt stung his eye. He didn't lift a hand to rub it away. Maxim waited for the signal.

He had a full day of plans with the underground illegal group. Once he returned from the raid, with the others in his smaller party, he would help categorize their supplies before they tried to take the capitol. Exhausted from the abuse, not only from their lower form of government but from the Ls, they wanted to be free. He'd be one of the main forces leading the riot and uprising against the capitol building in Central. They had to find a way out of the city.

Maxim made to move to the next location but stopped when he heard the telltale sound of feet marching on the dusty road. He froze and prayed he hid well enough between the sage brush. Through the cracks in the branches, he watched as several law enforcement officials marched past. Maxim held his breath to be on the safe side; he thanked his genetics for his tanned skin. It helped him blend in with the pale color of the dirt.

The tank top, stained and smudged with dirt, had rips in several places. He picked a sliver out of the material near his left pectoral before he scooted across the ground. His tan cargo shorts neared the same color as his shirt. Maxim pushed himself into a kneeling position and brushed away what dirt he could before he pulled the Glock style Lūminis Sclopētum from his waistband.

The weapons were a lucky find. Only the military had access to weapons—not even the police force used them. The people had no need for weapons. The underground found the crate mixed in with the usual supplies for the Uns during one of their warehouse raids. At the time, Maxim figured it was a mistake.

He shuffled to the corner of the warehouse and peered around it. Another member of his recovery team laid low a few feet in front of Maxim, eyes glued to the sky, waiting for the signal. Maxim glanced up and prayed it would come soon. They operated on a time crunch to get in and out before the capitol attack.

He heard a pop and recognized the start signal. The flare shot between him and the other team members. It sizzled across the ground with a similar sound to a rattlesnake before it stopped at Maxim's feet and nearly set the brush on fire. He stomped out the flame and moved. The other members of his team joined him, and they surrounded the small service door instead of the main roll up one.

Maxim stood off to the side as Qasim approached and checked the locked door. The quickest way to open the door would be to dismantle the lock. He pulled out a bastard file, with a flat head screwdriver style tip, and took the screws out until he could pull half of the doorknob unit off. Qasim laid the metalwork to the side while he used the file to remove the locking mechanism pieces themselves.

The knob clattered to the floor on the other side, and Qasim released the lock entirely. With a little pressure, the door swung open, and they peered inside cautiously. Maxim held out his hand and one of the others in his group put a can of black spray paint in it. He slid around the door and did his best to move in the blind spots of the camera before it turned to face the door. He reached up and covered his face with his other arm while he colored the lens out.

The group dispersed immediately among the stacks of food and utilities. They stuffed as much of it as they could into their backpacks, pockets, jackets, and trash bags. Maxim knew they had five minutes tops to collect what they needed and get out before the police arrived on the scene. One good thing about their current government, it kept a sharp eye on the people in case of any wrongdoing.

The holler of sirens in the distance signaled the end of their mission. They tied off bags and zipped zippers before they darted into the desert. The police force, while comprised of other Uns, received their supplies from the Ls. The hover cars veered off the path of the road and tore through the brush after the rebels. Traveling on foot, while inferior to a car, allowed them to hide easier. They also knew the lay of the land in ways the government officials didn't. Maxim split from his group, and he saw them branch off on their own paths.

His feet pounded across the ground, and he heard the officers trailing them shout as the rebels burst onto another exterior city street. He followed the familiar paths until he reached the back-alley to their underground headquarters. He reached the door at the same time as most of his teammates, and they entered the space together.

"You almost led them here, Maxim," a voice chided.

He passed his bag off to the others and let out a low chuckle. Esebelle sat with her arms crossed as she watched him from the main chair instead of the security camera footage behind her. Her bomber jacket crinkled when she shifted and revealed a small strip of skin above her own earth dyed tank top. She pulled her legs onto the chair, and her sweatpants rode up around her ankles.

"And you're supposed to be watching the cameras at the capitol. Or did you forget we're storming them today?" Maxim walked over to the screens. His accent almost vanished after years of not speaking any Russian. "On the other hand, you didn't see the food in the warehouse. You'll thank me after seeing the haul."

"Can't wait to see it—we'll be sending out the signal in about two hours from now." Esebelle had seniority as one of the oldest members of their group. She turned her chair with a loud scrape to the computer system. She typed a few strokes, and the cameras changed position.

Maxim grabbed one of the available chairs and swung it around until he could sit next to his pseudo-friend. "Is it enough to gather everything we planned on?"

Esebelle typed a command into the computer and didn't respond.

Maxim's eyes roved over the screens until it landed on the section connected to the warehouses. "Are you actively communicating with those in the capitol?"

"No ear pieces." She brushed back her dirty brown hair and tapped her ear before she flipped through a couple more cameras.

"What do you need me to help with?" Maxim ran his fingers through his curls and watched another foraging group black out a camera.

Esebelle directed him to his position in the small office space, and they went to work. After an hour, Maxim assigned himself to categorize supplies and make sure they would be ready to go when the signal went off. He created extensive plans on the computer of how they would ration what they had to hold out once the protests began. Two hours later, he sat at the computer, unconfident they would be able to feed the entire uprising for more than a few days.

Maxim watched as rebellion aligned government officials moved into their places in each of the frames. "Everyone is moving—it's almost time to start."

"Start the countdown when everyone is ready," Esebelle commanded.

He flipped through the screens at lightning speed, each image passed through his mind long enough to verify who stood where.

"Countdown initiating, we have thirty seconds."

"Launch codes entering database. Signal is aiming," Esebelle confirmed. "Riots are ready to go, door locks waiting to be engaged."

"Signal in five." Maxim stood and opened the cabinet in the corner. A firework exploded over the main part of the city. He strapped a smuggled rifle style Lūminis Sclopētum to his back. He tossed the same model to Esebelle, and she caught it deftly with one hand. She checked the safety before nodding.

The uprising began.

The Council Chambers, The Academy, Elementōrum Patriam

The Council gathered for lunch in the law room where they worked. Dwayne and Eilene showed Ethan what they did with proposed laws and laws in need of their collective signature because the people voted them into effect when their phones simultaneously flashed blue, and Luana picked hers up first.

"The Uns are reporting riots. They have weapons, and they've taken the city hall building hostage," she reported.

"They've finally risen up against their oppressors." Eilene leveled their leader with a heavy gaze. "Are you going to send us to suppress them—again?"

"I won't be sending you. Hans, Ethan, Scott, I want you to remind them who they're up against."

"Luana—they are our people. We don't want them to live in fear of us," Dwayne argued.

"Then what do you propose we do? Reward them for running rampant and stealing from those who follow the law?" she growled. "They're Uns— they don't have any of our abilities. They're a regeneration. They have no power over us."

Eilene opened her mouth to argue again, but Hans held up his hand.

"We'll take care of it." He stood. "Scott and I will show Ethan how we handle these events."

The other two followed his lead, their unfinished lunches left behind.

Ethan smiled when he saw the updated hooks for their cloaks. Knowing he had a cloak waiting for him with DEATH emblazoned on the wall next to the empty SUPERNATURAL hook gave him hope for the future. It meant he had a place among the Council—future generations would have a known place among the elementalists.

Ethan donned the robes and followed the other two out of the chambers.

In the early hours, students milled around the main hallways and laughed with their friends or used their abilities to joke around and perform small tricks. It ceased as soon as they spotted the three Council members. One of the Air elementalists dropped to the ground. They darted to the edges of the hallway and stood at attention. The students knew whoever wore the cloaks stood as the strongest elementalists in the world. None of them wanted to challenge the Council's power by standing in the way.

"Where do you think they're going?" A girl on the younger side leaned into the other female next to her.

"Hard to say."

Ethan wanted to look around and see if he knew any of the students, but he couldn't turn his head much under the robe or he'd give up the prim and proper expectations of the Council. He focused on following the pattern Hans and Scott made ahead of him as they walked to the front doors. He heard the harried speculations behind them, and one word struck him through the chest. *Rogue.*

What will it be like when we go after my first Rogue? What if I'm required to kill them?

They stepped into the sunshine and Ethan realized he forgot the beauty of the Academy lawn. It spread out in triangle patterns, lined with hedges of flowers, between the marble pathways until it led out to the City of Garden. He took a deep breath of clean, crisp air. He sensed the other two ease—despite what their task would have them do, far from the capitol.

The trio fanned out across the steps and descended in a line. Each of them took their time to take in the sights as they passed maintenance workers. Their path led them past one of the deep pools of water, and the droplets shone like gold when an elementalist burst free and soared into the air. Ethan nearly tripped, and Scott turned to check on him.

"How are we getting there?" Ethan whispered lowly.

"Bullet," Hans supplied with a similar volume.

At the end of the long path, they passed through an archway and over a small bridge into the Academy gardens. The garden portions above the houses swarmed with insects and blossomed flowers Ethan couldn't dream to name. A butterfly with blue wings brushed past his face, and he wished he could take off the hood and protective mask to enjoy the outdoors. He loved the view of the sprawling lawns of the Academy.

Hans put a guiding hand on his arm and kept him on the path to the train station. They waited on the platform, and the others riding the train stood far away from them. The front compartments would be near capacity from nervousness rather than excessive crowds or commuter rush hour.

The train pulled onto the platform and the three stepped into the end compartment. The elementalists already sitting on the train scattered as soon as they saw who boarded. They huddled up together, cramped onto the front end, while the Council took three of the four available seats in one of the back sections.

"Why doesn't, uh, you-know-who like the Uns very much?" Ethan asked.

"Fire has a lot of opinions we don't necessarily agree with. It's easier to take the task she dishes out and complete them our way than it is to fight her on her opinions," Hans said. "I don't agree with her views on the Uns, but it is something we need to address immediately. Taking the job without complaint means I get to solve it the way I want."

"She's strait laced," Scott said.

"What do you mean?"

"She's stuck in her own head and her own ways. Inflexible. Getting her to branch out and understand how our country is multi-cultural is almost impossible. The weirdest part about it is she's been on the Council since she was eight." Scott turned his head to make sure they had no eavesdroppers. Those who dared to look at them immediately dropped their gaze.

"Maybe she was brainwashed by other Council members? If they raised her in this system, she'll stick to what she knows," Ethan suggested.

"That is a likely explanation." Hans shifted in the seat. "Either way, there's certain days and subjects which make her harder to work with. This happens to be one of those times."

"What will we do in City of the Uns?"

"That's dependent on what we observe. Stay behind us as much as possible. If it comes down to it, we'll use scare tactics to make them back off—then we can work on finding a temporary solution."

"And if we can't find one?" Ethan turned his head directly to Hans, and Scott tapped him on the knee, telling him to move back.

Hans shrugged. "We can't make everyone happy. We have to fall back on written policies and work to revise them in the Council."

"Which is hard to do with our favorite person around," Scott said.

"How come no one stands up against her?"

"We try—you saw Water and Life. She only became fiercer and locked down harder on her opinions. We thought, after what happened to you, she might realize her opinions hurt more people than it helps—but a person doesn't change overnight. She needs something more to rattle her, and I don't know that is. I do legitimately want to help her see the country from a different perspective."

"She's blind," Ethan said.

Scott nodded.

The three of them rode the train up past the City of Uns into the City of Ricci. If they stopped in Vasha, they'd have to walk the entire length of the city to reach Central, the Uns capital. The City of Barren also crossed right above Central, but the closest stop put them too far northwest and on the edge of the country.

Hans pointed out the Meeting of Fate to Ethan as they passed. The Meeting of Fate. The only point in the country where four cities met at their border. Uns, Vasha, Yahav, and Ricci.

From the station in City of Ricci, they could hear the riots—though they sounded like a muffled roar. People on the platform looked around curiously for the source of the noise, but when they saw the Council members heading for the Uns, their curiosity dropped.

The southward path brought them to a high fenced border around the city. Ethan inspected it curiously. *A measly invisi-fence can keep the Uns from escaping the city?*

"It's electrocuted—it registers genetic makeup," Scott whispered in his ear.

"Ouch."

The gate into the city opened for them as they approached. Hans returned a small clicker, like a garage door opener, to his pocket. Only certain people would have access to opening the gates. The houses when they first entered the city had no foundation. Most of them consisted of boards leaning on each other like a teepee, while others were lashed together with twine and held up by a single log in each corner. They hardly resembled living spaces.

The structure of the city had nothing. Open dirt fields and tumbleweeds sent the sound of hooves beating against the ground through Ethan's mind for the first time in months. The scorching heat bled through his Council robe. Ethan resisted the urge to tug at it, but he couldn't help panting. Even in January, the Storm elementalists gave them no new weather. From the cracked patterns in the dirt, Ethan would be surprised if it ever rained in City of the Uns.

Even far from the center of Central, people fought and shouted. One Un shoved another out into the street in front of the elementalists, and the man fell to the ground. He jumped up without noticing the passerby and lifted a fist to hit the person who pushed him. Scott's gloved hand wrapped around his wrist.

He froze and turned wide eyes on the three.

The street in front of them fell silent as they noticed their visitors. Scott let go of the man's wrist, and they moved toward the main part of Central. With some of the braver Uns, Hans shifted his foot across the dirt, and small rift opened. The Uns stumbled and fell into the pit only to find themselves sealed in the dirt up to their necks. Scott lifted a few in the air and placed them back on the ground when they begged. The houses closer to the city resembled something more like a house Ethan knew, but most remained rudimentary—they didn't have multiple floors, let alone a solid foundation to build one.

When the side street met the main street in Central, they found the road blocked by an amateur barricade. Hans flicked two of his fingers into the air and the earth under the barricade rocketed into the sky, sending the scrap metal and furniture flying. Scott tamed the airborne debris and lowered it to the ground. The raised earth dropped back to its expected elevation with a flick in the opposite direction from Hans. In the square, shocked faces greeted them. Many stood frozen in the middle of fights.

Rioting signs clattered to the ground and echoed between the buildings while the three Council members made their slow approach. On the side of one building, the head of the Uns government, Marcis Berzins, hung strapped and suspended upside down. The redness in his plump cheeks, and the open-mouthed gape showcased his equal fear of the Council and the rioting Uns. His round belly followed gravity toward the ground and strained at his shirt buttons.

Hans put out his hand, palm up, and lifted it into the air. In the middle of the square, a makeshift platform appeared. The people on top of the stage scrambled off and the Council members ascended it instead. Ethan glanced around the main part of Central and found, to his surprise, a lush oasis with plants, grass, proper houses, and trees.

Is this a result of a corrupt Uns government or are we as a Council not giving them enough support to function?

Scott lifted his own hand and used several gusts of wind to free the man from the side of the building and lower him to the ground, where he promptly vomited.

"What is going on here?" Hans called out with as little accent as he could muster. They needed to disconnect themselves from any locational ties or people might discover their true identities.

"It was the rebellion, sir!" a government worker said with a slight shout heard around the square. "They attacked us suddenly—a firework was all the warning we had. They've been after our storage buildings for weeks, taking what is ours and hoarding it for themselves. Today, they took us on directly."

"This has been going on for weeks, yet you did not contact the Council sooner?" Scott said coolly. He turned to the porky leader on the ground, kneeling by a tree.

"We didn't—we thought—"

"Clearly, you didn't think at all." Hans kept the same tone as Scott. "We're here to settle this dispute. We want to hear from both sides. Will any of you from the rebellion strike us before we can carry out our duty?"

The crowd remained quiet.

"Good—then we can move on to solving this situation."

"I'll stand against you," a woman spoke suddenly from the crowd. The people parted until it gave the Council a clear view of a dirty-haired brunette. She held her Lūminis Sclopētum in a ready to shoot position. She activated the sight with a short whisper of "cōnferō".

The man at her side had his own weapon, but it rested at his side. Hans' breath hitched as he took in the familiar build and facial features of his brother—he took after their father, Yerik. Ethan's gaze snapped between the two as subtly as he could—the Un looked like an older version of Hans. Scott also noted the change in his companion's stature and took a step forward.

"We're the leaders of the rebellion. Your laws are oppressive and don't understand the world we're forced to live in. We're fighting for a normal life," the woman continued.

Hushed murmurs of agreement traveled through the crowd.

"What is your name?" Hans asked.

"Esebelle." She swallowed and straightened her neck into a haughtier position. "It is polite to give your enemy your name."

"We have no names on the Council." Hans' practiced answer was obvious to the crowd. Not one person in the world knew the members. "What would you consider a normal life, Esebelle?"

"Proper shelter, food and water. We live ration to ration on nothing except scraps most days. We steal from the warehouses, so we can have an actual meal."

"She's lying!" Marcis shouted.

"It is not yet your turn to share." Hans' pinkie twitched and a rope of dirt wrapped itself around the man's mouth. His screams of panic and anger muffled drastically.

Ethan glanced around the square and took note of the ornate decorations and sprawling lawns. He lifted a hand and imitated the tone. "Esebelle, who lives in those houses?"

"The government officials."

"I see." He took a step back toward where they came into the city from. "And who lives in these lesser versions?"

"Everyone else—the ones with money have the nicer ones."

Ethan turned to Scott and Hans. "Do you mind if I even the playing field a little?"

He heard a small laugh escape Scott's mouth before he received an affirmative nod from both.

Ethan never used his powers with his own will before. He didn't want to hurt anyone, but he also had same the distinct feeling he could do it. He had to concentrate. Ethan raised his arm and held out his hand toward the lush houses. The people watched, uncertain of what would happen. For a long moment nothing changed, then the grass wilted, the leaves fell from the trees, and the flowers dropped to the dirt, dead. Every house looked the same. Brutalized. Dry. Broken. They matched the desert they lived in.

"What have you done?" one of the politicians shouted.

"I'm sure you can bring it back to life, along with the yards of all the other Uns, too." Ethan grinned under his mask.

Hans touched Ethan's shoulder and pushed him toward Scott. "Are there any neutral parties here today?"

A shaking woman raised her hand.

"Come forward and tell us your name." He waved her to the stage.

Her skin glittered in the sunlight and Ethan wished he could identify her origin deeper than Asian.

"What's your name?"

"Hwangbo Sang-jin."

"Hwangbo Sang-jin-ssi," Scott startled her with the polite formal tone. "What's your reason for being here in Central today?"

"I live in the more southern part of Uns, and I wanted to visit with the government to see about raising my food allotment. I get two single cans of soup daily and a gallon of milk per week. I'm starving because I have no fruits or vegetables—or anything except canned soup. I wanted to talk with them about what it would cost to be provided with better stock."

"And what do our politicians say to this?" Hans removed the mouth guard from Marcis, and he spat out mud.

"You don't send us enough money to supply our people with more," he argued. "You abuse your post and think yourself superior."

Hans produced his phone from his cloak and flipped through the apps. He asked for a piece of paper and wrote a few numbers on it before he did the math alongside the reported population.

"The report I have here shows we send over enough money to your offices on a weekly basis to supply all persons with a livable wage and enough money for groceries based on how many are living in a household—not to mention the money is meant to go toward construction projects such as building new housing for incoming Uns and utilities for all houses and work buildings."

"And what are the numbers you're calculating from?" Marcis sneered as if he had something to hold over the Council.

"Each working class Un is to receive a stipend of one hundred chrono electrum weekly as sub-service for the work they do. Two hundred and fifty chrono electrum is allotted to each single Un in the territory for food. Four hundred to couples, and seven hundred to families. This totals between three-hundred and fifty to eight hundred chrono electrum to each registered family on a weekly basis. The population of the Uns is currently a quarter-million. The stipend for housing and utilities changes week to week and should be reported on Mondays. The last reported housing and utility costs totaled—that is a low number!" Ethan read out from the page over Hans' shoulder.

"Does any of this sound familiar to you?" Scott turned toward the portly man.

"I—I can't say it does." Marcis adjusted his necktie.

"We're supposed to get one hundred a week?" Maxim's jaw dropped. "We're lucky to make seven."

"Marcis, would you care to answer where this money is going?" Hans lifted a hand, ready to attack the man if need be. "Or will we need to pull an audit on all government and government employee spending?"

"It wasn't the Ls," Esebelle whispered. "We were going after the wrong people."

"Uns, it is going to take a while for us to resolve this issue—we will be getting rid of all current government employees and government officials. If you would like the chance to speak for your people, consider campaigning. Remember to submit official forms through to the Council. We appreciate your cooperation," Hans announced with widespread arms. "You are our people too—we do care about your well-being."

"You can't do this!" Marcis grabbed a gun off one of the rebel Uns and ran with it. He pointed it shakily at Ethan. "You can't take this away from me—I won't let you!"

Before any of the officers could get to Marcis, he pulled the trigger. The Lūminis Sagitta sailed through Ethan's head and tore through the fabric of the robe at the back, but his body didn't fall to the ground as everyone expected. He took several slow and steady steps toward Marcis who dropped the gun and shook himself into a puddle.

"That doesn't work on me," Ethan spoke lowly, but the entire square heard him. Whispers passed through the crowd like a wave.

"Marcis, I hope you enjoy isolation," Hans said.

Two officers retrieved the gun from Marcis' side and hauled him to his feet before they handcuffed him and led him away.

"Anyone else like to stand against us?" Scott asked the crowd. Silence answered him. He waved a hand, and the resistance's weapons swept into the air and settled in a neat pile on the stage. He gestured for the officers to collect them for proper disposal. "Clean up this mess—we'll send in a few governmental representatives to assist in your transition this evening."

As they made to leave Central and head back to the Academy, a hand caught Hans' arm and stopped them. They knew of no one brave enough to get closer than a few feet. Hans stared into Maxim's unknowing face and tried to ease his racing heart.

"I just wanted to say thank you for today. We've been struggling for a while, and I know we came off as the bad guys, but we wanted a better life here—since we're stuck here."

"We understand," Scott inserted. He gently pushed Maxim back until he let go of Hans' arm. The latticework of scars glimmered in the sun.

"I'm sorry I had the wrong impression of you Ls," Maxim said.

Ethan smiled under his hood. "Next time we meet, I'm sure it'll be under better circumstances."

Maxim left them alone, and the group of three continued on their journey home. Neither Ethan nor Scott felt in a position to ask Hans about the rebel Un. They could see the family resemblance.

Luana waited for their return in the main entryway, but Hans brushed her off. Shocked by his cold attitude, she received a rundown of events from the other two.

Inside his room, Hans threw himself onto his bed and fought off the tears threatening to fall. Maxim stood in front of him. He reached out and touched his arm. Eighteen years passed since he last saw his brother. He didn't expect their meeting to roil with emotions—ones Maxim wouldn't feel on his end.

Maxim joined the rebellion; he pushed against the elementalists and blamed them for his problems. Hans wished Ethan did more than destroy their prized lawns—but they couldn't kill people without court ruling. Death gave them a quick way out of punishment.

Hans pushed his fingers through his hair to get a grip on the situation, but his mind whirred with unconnected thoughts. Maxim thanked them for their help.

Hans pulled the box of tissues closer to him from the nightstand and blew his nose. He crumpled it up and tossed it onto his bed sheet as the closest trashcan was in the bathroom. He stared at the open sky of a Russian countryside projected on his ceiling and smiled.

A knock at the door interrupted his reminiscing; Luana didn't surprise him when she opened the door. She watched him from inside the doorway.

"You, okay?"

"My brother stood there—in front of me. He talked to me. He thanked us for righting the wrong being done to them."

Luana frowned. "He's not your brother, he's an Un. You three also didn't do as I asked."

"You have no right to say that to me," Hans snapped.

"We're Council members—we need to protect the people. Uns are an entity we have to control."

"We don't need to control them if we're showing them common curtesy." Hans bore down over her. "You have no siblings—you do not get to tell me he is no longer my brother because of a piece of degenerative DNA."

"You were supposed to scare the Uns into submission."

"And leave them on the verge of dying under a corrupt government using the funds for themselves? Luana, you're treating them like they're animals. They're as alive as we are. You can't tell me to abandon my ties to my family."

"When you joined the Council, your family became us. You renounced any ties you have outside of us."

"When I joined the Council, we had to tell my parents I was a Rogue and killed—just like my older sister. My father killed himself in shame. My mother is out there living with no children, no husband. If I told you, I didn't feel upset about them, I would be lying. Maxim's been living day to day on no food because the money we sent to the Uns for years was never going where it was supposed to. The Uns shouldn't be separate from us Luana. They're trapped in a cage because of us." Hans breathed heavy and rapid, the expression on his face thunderous. Luana stumbled away from him. "If I can give even one of my family members a little bit of peace because of my position, then I will be doing something right. Until you've faced one of your family members as a member of the Council, you can't say anything to me. The Council is my family—but Maxim and I are bonded by blood. I'm done playing your little games and continuing to ruin the lives of people who never deserved it in the first place. We are supposed to be helping our people."

"Hans," Luana wanted to calm him down, but she didn't know what to say. If it came to a physical fight, Hans was stronger than her—not only in bulk, but in element.

"Just get out," he said. He turned away from her and clenched his fists.

Luana did as told and leaned against the wall outside his room. She brought her hands up to her face and pressed against her eyes. She didn't know what to do.

CHAPTER ELEVEN
Ruin

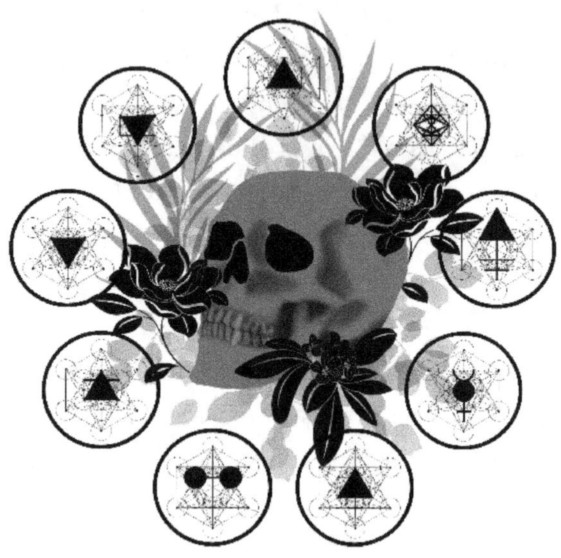

March 5, 2306

Hónghú, Jīngzhōu, Hubei, People's Republic of China

A jeering catcall followed Lí Scarlet as she walked home from school. With another annoyed huff, she increased her pace. The whistles started two years previously when she turned twelve. Although she wouldn't be fourteen until October, her body developed quicker than the other children her age, and it took a toll on her. Scarlet felt more guarded than most teenagers her age, and she made sure to wear baggy sweatshirts to hide herself.

Her black hair fell in waves against her shoulders. Scarlet didn't like spending much time outside, so her skin had a paler quality over her parents. When she did go out, the older pedophilic men tended to try to pick her up. The boys her age wanted her for status; she ignored them. Of all the people in Hongu, she liked the women in their forties and fifties the most, and sometimes sixties. They often told her she looked like the Chinese version of Aphrodite. Scarlet didn't hate the idea—but she preferred the comparison to

Mulan.

The women liked to ask her about her plans. With their short life-spans—humans and elementalists alike barely lived to see a day past sixty—they expected to meet their significant other young and marry before twenty-seven. If they didn't, they'd be an old maid with no children and certainly no grandchildren. Scarlet had no interest in any of it. The women told her stories of times when both groups used to live well into their nineties and hundreds. They often mused how Scarlet might be the first to bring it back.

It didn't take long before the compliments grew old, and Scarlet hated how she looked.

She turned her attention to the horizon and saw storm clouds rolling in. Scarlet cringed and prayed there wouldn't be lightning. Her fear stemmed from a disastrous experience as a child. A lightning strike hit and killed her grandmother. After weeks of unyielding shock, her parents took her to the doctor, and he diagnosed her with mild PTSD and anxiety. Scarlet spent weeks in counseling, and the other students bullied her when they found out. To help comfort her, her parents commissioned one of her close friends for a painting. Her friend painted a gorgeous picture of Scarlet as Mulan.

While the anxiety continued, she mostly recovered—except when lightning came too close. Scarlet's eyes flashed yellow for a moment as the storm approached, but she felt comforted when the clouds dropped the wall of water without clashing. She turned the corner to her street and ducked from building to building with her school bag held over her head to stave off the rain. She glanced down the street to find a silver transportation pod waiting outside her house.

Scarlet stopped on the sidewalk and let the rain pound on her skin. Each drop echoed a rising drumbeat of panic in her veins. She continued down the walkway until she stood in front of her house. Two figures in military attire sat in the main room, and she swallowed hard. Scarlet darted past the main fence to the front door. She prayed she could slip past the living room without her family noticing, but her mother stepped out to visit the restroom when she slipped off her shoes.

"Zhū Hóng, you're home." Her mother smiled, but no genuine emotion showed. "You're all wet. I'll get you a towel."

She turned stiffly away from her daughter, and Scarlet had the sneaking suspicion her mother wouldn't be as fond of her anymore. She ran a hand through her hair and tried wringing some of the excess water from the strands. When her mother returned with a towel, she took the fabric and quickly dried the rest of her body from the rain.

"We have guests. I expect you to come meet with them when you're dry." Zhang Fei Hong, a beautiful woman with the same shade of black hair as her daughter, returned to the living room. Scarlet hung her bag on the hook by the door and tried to dry some of the water from the fabric so it wouldn't drip. She hung the towel on top of the bag strap and put on her slippers before stepping up into the rest of the house. Scarlet entered the first room on her left and immediately fell into a bow from her shoulders. The representatives stood and nodded their heads in acknowledgement. They wore large red patches on the sleeve of their military uniform that advertised their alignment with the Council and Elementōrum Patriam.

"Hello esteemed representatives, I am Lí Zhū Hóng," Scarlet greeted.

"Miss Lí, it's a pleasure to meet you."

She appreciated that they spoke Mandarin.

"I'm sure you know why we're here today."

"You think I am an elementalist," Scarlet said.

"We do not think, Miss Lí. We've come to collect you for your education at the Academy," one representative said.

"We'll give you time to pack what you might need. Keep in mind, we provide all necessary technology and study materials for you." The other representative gave a respectful bow at the shoulders.

Scarlet closed her eyes. When she opened them, the representatives sat and sipped the tea her mother served. She headed out of the room and up the stairs to her bedroom—the third door on the right. She pulled the outfits out of her closet, disposed of her damp school uniform, and shoved the things she needed into an available duffle. Scarlet looked at the ceiling and examined the Mulan painting above her bed. She climbed onto the furniture and pulled the painting down before she safely tucked it away in a poster tube.

With the duffle, tube, and stiff pillow she loved, Scarlet convinced herself she could leave her childhood home.

The representatives moved to the foot of the stairs by the time she finished packing. They immediately replaced their guest slippers on the step before walking out the front door, and Scarlet started to follow them when her mother's voice stopped her. Fei Hong and her husband, Wang Lei, stood in the doorway of the living room.

"Zhū Hóng, we will miss you."

Scarlet nodded stiffly. "I'll be fine, Āmā."

She walked out of the house.

Scarlet pressed her face against the cool glass of the transportation pod; the representatives of the elementalists sat quietly—their attempt to make the event less painful. She sighed and watched the crowded streets, shops, and skyscrapers slip away. They turned into a wide expanse of ocean. Her eyes slid closed

Scarlet awoke hours later from a peaceful sleep to the sound of a crinkling wrapper. The representatives shared pre-prepared food and spoke in low whispers. She recognized it as English, but she couldn't pick up on what they said. When she saw the salad, her hand flew out for some. They handed her a plate, and she thanked them. When she looked outside, a strip of something winked in and out of view on the horizon.

"What is that?" she asked.

"America, it'll be another three hours before we reach the Academy. You can sleep some more if you'd like."

Scarlet nodded and pushed another lettuce leaf into her mouth. The Council members passed her a can, and she looked at it suspiciously. She could make out the word *BEER* imprinted on the front with another word she didn't recognize.

"Is this alcohol?"

The pair looked at her in surprise.

"Of course not, alcohol is a human enjoyment, not elementalist; this is a soda known as Root Beer."

"Elementalists cannot consume alcohol, or they will die."

"Does someone kill them?" Scarlet turned the can and popped the tab on top.

"No, the alcohol will."

"Why is our body not tolerant of the same things humans are?"

"Alcohol does destroy the human body, but at a much slower rate. Elementalists are a more evolved form of humans. We come from various genetic mutations in the human body which have existed since humans gained a form themselves. We have more tolerance for certain diseases and can often cure ourselves, but others are much more destructive to us than they are to humans. Whether either has built up a certain immunity toward it is undefined as we are not willing to put up subjects for testing of hypothesis."

The pod turned sharply as it prepared for its vertical ascent into Elementōrum Patriam. They flew over the west side of the country, and Scarlet examined the interworking of rivers and forest across the land. The Academy caught her attention, and she pressed her fingers to the glass. She ached to touch the city. The pod descended to the parking garage and waited for its passengers to exit when it arrived at the main doors.

"Welcome back," a few of the workers greeted quietly in English.

They stepped through the double doors where a waiting line of elementalists stood in a hallway lined with huge windows.

"Shannon, will you please escort Miss Lí to the check in for new elementalists studying at the academy?"

"Of course." Her skin, a lovely dark brown, sparkled; her bright blue eyes and styled black hair made her angelic in the sun. "Come with me, Miss Lí."

Within the blink of an eye, they whisked Scarlet away.

January 1, 2311

The Council Chambers, The Academy, Elementōrum Patriam

The first day Scarlet spent as a Council member immersed her headfirst in her duties. The Council members with seniority requested she help oversee the laws and bills portion of the government because they wanted her input. Despite giving her own personal feelings regarding the information presented, she didn't feel like she did much during the day.

Her first few hours working side by side with Luana made her realize the woman had a superiority complex no one on the Council acknowledged. Several arguments led to looping circles and no progression; Scarlet gave up and went quiet for the duration of the shift. It allowed her more time to examine her surroundings and become familiar with the Council chambers.

At the time she accepted the position, only three of the Council members from 2317 served with her. The others close to her age, Hans and Scott, told her Luana served with the Council the longest; she saw the evidence in her attitude and the way she took control of the work on a particularly cloudy morning.

Hans sat in the room with them and watched Luana instead of inputting his own opinions. Scarlet let a small giggle escape and ended up being scolded by Luana for not listening to the presentation. She rolled her eyes once Luana looked away and caught Hans' curious gaze. Scarlet did her best to give a non-verbal communication to show she knew he liked Luana romantically, but he didn't seem to understand the gesture.

Once Luana's speech ended, the room remained mostly quiet until they released for lunch. Scarlet grew excited to be with the other elementalists and engage in conversation outside of *"This is how the Council has done it since I was eight, and it's not changing."*

In the communal dining area, she collected her own ordered meal from the dumbwaiter and took a seat at the table across from a boy dressed in dark blue skinny jeans, boots, and a black jacket. He had the hood up over his face, and she couldn't remember his age. Scarlet examined the American cuisine on his plate before she glanced around the table to see what the others decided to eat. The Council had a lot of diversity, but she would be the only one not eating any meat products.

"I'm Lí Scarlet." She gave a slight nod to the man across the table.

"Scott Everton."

"Oh, right, first name first." Scarlet blushed.

"It's alright to keep your culture here," Hans interrupted. "Elementōrum Patriam is a country meant to collect the world and merge it in the best way possible."

"Where is everyone from?"

"South Carolina—it's a state on the east coast in America," Scott said.

"City of Vasha." Hans grinned. "More specifically from the Russia sector."

"I'm from Tennessee." Luana rolled her eyes. "What about you, though?"

"Hónghú, Jīngzhōu, in the Hubei prefecture of the People's Republic of China." She glanced at her plate. "Hans, can I ask why you have a German name?"

"My grandmother was German—she always wanted a son named Hans, but she only had daughters. Since I'm my mother's second son, she named me Hans in honor of her mother's wish. It upset a few of the traditionalist Russians when they first found out." He took a bite of his meal. "What about you? Do you have a different name in Mandarin?"

"My name is Zhū Hóng, but I use Scarlet in English. It's close to the same meaning, so my name isn't really any different."

Luana opened her mouth, but Hans put a hand on her arm before she could vocalize any thoughts. He shook his head quickly, and she looked away with a scowl.

"When did you join the Council, Scott?" Scarlet asked.

"Last month."

"The older the Council members get, the closer they die together," Ruben Antonio Portillo-Benitez, the Water elementalist, said. "I doubt we'll see anyone else die this year, though."

Ruben was almost correct, as they didn't see any more deaths in 2310. When Scarlet first joined the Council, it took several weeks for her to feel like a helpful member. She learned how to work in the parameters of the expectations between those around her and the Council head. Scarlet also discovered the library, where she spent most of her free hours studying. She took the time to learn to speak Russian. After several months of practicing on her own, she felt confident to say her first sentence to Hans.

He stared at her for a long while before gently correcting her pronunciation. Hans tutored her in the language until they could have fluent conversations in Russian on any topic. Hans tried to learn Mandarin in return, but he struggled too much; Scarlet asked him to stop wasting his time. His gesture made her happy, and she preferred conversing in Russian when English wouldn't be available.

Luana often made rude comments when they had mini conversations during meals, and Hans always rolled his eyes and treated it as an issue with Luana, not with them.

Older members of the Council passed away and with each one, they collected a new member. The Life elementalist died in May 2311, and Dwayne joined their ranks. Scarlet didn't know what to think about the easygoing adult with nicknames for everyone and a joke in every situation. His constant smile made for a nice change, and the way he retaliated against Luana certainly kept them entertained.

He consulted each person about their nickname, except Luana who threw a fit over every small change. Scarlet wasn't sure what to suggest, but after Dwayne learned about her past, he dubbed her, Mulan. The nickname meant he paid attention to her and genuinely cared about what she told him. The name made her feel powerful and comforted.

Eilene joined them in 2312, a few short months before Series joined them at only fourteen-years-old. Luana and Eilene didn't get along from day one. She refused to shy away from fighting for her opinion and often challenged Luana on her policies for the country and international relations. On the other hand, Eilene and Dwayne stuck together, thick as thieves, and Scarlet wondered if the two would announce an official relationship. Then, one day, Dwayne came out as aromantic asexual to Scarlet with no desire for any relationship. As an Ace herself, Scarlet felt her heart break for Eilene who had no idea.

No one ever discussed relationships on the Council. The decision to join the Council created a lock on regular life. They couldn't have relationships outside of a professional one. If it led anywhere, the Council member couldn't build their own family.

January 10, 2317

The Council Chambers, The Academy, Elementōrum Patriam

Series sunk into her pillows and stared at the starry sky displayed on her ceiling. It reminded her of the open skies on the reservation in Northwest Arizona. Everything was open and on display, no pollution to block her view of the Milky Way. She could stare at the universe forever and never know if she saw the end. Series pulled the duvet higher over her body and curled her toes into the warm material. She turned onto her left side and tangled her legs in the blankets. The room slipped away, and she fell into a harrowing dream.

Memories blurred and moved at a pace where she couldn't track the events. It came to a stop in a small cabin in the woods and she shivered. Series knew the cabin stored blankets in the basement. She headed into the dark depths, but when she came to the foot of the stairs, her toes chilled, and a large lake awaited her arrival. In the middle, a rock protruded where a large frog, wearing a royal crown, sat on a tall throne made of spider webs and lakeweed. Series jumped into the water and swam toward the island, but a firefly landed in her hair and pushed her under the surface. When she struggled against the insect, the water turned to air, and she fell until her back collided with the center of a sunflower. She pushed herself out of the flower and came face to face with a man she didn't recognize.

He gestured for her to come forward and stand in front of a large mirror. She glanced at him before leaning in, but she saw no reflection. Hands landed on her back and pushed her into the glass. She passed through and collided heavily with a pool of silvery water. When she gripped the underwater weeds, it changed to grass and her body collapsed in a soaking heap on a hillside. The ground under her turned to mud. A mass of bodies surrounded her and moved through her as if she didn't exist. When she stood and turned to one of the clearings, Scott flew high above the ground in the middle. His eyes glowed a stark white that traveled to the rest of his body, and he wielded all the elements at once. She gasped, and the vision forced her away from the display when she caught a glimpse of herself in the crowd. The other Series fought off her own hoards, and a large ring of gold imprinted on the ground. She had the same mysterious glow of gold. Series moved through the crowd, but she lost her footing and rolled the rest of the way down the hill.

When she hit the bottom, a layer of fine sand coated her skin. Several tents waited farther away from the shoreline, and she headed toward them. Before she got there, two figures walking down the beach distracted her. Luana and Hans, their shoes in hand as the wind blew at their clothes—their skin lit up in different colors from the setting sun. Luana tossed her hair out of her face.

"I never expected to see him out here, fighting against us." Her voice cracked with tears.

"I think he was surprised, too, to face you that way." Hans pulled her into his arms and rubbed his hands up and down her back to warm and comfort their leader.

"How are we going to win this war?"

"By remaining strong when we see adversity."

Series continued to a temporary medical tent. When she pushed up one of the flaps to explore, a crowd of elementalist people confronted her. The Academy rose just ahead of them and poised on the marble steps, the eight current members of the Council with their cloaks bundled at their feet stood on full display to euphoric cheers.

Series jolted awake safely under her covers. Heavy breaths escaped her chest, and her mind raced to process what she saw. She tried to make sense of the scenes but decided to ignore them until she had a better idea of what they meant. She only knew four things. One, they would go to war. Two, Scott and she could wield the nine elements. Three, Luana met someone during the war who she didn't expect to see. Four, they would show Elementōrum Patriam and the world their true identities.

Luana would freak.

January 13, 2317

Series twisted and turned in her covers. She often struggled to get to sleep since she took frequent naps during the day, a terrible downside of her ability. Her throat ached, and she decided to get a glass of water, provided the sheet wouldn't continue to tie her to the mattress.

She groaned and pushed her face into the flat pillow as she attempted to caterpillar crawl out of the blankets. When she managed it, her feet touched the cool tile floor of her room, and she shivered. Series asked the room to heat the floor, but it would take a while to adjust. She tried to stand but lost her balance as her vision blacked out. She fell backward, but instead of hitting her bed, she fell into a pool of mud. The dark skies and stars occupying her walls and ceiling vanished, and in their place, dark clouds hung over the scene.

Pouring rain cascaded from the sky; her hair fell flat into her face. Her clothes were soaked and coated in mud. Series pushed herself out of the pool and tried to gain her footing on the wet grass, but the bodies writhing around her made it difficult. Gunfire rang out around her. A blast of air passed over her and several humans went flying. She heard a bomb explode nearby and saw the spray of mud into the air. She pulled herself up, despite the ringing in her ears, and tried her best to focus on the fight.

"You can't kill me. You don't know how many times I've tried to do it myself."

The shout surprised her, but it helped ground her in the vision. She turned and found a small clearing in the fighting where two men stood face to face, mostly covered in mud like her, weapons held out in front of them. It reminded her of her vision where Scott wielded the nine elements. *Perhaps a different part of the same battle?*

The younger of the two in the middle of the ring had hair pulled into a bun; she didn't recognize him. He held dual Lūcis Ēnsēs, a type of sword with a single-sided blade, in his hands. The other, she knew: Tyr Slattery. The father of the child most recently removed from the surface.

Series stumbled forward and shivered at the cold feeling of the rain on her skin. She had to see the fight—she needed to know what would come.

"I've been forging this for months," Tyr grinned; mud stained his teeth, *"it will destroy you."*

He lifted the weapon in his hand. It resembled a medieval style claymore made of a shimmery silver colored metal. Against the rain's every effort, blue flames spilled from the hollow core and through holes along the blade. Tyr pointed it at the man across from him.

Series pulled back to her bedroom in the Council chambers with a sharp gasp. It felt like surfacing for air after trying to swim in the depths of the pools in the Academy. She coughed violently and rolled off the bed onto the floor. Several minutes passed before she caught her breath and pushed herself to her feet.

In the past, she always had to sleep to catch any glimpses of the future. It was the first time she had one while fully conscious, and she could control her movements to a certain extent. A different experience. Exhilarating.

Before she desperately sought intervals of naps during the day in the vain hope of catching something. They all seemed worthless compared to that night. The glimpse didn't show her much, but it told them who would be a major part of the war on their doorstep.

Series grabbed her phone off her nightstand and made her way into the bathroom for her glass of water. The light clicked on, and her eyes dragged up to her reflection in the mirror. Her hair, a mess from her unease in bed, needed to be combed. Her sleeping tank top had one strap falling off her shoulder, almost far enough to reveal her breast. She pulled the strap back into place and reached for her water glass. She downed the cup of water in a couple of swallows and placed it where it belonged. Series gazed at herself for a long while in the mirror and willed her dreams to bring more visions.

She cupped her hands in the sink, caught the water, and splashed it across her face. She took the hand towel off the hook and pressed it against her skin. When Series' eyes met her own again, her vision swam; her legs gave out. She faintly recognized her back hitting the wall. Her head connected with the corner of the shower before she landed on the muddy field.

That time, the younger kneeled; he had one Lūcis Ēnsēs still clutched in his left hand, but the other on the ground, broken underfoot of the pressing crowd around them. A piece of the hilt stood straight up in the mud and made half-hearted sparks.

"I'm just getting started." Tyr laughed. He held his weapon to the younger's neck. Blood trickled down the younger man's arm. *"Once I kill you,*

I'll move to the rest of the Council. From there, the rest of your kind will fall at my feet. None of them have any knowledge of the real world."

The younger man lifted his weapon again and light stretched from the hilt between them. A couple of hard hits from Tyr parried the weapon across the crowd; it landed somewhere neither of them could see.

"You'll never touch them," he spat.

Series blinked and found herself back in her bathroom. She winced in pain and scooted across the floor until she laid comfortably on her back. She felt around the floor for her phone; when she found it, she noticed a small crack on the corner from where it fell. She pinched her lips to the side and opened her messaging app.

> **Dwayne, if you're awake, can you**
> **make a trip to my room?**

Series brought her legs up into a bent position and tried to decide if they would be strong enough to stay under her long enough to make it to her bed. She decided to brave a sitting position. She used the loosely anchored towel rack to pull herself from the floor until she could safely drop on top of the closed toilet.

She rubbed the point between her nose and eyebrows and tried to process what happened. As a member of the Council, she would be stronger than *normal* Fortune elementalists, but they had no record of anyone previously experiencing waking visions of the future.

When she closed her eyes, her mind settled on another scene—wildly different from the battles. Dwayne stood on a sidewalk, a jovial smile on his face, as he stared out to the street where someone she couldn't see stood.

"Want me to stand up and say I don't want you two to get married?"

Her phone buzzed in her hand and jolted her away from the scene. She stared at the return message from Dwayne without comprehension and pondered who he might know who would be getting married.

> **I'm not a cheap booty call.**

He paired the message with an emoji winking and sticking its tongue out.

> **I hit my head on the shower when**
> **I fell. Having a hard time walking.**

Series hoped he would hurry, but she also wanted time to process the scenes. She didn't receive a text back and settled for leaning against the shower wall for support. She didn't know what to make of her newfound power, let alone how to harness and control it.

Her mind started to slip into another day of fighting when she heard her bedroom door slide open. It kept her planted firmly in the present.

"Muuyaw?"

"In the bathroom."

Dwayne pushed open the door and crouched in front of her. He held out his hands, and they let off a faint glow as he assessed her injuries. "How'd you hit your head on the shower?"

"I had a vision while awake, and my body gave out."

"That's not normal." He held the back of his hand to her forehead. "When did it start?"

"Tonight. I don't know how to control it. It's like my body immediately tries to go into a sleep state to process the vision." She leaned into his touch, and her eyes fluttered closed.

Dwayne scooped her up into his arms and carried her back to bed. "What are you doing in the bathroom?"

"Getting some water. I was having a hard time falling asleep."

"It looks like you had quite the fight with your bed." He set her down and shoved his hands into his pockets and watched her curl up under the sheets.

"Does anyone really use the top sheet anymore?" She let out a low laugh and pulled a fluffy pillow under her chin. Dwayne took a seat on the edge of the bed where he could still see her face. "I wish my visions would just come in my sleep again."

"Do you need any more water?"

Series shook her head.

"What did you see in your vision tonight?"

She opened her mouth to respond, but another flash of the future caught her off guard. Her mind focused only on Luana's form. The woman stood with her back to the room. To the right, a large map of Elementōrum Patriam, and battle plans sketched on paper pinned over it in different places.

"*What are we going to do without him?*" Eilene's voice echoed from somewhere behind Series, but she couldn't turn.

"*We move on and win the war,*" Luana pushed her hair out of her face. Series didn't remember the dark strands being that messy; tear tracks stained Luana's face.

"Muuyaw?" Dwayne shook her shoulder, and her eyes rolled back to her bedroom. His face filled with concern.

"There's going to be a war. I keep seeing it," Series whispered.

"With who?"

"The humans. Tyr Slattery was there—the parent from the Fire elementalist extraction. He had this weapon. It's different from anything I've seen before. He was fighting someone."

"Someone is really descriptive."

"I don't know who it was. Their hair was covered in mud, but I couldn't make much else out about them. Tyr is coming for *us*. He wants to eradicate the Council." Series sat up and placed a hand on Dwayne's arm. Her grip left small crescent marks on his skin when he coaxed her hand away.

"We'll have to tell Molelo in the morning. We don't have much we can do tonight." He stood. "Promise me you'll get some sleep. I'll send you the bill tomorrow—it'll be pretty expensive."

"I'll try." She smiled and lay on the pillow. As he opened the door to exit, she stopped him with his name. "Dwayne, do you know anyone who is getting married?"

His eyebrows knit together. "No. Did you see something about a wedding?"

"In one of the visions you asked someone I didn't see if they wanted you to stand up and stop the wedding."

"Well," he gave her a small grin, "that one might just be a dream. As Council members, we aren't allowed to attend silly things like weddings. We'll talk to kgosi. Next time I'm here, tell me about a good dream you had instead."

"Sure." Series echoed his laugh as he closed the door.

CHAPTER TWELVE
Silence

January 14, 2317

The next morning, the Council assembled in one of the conference rooms waiting to hear about the situation going on with Series. Ethan stared at the empty spot to Luana's left where the Supernatural elementalist should sit. He recognized the warm presence and the crinkle of leather on his left as Scott took his seat next to Eilene. Hans took up residence on Luana's immediate right—the perfect buffer between her and Eilene. Directly across from Ethan, Scarlet sat at the end of the table next to Dwayne with Series on his right side.

"We are going to call this an official meeting," Luana announced. Once they sat in their appropriate seats, she stood. "Dwayne, I'd like for you to be in charge of minutes for this meeting."

Dwayne immediately pressed a button on the side paneling of the table, and a panel slid to the side. A computer screen emerged from the hole. It broadcast the keyboard across the table in front of him. He tapped the screen, opened a blank document, and started typing quickly across the page. His fingers quietly tapped against the table.

"The first matter of business is to turn time over to Series who is seeing flashes of our future as a Council." Luana sat down.

When Series stood, her height didn't change. She had the same stature, but it felt different. "To be honest with all of you, the visions started a while ago, but I couldn't connect them to any events and decided to wait until the situation presented itself. The time is now, and we need to address everything I saw and things I haven't." Series didn't waver under the intense stares from her comrades. "The first vision I saw involved Scott. In the dream, I landed on a battlefield. It was pouring rain, and, as I pushed through the throngs of soldiers, I found Scott flying above the field. People rushed him from all sides, but no one could touch him."

Scott's brows crinkled. He didn't think he made a particularly prolific warrior—especially against hordes of people.

"That's scary enough on its own, but his eyes glowed stark white, and he wielded all nine elements at once. A feat I'm not sure anyone ever achieved successfully. Not even Vasha could withstand it. Scott didn't have his robes on either—that's how I identified him."

Luana's eyes narrowed. Wearing no robes didn't bode well for them.

"Then, I saw myself. A group of enemies surrounded me. My eyes glowed like Scott's but in gold. When I tried to approach, I tripped and turned up on a beach. The dreams felt so vivid I could sense every part of the environment. The sand sticking to my skin, and the smell of the sea air."

"What was on the beach, Muuyaw?" Dwayne paused his notes.

"A temporary medical tent. Luana and Hans walked along the beach and they talked about seeing someone they didn't expect on the battlefield—though it came from Luana's side. I don't know who they saw, but they startled her. I saw Luana cry. When I tried to enter the tent to find out more information, the vision brought me back to the Academy. We stood on the steps overlooking the grounds and none of us wore our robes."

Luana bit her tongue, hard. She could taste blood in her mouth. Series' visions were never wrong—just as with any other Fortune elementalist. However, that didn't mean she had to like it. Ever since Ethan's appearance, rules started to break more and more among the Council members. Hans talked back to her about appropriate retaliation against the Uns. They had two new elements to look out for. Series told them that they would go before their people without their robes, without the sacred protection of secrecy afforded to them by multiple generations of elementalists.

"It doesn't end there—" Series took a shaky breath, "three nights ago, I started to have visions while awake."

"Is that possible?" Scarlet's brows furrowed together.

"Apparently, I never heard of it before." She licked her lips. "It's terrifying. They can hit at any moment, and I collapse because my body wants to go into a sleep state, but I'm also still awake through all of it. The visions from the other night—they showed a main contender in an upcoming war. We're fighting against the humans and the father of the child we retrieved the other day is at the front of the fight."

"Or, at the very least, he's taken the helm of this particular battle," Eilene said. The logic of her statement eased the postures of a few of the Council members.

"I can't see someone like him gaining enough of a following to start a war against us. We have accords with every single country. Those are not easily broken," Hans said.

"Did you garner any information we can use to stop him?" Luana's hands formed frustrated fists.

Series shook her head. "In the vision, he wielded a sword-like object. It imitated our Lūcis Armōrum. It's different, but I can't explain how since I didn't get a good enough look at its functions. I do know it had a gold coloring, and it generated flames not extinguished by the rain. Slattery fought someone I didn't recognize—because of the rain, mud covered everyone. I couldn't get close enough to look at his face, but Tyr put him at his mercy. He lost his weapons, our Lūcis Ēnsēs, during the fight because of the unknown weapon. I didn't get to see anything else because something jolted me back to the present moment. I do know he planned to kill them. The vision didn't continue until I went into the bathroom where I collapsed and hit my head on the shower before I called Dwayne."

"What did you see the second time around?" Luana scratched her nose.

"More of the same fight. The man ended up with one of his weapons destroyed, supposedly by the human."

Hans asked, "Is there anything else we may need to know to progress?"

"Someone dies. I don't know who. We never mentioned a name. They are male, however, and we are left with a limited number of options. I can't change the future." Series' lower lip trembled. She stared around the table at the faces of her friends, Scott, Hans, Dwayne, and Ethan. She couldn't imagine losing any of them.

"We don't have any control over who dies," Scott spoke up. "I don't think any of us will hold back even if we know we could die—that's a part of war. I'd be more surprised if we made it out unscathed."

"Scott makes a fair point." Hans nodded firmly. "Even if I knew I'm the one who dies, it wouldn't stop me from participating in this war. If my death is a part of what saves and brings peace back to our people, I'd die one-hundred times over."

"I think," Luana started with a slight tremor to her voice, "it may be best to avoid other wars until we're confronted with whatever this new force is."

"It's disappointing to think one person could cause so much chaos," Scarlet sighed. "Are we going to pull our current troops out of the field?"

"I think that is the best course of action." Eilene sucked on her teeth. "We can fortify here if we bring them home. We can make a call for people to join the army publicly. The more prepared we are, the better it'll be for our people in the long run. We should try to prevent as many casualties as possible—except our inevitable one."

"Since we know this war is coming, we need to prepare the best we can." Luana grabbed a stylus out of the cup at her desk and slid a slim panel of wood on her desk to reveal a screen. When she put the stylus to the glass, her writing appeared on one of the wall panels. "Things we should actively think about: Food Supply, may include rationing current food output. Write your own ideas down, and we can comment on and discuss them."

Scarlet leaned over to show Ethan how the panels worked and how he could flip to different ones and comment on them while someone else also wrote on the same panel. Series shared her writing pad with Dwayne, so he could keep the computer open. Eilene borrowed Dwayne's computer to pull up the census database and find the name of their suspected threat. On her wall, she wrote:

CONTACT FBI/CIA: PERSON OF INTEREST TYR SLATTERY

The Council flipped through panels and made notes until the walls resembled bad graffiti. Stars and arrows marred the writings as it connected points together and put emphasis on ideas or needs. Once satisfied with the content, Luana exported the files into a single panoramic image file and sent it to their phones.

"Hans and I will compile this into an easily read file with the order of events. I'll send it out with your personal work assignments when we're done." Luana collected a few papers and books scattered around the room she thought that she would need. "For now, relax. If you find some work to do, feel free."

Hans took what she carried and nudged her out of the door first. Once they disappeared, Scarlet sighed. "Are those two ever going to admit their feelings?"

"Probably not." Series leaned back in her chair. "I wish I could get a handle on these waking visions. If I could control when I see them, it'd make our lives easier."

"You're asking for a miracle," Dwayne chuckled.

"Can Council members date each other?" Ethan doodled absentmindedly on the pad in front of him and watched the little drawings come to life on the wall behind Dwayne's head.

"Yeah—though we don't usually." Scarlet fluffed up her hair with her fingers.

"Why?"

"Dating usually leads to marriage—which isn't bad, but who are you going to invite? So, you have a small ceremony with the Council—great! You share a room with each other even though you could before. Now you're married, you might think about starting a family, but if you have a child, you don't get to raise it. The Council is full of 'dead' people—if any of us have children, they must go outside the academy and be adopted. It's easier to stay single for your entire life. It doesn't complicate anything." Dwayne leaned back in his chair and propped his feet up on the table. "I'm proud every day I'm aro ace. Makes my job here a hundred times easier."

"You're asexual?" Eilene's eyes snapped to him. Her face lit up in several shades of pink.

Dwayne's mouth parted as he realized he revealed his sexuality without talking to her first. He always planned to—he knew the depth of her feelings for him; he wasn't blind. Every time Dwayne tried to broach the subject, it never quite got there. He didn't know how to tell someone he would crush their dreams, but Eilene knew the realities of their work on the Council. He couldn't give her what she wanted, and her line of work wouldn't allow it either. Dwayne swallowed hard and dropped his feet back to the floor. The chair thudded down with him. He always meant to tell her gently.

"It slipped," Dwayne whispered.

Scott put a hand on Eilene's arm, but she shook him off.

"I'm the same as Dwayne, sorry boys." Scarlet quickly tried to cover for her friend.

Series picked up the hint. "Demisexual." She pulled her legs up into her chair and curled into the fetal position. "I have to agree. It'd be hard to be a sexual person with this job."

"I need to take some ibuprofen." Eilene headed for the door. "I'll see you guys later."

She took off running once in the hall. Dwayne stood and headed after her with a shout of, "Dickens, wait!"

Scarlet pushed away from the table and left without another word.

Series sized up the last two Council members left in the room. "Neither of you are going to flip out and cause drama, are you?"

Scott shook his head, and Ethan held up his hands in forfeit.

"Dickens." Dwayne caught up with Eilene using his gangly strides. His hand wrapped firmly around her bicep and drew them both to a halt. Eilene yanked her arm away and frowned. She didn't turn to face him. "I never meant to blurt it out in front of everyone. That's the last way I wanted everyone to find out."

"Yet, it happened," Eilene's voice choked with tears. "Did you intend to tell me?"

Dwayne reached out for her hand, but she slapped him away. His own throat felt blocked. He couldn't remember how many years passed since she acted like she did when she first joined the Council—scared of her own shadow. The remnants of what her uncle did to her. "I know how you feel about me. And I thought about telling you all the time—I wanted to tell you, but I could never come up with a good way to not break your heart. I didn't want to hurt you. You're always there for me, and I wanted to return the favor—turns out, I'm not as good at it as you."

She folded her arms and shivered in the dim lighting.

"I never said you weren't there for me." She picked out the flaw in his speech. "I don't think you couldn't not break my heart as soon as you knew I liked you in *that* way."

Dwayne took a steady breath. He reached out again and pulled her into a hug, her back cradled against his chest. "I'm sorry, Eilene. You're going to find someone perfect for you one day, you know? Someone who can give you the entire world."

Hot tears spilled down Eilene's face and dripped onto his arms. He kissed the top of her head. She tilted her head back into his chest. She liked and hated the sound of her name on his lips. It didn't fit him.

"I thought I was 'Dickens' to you." They both laughed. "I'll never find anyone like you."

"And that's a good thing." A smile crept back onto Dwayne's face. "I'd be pissed if you fell in love with someone else, and they broke your heart like I did. You've gotta find someone better than me—there's tons of men out there."

"People I don't know," she sniffled. "I don't exactly want to date Ethan."

Dwayne pursed his lips, surprised she didn't recognize Scott as a viable option. "If Muuyaw's visions are true, you might be able to meet a whole world full of people."

"I hate you for what you did to me."

"I can accept that, Dickens. Although, if you tell me you hate me for anything else, I'm not going to believe you."

"Shut up." She gently pulled away. "I'm going to spend some time alone."

June 23, 2313

The Council Chambers, The Academy, Elementōrum Patriam

Dwayne spread himself across his bed and held up the remote to the old boom box in the corner of his room. He skipped to the second to last song on the disc and leaned back where his head dropped off the edge of the queen-sized bed. Blood rushed to his head, and he liked the lightweight feeling it gave him. Snow Patrol's lyrics wrapped around him like a weight pulling him below the waves; the heavy anchor of Council responsibilities removed the *human* side of him. His cracked and strained voice joined the singing.

"What happens if my eyes are already open?" Eilene asked from the doorway. Dwayne shot up from the bed, and he felt dizzy as all the blood rushed away from his brain. He held a hand to the side of his head and waited for his vision to clear.

"Huh?"

"The song, *Open Your Eyes*. I'm questioning the lyrics."

"Do metaphors escape you, my dear, Dickens?" He dropped back onto the bed again.

"You're a mystery to me, Dwayne." Eilene batted at his legs until he pulled them in where he no longer starfished across the bed. She lay opposite him, her feet at his head. He raised his head above the edge of the large mattress to glare at her. "I get your feet. Deal with it."

"You're ruining a perfectly good song."

"It's the same sixteen beats which go up and down single notes after three measures."

"With a harmony and beautiful lyrics that make you think."

"I'd prefer not to think when I'm lying on my bed."

"I like thinking in my room. Allows me to get work done. Don't worry, I won't tell Molelo you're skipping out on work."

"You know, I think I'm falling into those lyrics a little bit. How about we sit in silence."

"Are my jokes too good for you, Dickens?"

"Shut up."

They sat in silence during the middle minute of the song. Their breathing matched the same pace, and Eilene let her eyes trail the sky of Botswana. She loved how their rooms adapted to their personal tastes.

"The sky looks different in the southern hemisphere."

"I think it's better." Dwayne wiggled his hips across the bed, so his head didn't hang off the edge. "What'd you come in here for, anyway?"

"You looked sad the last few days. I set up the game room with all types of games for us to mess around with. Even brought up *Fantasy Wars* on the computers so we can dick around and kill spider spawns. Or *Blockcraft*—we have that server."

"I kind of want to stay here and wallow in my own pity party."

"I'm okay with that, too."

Dwayne stopped the CD on the last song and restarted the disc in the player with the remote held over his head. He skipped several songs into the album.

"A true classic, *Chasing Cars*," Eilene teased.

"You know you love it."

"If we're going to wallow in self-pity, we should listen to some *better* music."

"Shhh, you wallow with the sad tones of my music if you're going to be in here."

"Are we allowed to talk about our problems amidst the depressing music?" Eilene tilted her head up to see Dwayne's face. He nodded. "I wish my parents would've believed me when I told them what happened with my uncle."

"I wish that, too."

"I found out through Council avenues he was injured badly during my escape."

"He deserved it."

"No doubt," Eilene paused, "it pissed me off, though. I found out because of his injuries he was found to be unfit for work, and he lives off money we send him every month."

Dwayne winced.

"He gets to stay at home all day and do nothing because I got revenge. Charges were never pressed against him, and I can't do anything about it. I'm stuck here on the Council and every month, one of us signs the check he spends to keep living another day." Tears stained her cheeks. "I wanted to prove he no longer had any power over my life, but here I am crying over the fact I occasionally sign his check. I wanted to be happy, Dwayne."

"Hey," Dwayne sat up and held his arms out for her. She darted into the warm embrace and pressed her face into his chest.

"If only one of my parents would've believed me when it first happened— but they thought I was an Un. The older Council members said they didn't even react when they informed them of my Rogue status, or that I was killed."

His grip tightened around her shoulders. "I'm going to keep you safe. No one is going to hurt you again, you hear?"

Eilene nodded into his shoulder. He ran a hand up and down her back to help calm her down.

"Now we've got a problem," Dwayne pulled away. She copied the motion, her eyes red and puffy. "I planned on spending the day alone celebrating my birthday, and now you're here."

Eilene snorted. "Oh please, it's not your birthday. You don't tell anyone when your birthday is."

"Then humor me a little."

January 17, 2317
Torii Station, Yomitan, Okinawa, Japan

Mason Ford watched the men and women march into the courtyard for morning line-up. Stationed on the military base, they would return home for an unknown span of time at the end of the week. He didn't like how quiet his home in Tennessee would be. No one lived there while he served outside the country—he didn't need hired help after the elementalists collected Luana from his home at age seven while he was on active service.

At eight, he received word of her classification of Rogue and her untimely death.

While he called the city, and the house, home—it no longer held any appeal.

"Alright, soldiers." Mason's voice echoed across the yard. "We're running drills for the first half of today. This afternoon, we are on cleaning duty."

"Sir, yes, sir!"

The days when they complained about their duties vanished, and on the blow of his whistle, they immediately went to work. Mason followed behind them to watch their drills and participate himself. He needed a good workout to keep his mind off his inevitable return home to the states.

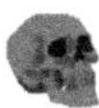

Key West, Monroe County, Florida, United States of America

"I was beginning to think you wouldn't come." Tyr said when he opened the door of his apartment to Ryan. "I'm just finishing packing a few boxes. I'm moving in three days. Going to try a new area, I think it'll be good for me."

"I don't quite get the proposal here. A. You think my son Scott is alive and serving on the Council because of the evidence presented in these pages." Ryan had to admit, the evidence looked sound, but he wasn't sure how they got their hands on school records. That was the piece throwing him. School records could be faked, no matter how much some person online claimed they were legitimate. "B. You're suggesting genocide because of a genetic mutation. There's no way parents are going to agree to kill their child simply because it came back positive with the elementalist mutation."

Tyr gave him a knowing look. "Won't they? Are you trying to tell me the habits of humans are going to change when it comes to the elementalist race? Have they yet to stop themselves from aborting a child when they find it has some other kind of genetic disease? Down syndrome? Autism? Other learning disabilities? Have they ever stopped to think about rearing a child when it is born with blindness or deafness, instead of seeking a cure? No.

Humans always look for cures for everything. They are obsessed with having a generation with no 'mistakes', no 'deformities.' They don't want anything wrong with a child which could affect the world they live in. If an elementalist child is born, they will seek to get rid of it. It's part of their nature. I'm sure once they know their child cannot live separately or receive training over their powers, they will no longer allow them to exist. Our cure is simply death to all who do not fit our human race." Tyr waved a hand through the air. "Besides, genocide isn't necessarily the right word for it. I'm simply willing to kill any elementalist who doesn't want their genetic mutation erased. That's how this works. We have to get rid of the mutation."

"You're exploiting the fear and weakness in humans and encouraging genocide for generations to come." Ryan cleared his throat—aware of the severity of what Tyr wanted to achieve. He stared down at his notes. "And if my son is on that Council?"

"If there was a different type of cure," Tyr continued, "if we knew how to rewrite their genes. Insert a repair to that chromosome—something that would remove their elementalist ability. How many parents do you think would do it?"

Ryan swallowed hard but didn't reply. Tyr didn't answer his question about Scott. *Does Tyr plan to kill the Council? Can I stop him?*

"If you were given free testing before your son was born, and he showed up as an elementalist—and with this fix, you could take it all away and keep him with you. Would you have done it?"

"Take away the part of him that made him special?"

"Take away the part of him that led others to kill him. He wouldn't be dead. You'd know that for a surety." Tyr held his hand out and counted on his fingers. "He'd be twenty-three now. Probably married. You could have a grandchild. You'd be happy."

"Can you do that? Fix the gene."

Tyr grinned. "There are several who are willing to fund such testing—if we can prove results. With your background, we could make that a reality for many other parents. We could put an end to the mutations. When I get my daughter back, I'll fix her, too. I'll offer the same to your son if he is alive."

Ryan extended a shaky hand. "You have a deal."

February 13, 2317

Milan, Gibson County, Tennessee, United States of America

Mason ended up being retained in Japan for almost a month longer than planned. Looking around his home left him with a sense of dread. The house was freezing. He didn't leave the central air on while on tour—it would cost a fortune. To top it off, a thick layer of dust covered every surface. He'd need his own brand of cleaning troops to get the house healthy again.

He kicked fresh dust into the air as he hauled his suitcase over the threshold. It filled his lungs, and he entered a horrible coughing fit that only revived itself when he walked outside in the cold winter air a second time. He used his shirt as a mask as he navigated the space. He left his case in the middle of the living room for the time being.

Mason retrieved a brand-new filter for the central air and replaced it before turning the unit on. After a trip around the house with the vacuum, emptying the container several times into a garbage sack, he felt comfortable enough to live for the time being. Only one room remained untouched.

He stepped into the kitchen and came across a new problem he needed to resolve. Inside the fridge, he had a few water bottles, all flavored. The cupboards offered him a box of stale crackers and cereal. Nothing he particularly wanted to ingest—but fast food didn't sound appetizing either. Mason shuffled out of the house again to his vehicle and programmed in the address for it to take him to the local grocery store. Being back in the house reminded him too much of Luana. Walking around the house felt like living with a ghost. He couldn't stop the flashes of his child walking the halls.

Mason stared blankly out the window and considered the what ifs. Luana would be twenty-five, quickly approaching twenty-six if the Council didn't kill her at eight. He could be a grandfather. Even if he would never meet or see them—they'd live in Elementōrum Patriam where he couldn't go. He wondered if he could send them gifts.

Mason spent the next couple of hours traipsing up and down the aisles as he restocked his entire kitchen. He didn't have the will to cook, but he knew buying fresh ingredients and fixing his food would be healthier for his body in the long run. He found he didn't mind the long weekend checkout lines even with perishables in his cart. The moments outside of his empty house were like paradise.

Unwilling to stay in his house longer than it took to put away the groceries, he headed into the cold again, dressed in a winter work-out outfit.

February 23, 2317

Mason returned from his run out of breath and ready for a nap, except two unfamiliar men stood on his doorstep looking through the open front window. Uneasy, he hesitated and considered going for another lap. One of the men was close to his age, late forties, while the other looked closer to his late twenties.

He hoped they weren't salesmen. Not many people went door to door anymore, but a few showed up every so often. He certainly hoped they weren't there to proselyte a religion. He'd turn them away in no time.

"Are you Mr. Ford?" the younger asked upon his cautious approach.

"I am." Mason stopped halfway up the driveway. "Is there something I can help you with?"

"Can we speak inside?" he pushed.

"I don't invite strangers into my home. I could call the police for trespassing."

"I'm sorry, sir, we don't mean to be a bother," the older one cut in. "It's just a rather sensitive matter. We hoped to ask a few questions about your daughter."

Mason's eyes narrowed further. "I don't have a daughter."

The pair exchanged a glance. The first continued, "We understand. Sorry for bothering you." He settled a folder under his arm before they left. A sheet of paper slid out and dropped to the ground.

Mason picked it up and started to call out, but he stopped when he saw the text on the page.

Luana Ford

Top of the Class in Fire instruction

Reportedly Killed: August 19, 2306

Pictured: October 2306 Fire Council member approximately the same height as previously named.

"Where did you get this?" Mason held up the sheet. Both stopped at the end of the driveway.

"From an online forum." The younger licked his lips. "I'm Tyr Slattery, and this is Ryan Everton. We're gathering information on the elementalists to find a way to cure them."

"What do you mean 'cure'?" Mason ran his thumb over the picture of Luana as a smiley child on her school ID.

"Well," Tyr bit his lip, "I want to find a way to reverse the gene mutation, so we can put an end to the elementalist people. Ryan agreed to help me because if something like this existed, his son wouldn't have been killed the same as yours. We hoped you might be willing to join our research."

"Who is funding this research?"

Ryan shuffled his feet. "A few different parties. We're still drawing connections to various groups."

"What stakes do you have tied up in this?" Mason nodded to Tyr.

"My daughter was taken recently. I hope to rescue her and fix her gene, so I don't have to say goodbye to her forever like you and many other parents do."

"So, you're building a terrorist organization."

"Only against the elementalists—I only want to help the human race." Tyr spoke with such calmness that it startled Mason. "I want to build a society that won't tear parents from their children."

Mason folded his arms. Terrorism would put him directly in opposition to his ranking with the U.S. Army. However, he never said a proper goodbye to his daughter. The seventeen years of silence flooded the gap between his heart and mind. A seventeen-year-old promise to see her on the next break in his service. A promise he had no choice in breaking. He felt her tiny hand slide into his.

"What do you need help with?"

CHAPTER THIRTEEN
Collapse

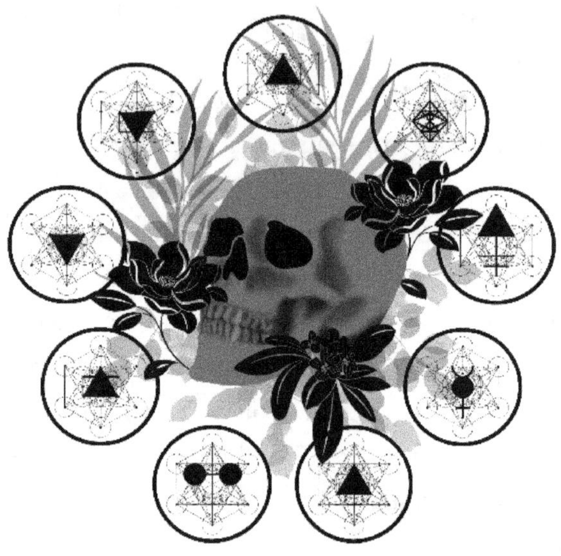

April 22, 2317

Lake Michigan, Leelanau State Park, Northport, Leelanau County, Michigan, United States of America

"Hey, Ralph! Time me to see how long I can hold my breath underwater!" Matt called to his friend on the shoreline. Both their families took an early season camping trip and allowed the boys to visit the lake. Matt decided to swim despite the frigidness of the water. He claimed he didn't feel it.

"I already timed you several times. I'm not doing it again—I get it, you're a freak who can hold your breath for over ten minutes." Ralph tightened his jacket around him and shivered as a blast of wind crossed through the valley. It rose a choppy wave in the small inlet and washed over Matt and lapped at Ralph's shoes. When Matt surfaced again, Ralph said, "It's unnatural. We should head back."

"You should race me, just once." Matt turned over onto his back and floated across the top of the water.

"Not in this weather. I don't know how you aren't a popsicle."

"Come on, one race can't hurt you."

"It will if I catch hypothermia." Ralph stood. "I'm heading back and telling your parents you're swimming in the lake."

"Don't!" Matt lifted a hand in terror; a wave followed the motion and pulled Ralph into the lake with Matt.

He laughed.

Ralph didn't resurface.

Matt struck out from the shallows looking for his friend before he dived under the water and found the other boy tangled among the lakeweed and rocks.

Matt rushed through the water to Ralph's side and dug at the biome trapping him underwater. By the time he managed to cut his friend free, his lifeless body floated to the surface.

Matt screamed when he broke the cresting wave.

He heard their parents running across the gravelly beach, but he didn't have an explanation for what happened.

He killed his best friend.

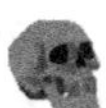

April 23, 2317

Jackson, Hinds County, Mississippi, United States of America

Kristen cursed her inability to catch the right bus on every public transport system she encountered. She ran, desperately, arms flailing and feet slapping against the pavement. Her body slammed to a stop and impacted the employee entrance door. Kristen peeled herself away and belatedly realized she could use her powers to arrive on time. She pursed her lips and opened the door to the restaurant. She accepted the glass of water and the apron her supervisor offered her.

"Right on time, Delavida."

"I try my best." She gasped around a mouthful of water. Kristen tied her apron around her waist and passed her cup to the dishwasher. If one more dirty, old man grabbed her butt again while she worked, she would lose it.

As far as customers went, the worst ones congregated around that job. She never experienced lurkers as a waitress previously.

She collected her table schedule from the front podium and checked into the computer system to see who sat where. A table with three occupants waited in her section. Three men. She frowned. Kristen pulled the electronic pad and stylus from the pocket of her apron. She did her best to hide her disdain as she asked, "Can I get any drinks started for you gentlemen today?"

"I'll take a sprite," one of the older gentlemen with brunet hair told her. She hid her surprise behind a cough. The older patrons typically ordered alcohol, and the request threw her off.

"The strawberry-banana smoothie is calling my name." The other older gentleman chuckled; his blond hair shimmered under the low lights of the bar area.

"Just a beer will be fine, and a glass of water on the side," the youngest said.

"I'll bring those out and give you a few more minutes to consider the menu." Kristen scrawled a couple of notes across the ticket and sent it to the bar.

"Wimp," the bartender muttered under his breath as he reached for the smoothie mixer, "has to have water with his alcohol to stay hydrated."

She laughed. John, the bartender, was always incredibly vocal. He made fast friends with everyone who worked in the restaurant, and no one could put the fear of God into crappy customers like John.

"Wouldn't it be the other way around? Not ordering alcohol?" Kristen took the drink from his hand and put it on her serving tray.

"A real man knows what he likes." John shrugged. "Anyone confident enough to choose a drink they like over the one society chooses deserves mad respect."

Kristen hoisted the tray into the air. Before she returned to the table, she checked the screen next to the bar for occupied tables. She had no other customers. At their table, as she started to unload the tray, it tipped and fell. Eyes wide, and without thinking, Kristen slowed down time around the drink and grabbed it before it had a chance to spill. She set it gently on the table in front of the shocked men.

"Fast reaction time you have there," the younger man forced a laugh.

"I've had lots of practice working with drinks." She tried to pass it off with a smile, but her shaky voice gave away her nerves. She couldn't reveal her ability—but her subconscious got the better of her again. Her control slipped because she had no professional training. She shakily reached for her pad. "Can I get you started on any appetizers?"

Relief washed over Kristen at the end of her shift. She rolled her shoulders and dropped into her usual bad posture—curved over at the top of her spine. She collected her things to leave and noticed the three men from the first part of her shift sitting on the main bench outside the building. Kristen swallowed and turned back to the break room.

"John?"

"What is it, small fry?" He appeared in the doorway with his jacket half on.

"There's some men outside. My customers from earlier today. I don't want to walk out there alone."

"Well then, come on, little lady." John offered his elbow. "Where am I escorting you tonight?"

She took the offered arm, his dark skin warm from the heat of the bar lights. "I am off to the bus stop, good sir."

The music at the bar still played over the speakers, and John waltzed her across the floor to the exit. He smiled. "I think I could be a movie star with moves like these."

Kristen broke into a fit of giggles. John, already in his late fifties, approached death's door every day. As a kind and gentle man—divorced, with two kids around Kristen's age—she knew he wouldn't let any harm come to her.

They had light conversation until the bus arrived to pick up passengers. John stuck around long enough to make sure the three men didn't follow her onto the bus line.

The next few nights followed the same pattern. The older men seemed reluctant to keep visiting, but Kristen saw the animal like lust in the younger's eyes. He watched her walk around the tables as she waitressed. She switched serving areas with the other servers every night they came in. John's frustration with the wannabe stalkers grew daily as well. Several of the other employees noticed their fascination with Kristen and did their best to keep throwing them off.

Kristen kept counting down the days until she had enough money to get into Elementōrum Patriam—at least to the visitor's center. The night of her final workday, she promised her coworkers she would come visit or return to work there if her new location didn't work out. She hoped to break the rules and find a place among others somewhat like her. She wanted answers.

Kristen entered her apartment and the familiar tingles of someone watching her spread across her arms. She did her best to shake it off as she locked the door. She dropped to the floor and crawled over to the window. Outside, she spotted a large off-roader Jeep. She caught sight of the man sitting in the passenger seat and nearly choked on her own heart. Kristen crawled away from the window and shoved her belongings into her hiking backpack. She wrapped several jackets around herself to help brace herself from the weight and save space in the pack for water.

She wouldn't be able to leave through her front door. Kristen took the time to check out the fire escape but found they could see the route from their vehicle. She frowned and searched her apartment for a window facing away from the parking lot. One of the bedroom ones provided her with the perfect opportunity, and she pushed the window open. It took her only a few seconds to remove the screen. She moved the backpack out first and hung it from the drainpipe.

Once Kristen pulled herself out and balanced on the windowsill, she retrieved the pack and moved herself slowly across the brick exterior of the building until she had a lower point to jump from. Free from the second floor, she headed into the night. It would be a long trip to the airport on foot, but she had no other options for escaping the stalkers.

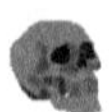

July 2, 2317

Hattiesburg, Forrest County, Mississippi, United States of America

The Council itched to get out of their chambers. In times where they had a lot of stress, they sought any escape they could find. They heard nothing in their probing regarding Tyr. The FBI had no luck pinning him down. He managed to evade their top security systems and disappear. They suspected he stole IDs and credit cards to keep his cover—or he worked with others who fronted any operations and progress he made.

The Council had access to everything they needed behind their locked doors, except freedom. After Eilene's third panic attack, strictly behind closed doors and safely with Dwayne to walk her through it, he recommended she take a trip somewhere to cool off and relax. Series and Scott were assigned to go with her. Series desperately needed the break away from the Council because Luana kept pushing her to see more information. Except, her Fortune ability wouldn't cooperate, causing more tension. Dwayne thought the break would do her good as well. They chose a simple mall trip to shop for new clothes. Since they couldn't be in public on Elementōrum without their robes, they voted for a location close to the border of their continent. The Southern States provided a lot of opportunities for quick escapes.

"Are you sure you won't get bored escorting us around the mall?" Eilene asked Scott in the parking lot. Scott shook his head and watched Eilene pull her hair into a preppy ponytail and place a pair of sunglasses on her nose. She strung a bright pink purse on her shoulder.

Series smiled softly as she strung her own navy purse across her chest. "We have a list from the others on a few things they want as well. I'll have a hard time remembering to look."

Scott pulled the hood of his jacket over his head. The girls talked comfortably about next to nothing as they walked around looking for stores to shop in. Scott volunteered to juggle the bags.

Eilene took pity on Scott part way into their trip when he appeared overwhelmed by the amount of shopping. They found a cart to rest the bags on and returned to Series' side as she gazed longingly through a window at a gorgeous ball gown. It had a matching jacket with small bead embroidery around the gems. The bodice of the gold gown had the most embroidered gems in straight line patterns down the boning. The champagne tulle of the skirt flooded the window display and small pearl gems littered the edges of the fabric.

"You'd look beautiful," Eilene complimented. "You should buy it if they have it in your size."

"No, I couldn't. I would never have a use." Series turned away from the dress.

"You should get it," Scott said. They both stopped and Eilene lowered her sunglasses to look at him clearer. "You should both buy a dress."

"Alright," Eilene agreed.

They went into the dress store, and Series headed over into the ball gowns. Eilene searched her way through rows of dresses and only pulled options from the pastel colors. They both spent a while in the dressing room, but Series finished first. The color suited her skin tone, and she emulated the presence of a princess.

"I know the color is my element, but it feels more freeing this way." She smoothed her hands across the tulle.

"It suits you really well," Scott said.

"Thank you." She gave a little spin in the dress.

The curtain to the other dressing room opened and Scott couldn't pull his eyes away from Eilene. She wore a pastel turquoise color loose fabric style dress. It matched the summer weather with a flutter sleeve. Scott's eyes traced the V-neck. The waist was pulled together by a sash tie. The skirt had a mullet cut with the front barely reaching mid-thigh. The pull of the dress outlined her figure. He turned a faint shade of pink and tried to focus on something else.

"Wow," Series complimented with a grin on her face. She recognized the stunned look on Scott's face—the same one Hans gave Luana. Scott moved his mouth a few times like a fish before he stopped trying for words and gave her a nod.

"I kind of want to wear this one out of the store." She gave a small twirl. "It's incredibly comfortable."

"I'm sure they'd let you wear it out. Let me change back into my street clothes." Series hitched up her skirt and stepped into the dressing room.

Eilene decided to wear the dress out of the store, and Scott helped her remove the tags after they paid for it. She stayed quiet during the rest of their shopping experience, except when she chose a few clothing options for Scott and spent several minutes convincing him to try them on. He agreed on the terms he could choose his own jacket as he preferred function over fashion. Eilene complimented him on the choice when he brought it with him to the changing room. Despite his reservations, he had fun.

As they made their way toward the door, Series gasped and swayed on her feet. She threw out her left hand and grabbed Eilene's arm, sending a shock of pain that made her wince. Her nails left behind crescent moon shapes on Eilene's skin.

"Series?"

She fought for air as her vision swirled. The camera of her vision swung away from the second floor and drifted to the first. In front of her, entering through the doors of the mall with purpose, the humans opposing them in the coming war. She could see herself, Scott, and Eilene on the upper balcony. Her body swayed. The three men branched off in different directions and her vision returned to normal.

"Series?" Eilene held a ball of water against her forehead.

She mouthed uncomfortably for a while before she could find words. "They're here," she choked out.

"Who?" Eilene grabbed her other hand.

"The humans—the ones who are going to start the war. They just walked in through the front door."

"What do we do?" Eilene turned to face Scott.

"Spread out and look for them," he said.

Series ran toward the front door. However, a man materialized out of the space between two shops. He carried a golf club. Series skidded to a stop. She recognized the handsome older features. His messy, dark brown hair sent a chill down her spine, but she couldn't quite place him in her memory. She only knew him as the man next to Tyr when they walked into the mall.

"You," she said.

"I think you must have me confused with someone else." He held up his hands in surrender.

Farther along the upper balcony, closer to the center fountain, Tyr tore across the open space with a small girl over his shoulder screaming bloody murder. "I've got her!" he shouted.

The man in front of Series made to move away, but he halted. She burned a gold ring into the ground around her. A gold sphere erupted around her body and fluctuated until it fit her form perfectly. It reminded her of the path of an electron around the nucleus. The man, just inside the outer path, shuddered.

"Are you one of the kidnappers?" She took a defensive stance.

Behind the man, Scott flew through the mall and dived toward Tyr's path, intent on stopping him. The crowd of bystanders gasped and screamed. Some ran for cover while others pointed at the elementalists in their midst.

"I'm afraid I can't let you go any further," Series said.

"You'll do better to stay out of this because I can't," he said.

"I think you're taking me for granted. Your companion has an elementalist child, and I cannot allow you to get away with one of my own people. The minute you took them, you tangled me into your mess." Series smirked. "I'm glad to show you our true power face to face."

The man shifted forward. His movements sluggish as he raised the weapon. She placed her right hand against his forearm just past the wrist, and with her left hand she swung open palmed hard into the back of his hand. The inertia of the hit loosened the grip in his fingers around the club, and it clanged into the railing before it fell over the edge. The people below screamed as they dodged. The man stumbled away from her. For a moment, he stood, mouth open and loose-limbed. They clashed for a second time, but a good elbow to the man's gut sent him reeling back.

"How?" he gasped in pain.

"You've never fought a fully trained elementalist, have you?" Series laughed. "You are out of your league to go into a fight without being prepared against us."

A blast of wind passed through the entire building, and the force swept several people off their feet. Series' hair swirled around her, and she took a steady step forward, not bothered by the gust.

In the next second, she saw the man in front of her. Standing in a kitchen with Tyr and the other man. Shattered dishes on the floor and staring at a TV. The scene changed. He stood on a beach and stumbled against Luana who burned like an ember, her whole body alight. In another moment, she saw him distracting Tyr while his fellow carried a small child to safety. She heard him confirm the safety of the elementalist child when Tyr wasn't present.

Series swayed on her feet. The man in front of her would act against Tyr. "Run," she whispered.

The man did. Once past the golden barrier, a powerful weight fell off his shoulders. He turned back for only a moment. Powerful for her young age. He frowned and returned to his weak escape plan. He didn't know what he would do if she came after him. The thought came to him, *Does Tyr even know what he's getting himself into?*

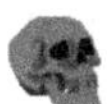

Eilene ran at full speed along the pathway when an unknown object collided with her side and sent her tumbling across the floor. The bench hit the glass railing above her and sent shards flying to the lower floors and onto Eilene's face. She pushed the bench away, and it fell to the bottom floor. People screamed as they ran from the scene.

Her attacker appeared like a shadow—much like Scott. She scrambled to her feet.

"You're one of the ones he shouted to." Eilene took stock of the people gathering to watch. She could tell they had no idea what happened.

"And if I am?" His voice gave away his exhaustion, and it nearly took her by surprise.

"I cannot allow someone to kidnap an innocent child. You're guilty by association, and I will take you down, here and now." Eilene held up her hands and glanced at the large fountain providing plenty of fodder for their fight.

"I guess this shall be our stage." His grin was manic and sad.

Eilene frowned; she didn't know what to expect.

"Though I have to ask: what can a young person like yourself do against me?"

"You shouldn't make hasty assumptions about your opponent." She cocked her head a little higher.

"Shall we make this a more traditional duel and exchange names?" The man made no effort to start the physical altercation. His blond hair glittered under the light from the sunroof.

"We have no other business than righting your wrong. The child does not belong to you, especially if they are an elementalist," she spat.

"And who is to say the child is not ours?"

"If you've taken an elementalist child, they are under the direct protection of Elementōrum Patriam as demanded by the legal accords of the United States of America."

"And so, I ask, how are they any different from us?" The man broke into pealed laughter. "The elementalists plan to rip the child away from their family the same as we would by kidnapping them. If you take them back, they will be reunited with their parents only long enough to say goodbye. And if they turn out to be a Rogue, the elementalists will kill them, and the parents will receive a notice of their child's death. You can claim the nation has its legal accords, but the elementalist's laws make them no better than the criminals on Earth's surface. Their kingdom may be on high, but they are not an exalted people. They and you are not any better than us."

"You have no knowledge of the danger a Rogue, let alone an untrained elementalist, poses against the human race," Eilene hissed.

"Now who is making the assumptions about their opponents? They killed my son." He charged forward like a bull.

Eilene jumped and braced her foot against the metal rail bar of the balcony. As she flipped, she extended her arms and spring boarded off the man's back with a blast of boiling water. He screamed in pain. His skin blistered under the heat.

"A Water elementalist," he managed to choke out as he straightened against the stinging of his burned skin.

"And a trained one—a dangerous threat to only those who oppose me." Her voice hardened, and her face morphed into a scowl.

The crowd of people backed away and disappeared into the safety of the shops. Security gates engaged and locked the bystanders inside.

"Just so you are aware," the man limped as he backed away, "the other one. He is looking for a way to end you. I didn't want to do this. I never wanted to kill you."

Tears flooded his eyes, and Eilene paused at the display of emotion.

"Your people may have killed my son and destroyed my family, but I came to peace with the terms. He has not. You should watch out for yourselves."

"If he is coming to end us, we will end him first," she promised.

The man tried his best to flee at a quick pace, but the burns stunted his movement. Eilene didn't follow. Instead, she held up a hand as a blast of wind shot through the building and several windows around her shattered. People screamed and held their hands over their faces. Eilene jumped onto the railing and looked around for Scott's fight. She needed to join his side and assist where she could.

On the main floor, she spotted him in combat with a familiar frame of a man. She jumped off the balcony and summoned the water from the fountain to break her fall and carry her to the next opponent.

Rage Scott didn't know tore through his body and set every cell on fire. The spark of emotion gave him hope; he could feel again. Even negative emotions warmed his soul as he did his best to keep from injuring the innocent child.

"You're an elementalist." The kidnapper's face filled with excitement as he faced Scott head on.

Scott skidded to a stop midair and took in the man and child before him. He recognized him as the father of the elementalist child who burned her house to the ground and killed her nanny. He held bitterness in his eyes. Scott gave him a slow nod of affirmation.

"Are you here to take this child back by force?" Tyr grinned. "I welcome the challenge."

The Air elementalist lowered himself.

"We are developing a way to rid the world of people like you, and that goes for your Death elementalists, too."

Scott's eyebrows furrowed together. Most humans didn't keep up with their news—nor did they know much about their race of people. They kept a lock on the information going out of the country.

"I'll be taking this child today, and you have no say in the matter." Tyr pointed a finger at him.

Scott responded by sending a controlled blast of air toward the man, and he pulled the child to safety in the same move. He spotted Eilene barreling toward them.

"The child is mine!" Tyr shouted, but his eyes darted to one of the other exits where Mason left the building with another kid. The elementalist followed his gaze and spoke for the first time in his presence.

"E! They went out the other door with the real target!"

"I'm on it!" Eilene changed the direction of her momentum and charged toward the door on her water steed.

Series landed at his side, and he felt the wall of luck hit them like a truck.

"Take the child and return them to their parents," Scott handed her the child, and she left immediately.

"You still plan to take me down when you know it is my accomplice who escaped with the child?" Tyr raised an eyebrow.

"I trust my friends."

"That's your first mistake." Tyr pulled out a gun and trained it on Scott. The elementalist put his hands in the air and watched as the man backed toward the exit. When he reached fifty paces, Scott moved.

The gun lifted out of the assailant's hands, and Scott leaped into the air to catch it. As he landed, Tyr vanished. He made a *tsk* sound and ran toward the door Eilene exited through. She stood on the sidewalk outside; a puddle of water soaked the ground underneath her. She pointed to the freeway when he stopped at her side.

"They took off on the freeway in a car. I can't do anything without destroying the area and putting humans in danger of injury." She looked at him. "Did you get Tyr?"

"He got away as I took the gun. I don't know where he's hiding, to be honest. I'm assuming those guys will come back for him."

"Or they have a second vehicle." She pointed to the car peeling out of the parking lot. It ignored the stop signs and nearly caused three accidents.

"Wow." Scott sucked in a harsh breath.

"On the plus side, we saved one child. We just didn't save the one we needed to." Eilene folded her arms across her chest. "I'm going to call D. We need to have someone from the Council come clean up this mess and none of us can disappear, or it'll be suspicious. Did you get a motive out of Tyr?"

He raised a single eyebrow at Eilene.

"Right, you don't hold conversations well." She laughed despite the grim situation. "At least this strengthens our case against Tyr with the federal government."

When they arrived back at the main plaza of the mall, several police swarmed the area and paid no attention to them. As they collected their things, the whole area quieted to watch them.

"Are you the elementalists involved in the altercation?" A detective approached them.

"We are," Eilene confirmed. "The Council is contacted, and they are on the way to help sort out this situation."

"We really only need a couple of statements about who you are and what happened."

"I'm afraid we cannot give you our names without the Council's express permission," Series stepped in. "The main man in the group of three is named Tyr Slattery. The Council has more information on him—but we do not have any information on his companions. We did manage to save one child from the kidnapping incident. It's unfortunate we could not save both."

"Did you even try?" The upset mother snapped.

"I could not in good conscious kill countless humans for the sake of one child," Eilene returned coolly.

"I think it's best we separate those involved and wait for the Council to arrive." The detective waved for the cops, and they pulled each group away into their own unit.

Scott raised a hand to Eilene's forehead. He rubbed his thumb against the skin hidden by her hair.

"What is it?" She raised her hand to the area.

He pulled away and showed her the blood on his thumb. "You're hurt."

Eilene turned a faint pink color. "I got thrown into the glass railing when the one I was fighting shoved a bench at me."

Scott wiped the blood on his jeans. "We'll have D check you over."

It took thirty minutes for Dwayne to arrive and all three could see his annoyed, tense posture under his robe. Eilene found it slightly entertaining, but quickly quieted when he passed an upset glare her way. She was glad for the first time she couldn't see his face.

"Esteemed Council, these three involved in the incident refuse to provide us with their names without your permission."

"Of course, it is policy for our country—especially when the incident involves humans." Dwayne nodded. "The man is Kaylan Dartmouth. The blonde is Claudia Jansen, while the brunette is Toski Lacapa."

"Thank you—we'll need to retain them only a while longer to get a witness statement. I'll give you a moment alone."

"Really? You named me 'feeble woman'?" Eilene hissed.

"At least I chose a Dutch name for you, Dickens," Dwayne laughed. "What trouble did you get yourself into?"

"Tyr Slattery showed up and kidnapped an elementalist child," Series said. "I saw him arrive in the mall, but we didn't have time to react."

"They distracted us from the real kidnapping with a secondary one. By the time I caught up to the real one, they escaped out of the parking lot. I couldn't go after them without risking casualties," Eilene continued.

"Kaylan saved the human child, but Tyr got away," Series offered.

"He pointed a gun at me. By the time I felt it was safe to take it away from him, it allowed him time to escape." Scott shook his head. "It was a shit show from the start."

"I see." He nodded. "New dress, Dickens?"

"Isn't it cute?"

"Yeah, yeah. Our shopping expedition was successful," Series cut in. "Tyr Slattery has a child who belongs to us—they are one of us. Do we have an update on the federal manhunt for him?"

"Paperwork is still clearing the government, apparently. Everything is approved on our end, but now it relies on the American side."

"Lovely." Eilene dropped her head to Scott's shoulder.

"Storm sent me with our account information—we'll have to pay for the damages obviously." Dwayne held up his phone.

"I blame Sco—sorry—Kaylan." Series returned to the bench with her shoulders low.

"What did I do?" Scott turned his head to give Series a glare, but instead caught a whiff of the citrus scent of Eilene's shampoo.

"I do believe you are the one who sent a shockwave of wind through the mall." Eilene failed to suppress her smile.

"Saving child, mall damages…" he pretended to weigh the two items with the former clearly winning.

"Whatever the motive, this is our issue to solve now." Dwayne pulled up a chair and took a seat. "Most of my job here is done. They'll put out an APB for Tyr Slattery and the child—I'm sure this would qualify as an Amber Alert, too. We need to finish our statements and settlement then we can return home."

"The next time we go shopping," Series started, "I hope we won't run into a kidnapper."

The Council Chambers, The Academy, Elementōrum Patriam

The group of four shuffled tiredly through the front door. The shopping bags garnered few looks because their arrival home occurred after curfew. Eilene pulled her phone out of her pocket once she had her robes off. An alert passed through their phones for an emergency meeting.

"How much did your outing cost us?" Luana asked as they sat down in the conference room.

"Only a few million. Repairs will go toward the windows and refilling the fountain Dickens emptied," Dwayne said.

"I offered to refill it for free, but they wouldn't go for it." Eilene folded her arms and leaned against the table. "The encounter with Slattery certainly could've gone better."

"But risking human lives is also a consideration. You made the right choice by not retaliating and trying to go after him. The metropolitan has too many people," Scarlet said.

"It's always a calculated decision working with the humans," Hans agreed. "At least we have confirmation of Slattery's plans. He wants to wipe our people out, and he's kidnapping elementalist children—most likely to run tests on them to see what works on us."

"Except he doesn't know about me, right? The Death elementalist?"

"He knows," Scott said. "He made a comment directly to me."

"So, war is on our doorstep." Luana folded her hands together and squeezed until her knuckles turned white.

"We can't declare an outright war against three people, can we?" Eilene pursed her lips in frustration.

"We've already done what we need to—the most important piece is contacting the human governments. Since it isn't the country declaring war against us, we can't do it. It'll look like we are starting a war with them instead of a large-scale manhunt for three people." Hans rubbed his face tiredly. The stubble across his chin scratched his palms and made him wince uncomfortably when it pulled his skin.

"We need to update the paperwork we already submitted—they violated the accords we made with the human governments." Luana grabbed a tablet and stylus.

"Where did we save the copies of the contracts? It'll be better if we can cite specific violations." Series triggered the computer at her desk and flipped through screen after screen of files.

"Should be in the legal file, potentially buried under a long file string." Scarlet reached for her own computer as well. "I'll help you look."

"Will the both of you be fine handling it on your own?"

"Of course." Series smiled.

"Dwayne, Ethan, I want the both of you to help me write and edit our formal letter to the world." Luana waved for them to stand and join her in the closer seats.

"What do you want Eilene, Scott, and me to do?" Hans pushed himself out of his seat and traded places with Dwayne.

"I'm trusting the three of you with delivering our letter and evidence to the humans. Get some rest until we call for you." She nodded confidently at them.

Several paces down the hallway, Eilene put her hand on Scott's arm, and he stopped. "Are you okay? I've never seen you lose it before—in the mall when you went head-to-head with Slattery."

He gave an affirmative nod and tried to turn away.

"I know you don't talk much, and I want you to know I'm okay with sitting in a room with you and keeping quiet if that's what you need." Her eyes searched his for answers. "You don't have to shut yourself away, Scott. You have people who care about you—we're just waiting on you to trust us."

His jaw clenched, and he swallowed hard before he found a voice to respond. "Trust is a two-way street, isn't it?"

She tilted her head into a forty-five-degree angle. "I want to tell you my story."

Scott's eyes went wide. Previously, Eilene only ever trusted Dwayne with her secrets. He was the only member of the Council who knew what Eilene went through before her arrival at the academy. Her offer showed him the biggest example of trust.

"You don't have to." His hand jumped forward to hold hers, but at the last second, he only hooked their pinkies together.

She smiled, softly at first, before she tugged his hand. "I wouldn't offer if I didn't want you to know. I think it's about time I talk about my past and accept it instead of running away from the horrors. I think I might feel better if I have others I can talk to—people who can listen when the nightmares become too much."

They walked, linked together, to the empty kitchen. They knew, when they exited the room, they wouldn't be the same.

August 30, 2307

Netherlands Sector, City of Barren, Elementōrum Patriam

Eilene adored how Charles Dickens used the English language. She loved his rich description of moments in history and the focus of his works. He addressed politics by staying with the poor, the people who suffered at the hands of the rich law makers. Eilene appreciated the novelty of his ideas. She absolutely despised what Charles John Huffam Dickens did to his wife, though. He had a loving home with his wife and several children. A brilliant father, but when they got older, Charles left his wife for a younger woman. Eilene did not approve of his actions. When she first found out, it caused her almost enough grief to keep her from reading his works again—but the lines of *A Tale of Two Cities* floated back to her, and she couldn't release herself from the French Revolution. She didn't want to let go of the ideal Sydney Carton who pined, yet supported, Lucie Manette who married another man, Charles Darnay. Eilene didn't care much for Mr. Darnay. Too weak for her standards and part of the aristocracy—the reason Sydney died. Eilene wanted Sydney.

Early in the afternoon, Eilene sat on her bed with a copy of *Oliver Twist*. The week before, she told her parents her Uncle Lucas raped her at a family reunion in the City of Joy. They didn't believe her.

Years before, they labeled her as an Un before the government made an official test. She still hadn't shown any signs of being an elementalist. Her parents put up barriers to avoid the hurt when she vanished. Eilene hoped Charles Dickens would give her some semblance of advice on the situation—it hadn't helped thus far. Eilene knew the reason why Lucas did it. He told her when it happened. She would be the first in over two-hundred years who had no chance of being an elementalist. Her family members boasted a proud line of elementalists. If she wouldn't become an elementalist, they could treat her how they desired until the Council came for her.

"Perhaps," he said, "if you get labeled as a Rogue, they can kill you for us."

There would be no funeral.

Eilene knew she had to bide her time.

Her mother used to tell her, "Passion is the most important thing in life."

Eilene didn't think it would ever be enough. She stared through the open blinds hanging in front of her window and tried to think of something else. Her memory wouldn't let her. When she first saw the familiar face walking down the street, Eilene thought she imagined it. He peered into her bedroom, and she *knew*.

Lucas waved at her from the street. He knew her parents wouldn't be home. Eilene's eyes widened, and she set the book on her pillow. Lucas walked up to the house and looked for a way in. She didn't have a place to hide. The space under her bed didn't fit her, and Lucas would look for her there. Her parents' room had a lock, but she didn't think that would stop him. He would tear down the door.

Eilene located her dingy school backpack on the floor and grabbed it. She pulled the homework and books out of it before grabbing the first clothes she could find. She stuffed them into the gaping hole and yanked the zipper up. The strap fell over her shoulder. A window shattered on the lower level, and she spun around. Eilene pushed the blinds to the top of the rail. She heard her uncle walk through the kitchen; his tennis shoes squeaked on the tile floor. She grabbed the lava lamp on her nightstand and hurled it at the window. Lucas' pace picked up speed downstairs. The bottom step of the stairs creaked.

Eilene yanked the twin mattress from her box bed and shoved it through the shattered window. It landed a story below her, not quite in a safe position for her to jump. Using the simple carabiner clip on her backpack, she clipped her half-filled water bottle to her items. She reached for the book on her pillow.

Lucas appeared in the doorway.

Eilene left the book.

She jumped through the window.

In the air, she managed to turn onto her side. Her right arm took the impact onto the mattress. Shards of glass danced around her and dug into her arm. Eilene jumped to her feet and ran before she recognized the sting of a gash on her forearm. One of the glass pieces sliced her arm open, and she left a trail of blood on the sidewalk. Eilene paused. Her breath came out in large puffs. Footsteps pounded behind her. She took off running again.

A hand grabbed her shoulder and made her turn around. Lucas bore down on her, and she fell onto her back. His hands jumped to her shirt, but Eilene's leg flew up and hit him where it counted. She managed to scramble back several feet before her uncle got his bearings and lunged at her again.

"Stop!" Eilene closed her eyes and threw her hands out in front of her. A startled scream joined her terrified one. She pried her eyes open, and Lucas clutched his face. Blisters formed across his skin.

"You!" he screeched.

In a panic, Eilene sent a second jet of boiling water. His skin turned red and boiled. She jumped to her feet before he could put his hands on her again. She held up her hands a third time. "Don't come any closer."

Lucas stayed on the ground. Eilene took several steps backward before she turned and ran.

CHAPTER FOURTEEN
Valedictory

July 2, 2317

The Council Chambers, The Academy, Elementōrum Patriam

"I came from a long line of elementalists," Eilene started. "A proud line. There's no record of the last time anyone in my family gave birth to an Un or a Rogue."

Scott made his way over to the fridge and pulled out the milk. He retrieved two glasses from the cupboard and poured their drinks.

"Coming from a prestigious line puts a lot of pressure on parents and children. I think. It's expected we will all turn out to be elementalists. When I showed no signs of it, everything went downhill." She took the glass. "My parents labeled me as an Un before any tests came out—they don't do tests. Everyone ends up an elementalist. There's no question. The problem is, I showed zero signs of it. I didn't reach any peak of powers until my teenage years. My parents, in turn, abandoned me. We continued to live in the same house and eat the same meals, but I didn't know them."

Scott watched her move to the small counter with shelving and seating at the raised bar area. She took a small book off the shelf.

"I like to read in here, so I hid a copy of my favorite book." She held it out to him. He took it gently and ran his fingers across the worn cover. "I spent a lot of time in my room. I turned to books to try and help fill the void my parents left behind.

"One day, I read *A Tale of Two Cities* by Charles Dickens, and it resonated with me. It's the story of a country at war with itself and how, despite the war, two people found a glimmer of love and hope. Sydney fascinated me, and the book changed my entire outlook on life." Eilene sipped her drink. "Somewhere along the way, I changed from an ignored child to a vulnerable one. I tried to spend more time with my family. Since I still didn't show signs of being an elementalist, I couldn't make any connections with my immediate family. Then came the connections to my extended family. My uncle took advantage of me."

Scott stepped up beside her and put his hand over hers.

"I tried to tell my parents what happened, that he—" she couldn't quite form the words. Scott squeezed her hand to say he understood. "But they didn't believe me. They shrugged me off, and my uncle convinced me I deserved it for failing to be born as an elementalist." Eilene bit her lower lip and tried to hold in her tears. "He kept coming after me, but one day things started to go too far, and I tried to run. Except, I couldn't. He caught me and raped me. When I returned home, with my clothes tattered and torn, my mother yelled at me for an hour. I tried to explain what happened, but she called me ungrateful and nearly threw me out of the house altogether."

She pushed a hand through her hair. Scott moved his arm around her shoulders and pulled her in tight against his chest.

"I wanted to prove myself as an elementalist. I thought if I could become one, they would believe me about everything else—I hoped I would magically have their support overnight." Her tears fell hot and thick against her cheeks. "My uncle came after me again. He broke the lock and entered our house when my parents were away. I managed to escape out the window, but he chased me. That day, in my fear, I awoke my powers as a Water elementalist.

When he pulled me to the ground, everything welled up, and I blasted him with boiling hot water. He couldn't move—third-degree burns—and I left him there in the street. I don't know who found him or what my family thought, but I came to the Academy and ended up here."

"That is why Dwayne calls you 'Dickens,'" Scott murmured against her hair.

"He is the first person I ever told," Eilene paused, lost in her thoughts, "I already mentioned Sydney Carton. He is the epitome of unconditional love. When I met him in the story, I realized I wanted my own Sydney Carton—but when I found him, fate knew it wouldn't be this way. You see, Sydney Carton loves this woman, Lucie Manette, except she is in love with a man named Charles Darnay. It's the French Revolution, and everything is in turmoil. After Lucie marries Charles, Madame Defarge turns Charles in for some false charges. Sadly, after some court battles and more charges, Darnay is sentenced to death for crimes his ancestors committed.

"Sydney is not okay with seeing Lucie upset over losing her husband, and he knows she will never love him back the way he wants. He switches places with Charles in the prison. He sacrifices himself to the guillotine. The book ends with Sydney happy with his choice and walking to the gallows. I decided then I would love Sydney back if he ever came into my life."

"Dwayne," Scott said.

"Yes." She let out a slow breath. "The problem is, I didn't realize there are multiple kinds of true love you can show a person. Dickens portrayed Sydney's love as more romance centered, but self-sacrificing platonic love is also completely valid. I spent so long convincing myself Sydney Carton is the right man to spend your life with, but I completely ignored the love between Lucie and Charles."

Scott stayed silent as he mulled over the story. "Are you content with living a story which is already written and finished?"

"What?"

"The story you told me about. It's already done. Charles Dickens told his story hundreds of years ago. Are you content with reliving the same story or are you going to write your own?" He dropped his arm and moved away.

"I am not." She gripped his forearms with her nails. "I don't want to live the same story over again."

"Then that's what you need to do." He gave her a half-smile, and she sat stunned on the chair at the uncharacteristic gesture.

She let go of his arms. "The people who wronged me in the past helped make me who I am today. I'm not condoning any of their actions, but without the fear of feeling trapped, I don't know if I ever would've awoken my elementalist powers. I want to keep moving forward. I want to prove we are meant to be here in this world. If it comes to a war against Tyr Slattery, then I'm ready and willing to be out there on the front lines, proving my worth."

Scott took the empty glass from her and walked over to the sink. A familiar set of arms not belonging to him wrapped around his waist, and he nearly dropped the glass.

"Thank you, Scott." Eilene took a deep breath as she hugged him; she recognized the tones of the cologne she picked out at the mall for him. One of his hands wrapped around hers and held her in place. She didn't know how long they stood there.

Scott let go of her hand and finished washing the dishes while she put the book back in its designated spot. She pressed a soft kiss to his cheek before she left. He dried his hands and retrieved the book from the shelf and settled into one of the bar stools for a few hours of reading. He wanted to see the story through for himself.

November 5, 2317
Bacon Level, Randolph County, Alabama, United States of America

"We were lucky to find this one—I wish we got the one in Jackson," Tyr growled as he worked on the model sword. He hoped it would be the last one he made, but every iteration of the weapon didn't touch the little girl. He convinced himself this one would.

"This one, you know for sure, is a Death elementalist," Mason pointed out from the kitchen table. He sat next to Ryan and pored over pages of papers and handwritten notes. "You merely have to find their limitations."

"You are right, as you often are lately." Tyr grinned. He held out the sword again. The research they accessed only mentioned extreme conditions affecting the elementalists, but as humans, they didn't have a good way of testing an extreme condition without their subject present. The child proved resistant to heat and cold in the locked room of the small house they broke into.

They had no idea when the owners might return, and every little noise made them jump. They couldn't use any lights at night because they feared it would alert the neighbors.

"I wish I could figure out elementalist limitations." Tyr frowned in frustration and bent forward. "Secretive bastards. I'm going to test this one."

Ryan followed Tyr into the other room to see him swing the sword futilely through the girl's stomach. Tyr let out a low and annoyed sigh as he inspected the edges of the weapon. They had a limited supply of items they could use based on their surroundings. The child gazed at Ryan sadly as she sat on the bed, completely motionless—devoid of life. She no longer flinched as the weapons swung her way.

Mason appeared with a milkshake and held out the glass to her. She took it wearily and pushed the straw into her mouth. She vomited any solid foods she ate.

"We don't want to kill you. I promise we'll find a way to help you," he whispered. "Drink up, for now."

Tyr walked into one of the other rooms and closed the door. The lock clicked.

"Didn't he want a cure?" Mason whispered into Ryan's ear.

"Yes," Ryan breathed out slowly and closed the door to the kitchen. "However, he thinks he'll need to kill the Council to get anywhere near the elementalists."

"He's not exactly wrong, is he?" Mason fetched a wet washcloth from the bathroom and pressed it against the child's face.

"Yeah, but he tried to convince us that both our children are serving on the Council then he turns around and wants to kill them." Ryan leaned against the dresser.

"That's how he's got us trapped." Mason used the comb in his back pocket to tend to the little hair the girl had left; he arranged it to hide the bald patches.

"I was supposed to help with a cure for the mutation."

"I doubt that'll happen anytime soon. His goals have changed." Mason stood. He put his hand on the handle of the door. "Our focus should be to do what we can for this child, to save her. The FBI is on our tail. It won't be long before they catch up to us, despite Tyr's thievery and tricks. If Tyr plans on raising his army, he has to do it soon."

Ryan swallowed around a lump in his throat.

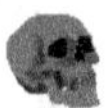

December 7, 2317

The Council Chambers, The Academy, Elementōrum Patriam

"Luana!" Series ran haggardly through the halls. "We have trouble!"

Luana met her in the hallway with the others crowded around them. Series held out her phone, the screen open to a news page.

WORLD LEADERS DENOUNCE ELEMENTALISTS—ANTI-ELEMENTALIST GROUPS DECLARE WAR UNDER LEADER TYR SLATTERY

"What?" Luana grabbed the phone and pressed it against the wall where the article blew up into a larger format for them all to read.

> Anti-elementalist rhetoric is at an all-time high in many countries around the world. While there are certain cities declared as safe-havens, or harbors, there are the same number of cities mandating genetic testing to remain an elementalist-free zone. Most recently, an American man, Tyr Slattery, kidnapped a supposed elementalist child from Hattiesburg, Mississippi. The United States original issued a warrant for his arrest in accordance with the agreements made with Elementōrum Patriam.
>
> However, the U.S. has temporarily removed this sanction in light of a video published online by Slattery where he demonstrated a weapon designed for use against the elementalists. Tyr is currently the face

of the online movement calling for action against those carrying the elementalist mutation.

In the video, Slattery explains how he developed a weapon to combat the elementalists after they took his daughter from him. The incident, as previously reported, occurred in Arizona and was the result of the five-year-old setting fire to their house and killing her nanny. The elementalists retrieved her according to their agreements with the American government and followed every legal procedure.

Slattery believes his daughter should still be in his care and plans to take the elementalists head-on in a battle for who is stronger—the elementalists or the humans. In his message, he proposes their complete eradication and practice of eugenics to keep the race from appearing again.

On the other hand, Slattery confirms he kidnapped the child from Hattiesburg to experiment on. In the video, he cuts the child, who he claims is a Death elementalist, with a flamethrower style blade, resembling the weapons the elementalists developed.

Some of the comments on the online video condemned Slattery for attempting to wipe out a race of people and human trial testing, while others celebrated his courage to stand up against what might be considered a higher power. Most radical online forums do not condemn his actions in kidnapping the child since the forums are generally anti-elementalist.

Many governments, including the American government, are taking Slattery's lead. They are pledging allegiance to his movement and have since withdrawn existing contracts with Elementōrum Patriam at risk of engaging in direct war.

Slattery's full video is linked below.

"Do we dare?" Dwayne reached toward the play button on the video.

"It's the only way we'll know." Luana clenched her jaw. "Either way, we have void contracts and will need to make a decision for the betterment of our country."

"Then we ought to have all the facts," Hans agreed.

Dwayne pressed the play button, and the video took three seconds to load. No one breathed. It felt like an hour had passed.

"How long must we remain oppressed? How long will we allow the world to remain under the control of a singular small country which chooses to live above us in the sky as if they are gods? I ask as a parent: how can they consider themselves to be more equipped to handle and raise our children? If the elementalists hold these powers, why don't they seek to assist humanity? Instead, they refuse to help us. Every year, more of us continue to die from diseases they eradicated among their own people. Why do they hide these secrets from us? Are we not deserving enough?

"We are burdened with debts to them as if they are great saviors of the world—when all they do is take our children from us. We are enslaved by a people with numbers smaller than ours. This is the beginning of our greater collapse. We have only contributed to our oppression by refusing to speak up—we humiliated ourselves, destroyed our honor, and denied everything which we held dearest to us. We stand as a trampled society under the foot of the elementalists. They look down on us with smirks on their faces.

"They know we live in fear of them—as witnessed in the Hattiesburg mall by the destruction they left in their wake. I faced them and won. Today, I sit before you with a message. The day will come when they claim we are no longer meeting our quota, no longer meeting our share of the work in populating their country. They will push us for more—they will take more from us. How long can we remain silent while they push us to the brink of despair as we hope for a better future?

"We are bound by the voice of our government. Many countries worldwide scream and cry all day long they are governed by the people, but the people do not have a voice! Those who sign the accords with the elementalists are the government. They cosigned away our children and told us it would be better this way. I have a better solution. Had we never had the elementalists, we would not be sitting in our inaction. No, we would be with our families around a table experiencing the trials of life as they come without fear of a mutation ruining our dreams and expectations.

"If we practiced caution and good sense, we would not be where we are today. There are cities around the world which ban elementalists for fear of the destruction they will reign upon us. We could have avoided this altogether by refusing to reproduce elementalists. Of course, what I'm suggesting is not easy for those who decide to follow love over common sense. If we had not reproduced with, or allowed the elementalists to reproduce, our lives would be quiet. Most likely, we would still be on Pangea—a happy continent where we are one with our fellow man instead of separated by a grand design of those who oppress us.

"Freedom comes through revolution. We can ask who is responsible for our misfortune and inquire as to who is profiting from our collapse—an eternal evolution into the elementalists. If they continue to be born, we will remain under their rule, terrified of the unnatural power they wield. Throughout time, the elementalists have not grown poorer and weaker as we convinced ourselves. Instead, they grow stronger and richer with every child born into the world. The day will come when they outnumber us and wipe us from the earth in their conquest for power.

"Do you think these people would be capable of ending a revolution if the world united against them? Even with the accords broken, we outnumber them. We have the chance to seize the moment when we take back our world. We take back our children. We take back our rights. We take back our choice. This stream of opposition we create as we carve out a new path in the mountains of the world's struggle shows our recognition of how the system manipulates us. We can take this system down by bonding together. If the masses come into action, the leaders of the elementalists will recognize the facts and come to their end by bowing down to the superior, more populous race.

"Their lies about separating for the betterment of humans will no longer persist. Let me show you why I can say this with such confidence." Tyr stood, and the camera followed him. "I have here a child who is a Death elementalist. I can confirm this through several methods. This is a regular knife. When I try to hurt her with the knife, her body reacts and doesn't allow her to take any injury." He showed them how her wrist turned to smoke for only a moment, the same as Ethan's.

"She's like me," he whispered. "There's more than just me."

"She isn't injured, but I am developing a weapon which will. It's a way we can take down all the types of elementalists, should they be mass manufactured." Tyr held a different type of hollow tubular weapon in front of him. The tube's edge sharpened to a point, like a knife. Along the sides, the weapon had holes in the silver-colored metal. He pressed a button on the hilt, and bright blue flames burst from every orifice. "When it is perfected, it will touch even these abominations."

"I can say, there is no doubt in my mind people will be roused to victory when they see the truth. The elementalists can be killed by the likes of us. Perhaps some remain apathetic, but I know this seed of hope will ferment in their hearts. Passion for the right is driven through distress, and since they unjustly took my daughter from me, I have lived in the deepest wells of distress. This is the faith you can cling to. This is your opportunity to do something right and change the course of our world as we know it. My movement going forward will create the torrential tsunami waves needed to maintain reform. Do not fail in the hours of confusion as the elementalists hope to win back your loyalty with their false promises." He held the weapon in front of him in a tight grip and the camera focused on it instead. "This is your future. You know where you can pledge your allegiance to. Put your faith in me and help to build the foundation of the new world where you will only find calmness settled into your heart.

"With these words, I announce my official declaration of war against the elementalists. Countries who wish to find a better future; join me and denounce our oppressors."

The video ended, and the website brought up automatic recommendations for other videos they could view next. They didn't move.

"The war Series foresaw. It's this one. A war threatening to end our race entirely." Luana took a shaky breath. "What is our first move?"

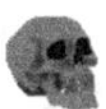

The Council barely broke for dinner amid their harried planning session. When they couldn't ignore the growling of their stomachs any longer, they sent their orders as one set to the kitchens. The plates arrived, and they set them in the middle, allowing everyone to pull their orders closer to them as they worked. Luana had army schematics pulled up on one wall, and she moved them around to represent the dissociated countries alongside those still allied through their unbroken contracts.

On another wall, Series and Scarlet worked with Hans and Ethan to write an appropriate response letter for the declaration.

Eilene worked close to Scott and Dwayne on securing plans to shut down Elementōrum Patriam if needed. She leaned over to whisper in Scott's ear, and he nearly jumped back in surprise from the sharp breath against his cheek.

"Before I forget, happy birthday." She smiled and pressed something into his palm.

His fingers wrapped around the object and her hand before she pulled away and reached for something to write on. Dwayne didn't appear to notice the exchange, and Scott lifted his hand. Between his fingers rested a small pin with a depiction of the wind element embossed into the metal. He didn't wear pins, but it came from *her*. He removed the backing and lifted it to the collared edge of his leather jacket then pressed the pin through the fabric before he reattached the back and returned to work.

A smile rested on Eilene's lips as she wrote a few notes onto her computer screen. In a brave move, Scott reached forward and stole a few of her fries from the plate. Her gray eyes pierced him with curiosity. He replied by pushing the bowl of ice cream closer to her.

"Do you think we'll need to make a nationwide call for volunteers to join the army?" Scott asked as Eilene helped herself to the sweet dessert.

"That's not a bad idea." Dwayne made a note of it. "I'll add it as a section in our plans for combatting the humans and their numbers."

"On that note, we need to let our troops know to mobilize as soon as we release the command if possible." Eilene brought her thumb away from the bowl and licked off a bit of chocolate. "Do you want me to work on the announcement? It'd probably be ideal to release it before morning."

"If you would, Eilene," Luana pitched in. "Your decision is for the best."

"Give me twenty minutes tops to have a draft."

Lakeland, Pointe Coupee Parish, Louisiana, United States of America

"You want to kidnap another child?" Mason nearly dropped the plate in his hands.

"The woman in Jackson, I'm sure she is one of the lost elements. We were lucky to find a Death elementalist shortly after her escape, but we haven't tested this weapon against the other. I'm sure it'll be fine against the seven elements since the other children are injured by normally devised weapons. I watched this new child—he had the same habits as the waitress. If we can't rid the world of all the elements, it does nothing for our cause." Tyr paced the length of the living room.

Ryan looked over at Mason. They still had the Death elementalist with them. Another child would make it harder to get them out of the hostage situation.

"I think it would be best if we develop corrections after seeing the weapon act in war against them," Ryan tried to placate. "We are trying to primarily work toward a cure—not destruction."

"No, it'll be too late then. If we go up against them without being fully prepared, we could be killed on the battlefield. Where would the fight for justice be, then?"

"You've made your point." Mason crossed his arms. "We'll agree—but you need to promise to keep both children alive and to return them to their families."

"What?" Tyr snapped like a vicious dog.

"You know what it's like to have your child ripped away from you. These children are not old enough to make their own decisions—they don't know what their people have done. They deserve to be returned to their home." Mason's voice remained calm and quiet.

"Where is the Council's consideration when they take our children away?" Tears gathered in the corner of Tyr's eyes. His breathing picked up pace, and he choked. "How can you say any of our children were old enough to make their own decisions about joining those *elementalists*?" he spat the last word. "Perhaps your children were old enough to think for themselves, but my daughter was five. Much closer to the typical age when they discover and take our children from us."

Mason's and Ryan's lips thinned. Mason bit his tongue to bite back the retort he wanted to say. Tyr's daughter was the only one with the true power of an elementalist. The Council had no reason to kill her like they did for their children.

"Do you honestly think they deserve to be returned to their families just to be torn away again?" Tyr asked. "We have to eradicate them as a steppingstone for their whole race."

"You promised a cure not genocide," Mason said.

"Fine—but let it be on your heads if one of them grows up to revive the mutation."

Ryan sighed. "They won't if you put your focus back on the cure. You can't kill your own daughter, Tyr."

Tyr didn't appear to hear him.

December 8, 2317
The Council Chambers, The Academy, Elementōrum Patriam

Ethan pulled the robe over his head. The Council spent a full twenty-four hours without sleep as they formulated their plans to move forward. In their tiredness, Series reached a moment of clarity and experienced another waking vision, telling them how to proceed. They would have to go before their people for the first time as a unit, ready for their judgement, and beg for their help.

Luana was convinced Ethan would need to be the one to face Tyr Slattery on the battlefield. She claimed, with the Council's backing, he would be able to train to become immune to the weapon he wielded, but Ethan had his own doubts about the plan. He simply felt too exhausted to argue. He wanted to finish their task for the day then sleep, but he didn't know when their next chance to rest would be.

In the meantime, they waited in the entrance hall for everyone to assemble and finish their measly breakfasts. Scott already had his robe on, but the hood rested on his shoulders as he watched Eilene. She inhaled a glass bottle of apple juice, but Ethan had a feeling she didn't register anything past the sugary taste. Dwayne laughed at something Scarlet said, but Ethan's brain refused to process the words—he couldn't say if they conversed in English, in the first place.

"I don't think this is cranberry juice," Eilene said. She held up the bottle for scrutiny, but her eyes kept drifting shut, and she couldn't comprehend the label. Dwayne gently took his apple juice back from her and replaced her drink with the correct one. As he took a sip from the half-empty bottle, he noticed Scott look away forcefully.

"These are kind of itchy." Ethan scratched at the robe just under his chest and tried to adjust the fabric.

"You'll get used to it," Series said.

Luana watched a small screen near the door. One of the squares shone bright red while the other eleven glowed green. They had to wait for an all-clear signal from the twelve feeds before they could leave the safety of the Council chambers. "As a reminder, the speech Scarlet and I prepared will be delivered to the entire world, not just to our people. We are hosting a live video feed, and I'm sure many are already tuned in. There are many speculating we will bow out of the war, but that would mean admitting we shouldn't be alive either. I'm sure there will be an uproar among all peoples. I want our people to trust us—which means we need to trust them. We need to be a part of them."

"We understand." Hans placed a hand on her shoulder.

The last light turned green. They lifted their hoods and donned the black face plates. The door opened to the brightly lit corridor. Eilene straightened but drifted several times along the wall. Dwayne put a hand on her shoulder and passed her a sour candy to help wake her up. She made a grunt of acknowledgement and quickly slid the candy into her mouth through the mask. With everyone gathered outside for the press conference, they didn't run the risk of someone seeing them, but they still wanted to take precautions.

At the front doors of the Academy, two security guards waited for them. The Council stopped per protocol, and the personnel used a walkie on their wrist to talk to those outside. It took a few minutes before security cleared them and opened the doors. They bowed in respect as the Council passed. Their people outside bowed in a similar manner.

A translator for Elementalist Sign Language waited on their podium. They gave a short non-verbal greeting before turning to the waiting crowd. One camera remained focused on them, so the translator would be broadcast through the entire feed. They didn't move as they waited for one of the Council members to speak. The eight took their place on the stand before Luana broke away and stepped up to the main microphone.

"As the Council, we come before you today to address the accusations and war cries sounded against our people. Since the announcement, we found ourselves stuck in a dizzying loop of pressure. With our discovery of lost elementalist history, there are many changes coming to our country and to the Council. As you see, we now number eight and hold out hope for us to be nine again. While this is happy news, the threat to our wellbeing is not." Her words echoed and weighed heavily on the people's hearts. Muttering passed through the crowd below them. Luana certainly caught their attention. "A human dared to threaten our existence as a people. They garnered the support of many countries we once considered allies in their protection. They called for the practice of eugenics to eradicate our race permanently, seeking to erase us from the history of the world. Their plan is to destroy everything we have built since being driven out of their lands thousands of years ago with the first Council. Vasha tore apart of the world and gave us our freedom in the sky. We cannot let her sacrifice die in vain.

"We naïvely believed we would be safe from the humans. However, we continue to live in fear and separate ourselves from them, but this is a futile solution. We will no longer bow to the will of humans. Yes, for years we refused to use our abilities to assist humans, which may cause some resentment, but let us not forget we helped the human race for centuries before they turned on us. Humans persecuted and killed our people for our powers. Thousands of years have passed, but we are in the same place, fighting the same war.

"We no longer wish to remain subjugated to the human population. For years we painfully tore children away from families to keep them from injuring or killing their parents and siblings while still unable to control their abilities. This is an agreement we made between all the countries of the world. We do not want to kill humans. We want to protect your race, but you denied us from helping you. Now, you come to us claiming we have not offered while you drove us off your lands.

"We come before our people with a plea. The world is revolting against us. They doubt our strength. They plan to kill us—they plan to kill our children before they have a chance to live a life which they have a right to live. We are not to blame for our abilities or our differences. As the Council, we strive to protect you and make a country where we are accepted for who we are. Instead, it provided a target which the world can hit easier than ever.

"As part of the Council, we needed to keep our identities hidden. We did not want the power to influence our decisions when it came to family members we ceaselessly love or friends who we deeply care about. We see it as one of our duties to disappear from the lives of those we care about to better protect them, but in doing so, it hurt them. So today, as a part of our plea to ask for your support, we made the decision to trust you. We are prepared to do what is right, even if it costs us our own lives. For you to trust us, there cannot be any secrets between us. We lived in hiding for countless centuries. This will be no more. Our shrouded identities will no longer exist. We hope this will gain your trust. We wish for you to join our fight against those set to destroy us."

The Council reached up and removed the face plates from their masks and threw the material onto the ground in front of them. They pushed the hoods down and gasps and murmurs passed through the crowd as they recognized the Council members who they believed to be dead. They pulled the robes free from the rest of their body, and the red fabric joined the masks on the ground.

Luana ran her fingers through her messy hair and smiled. "I thought it would be more upsetting to reveal ourselves when we lived hidden for so long, but there is something freeing in this action. It makes me feel closer to all of you. My name is Luana Ford, from Tennessee in America. I am the representative of Fire on the Council." She snapped her fingers and the robes burst into flames. They had new ones without the fire-retardant material, commissioned overnight for Luana to put on a show. "I've acted as a part of this Council since twenty-two-ninety-nine. I would like to take a moment to introduce you to my friends and fellow Council members."

She stepped away from the microphone and the others lined up to take their turn.

"Hans Aliyev, the representative of Earth. I joined the Council in twenty-three-oh-six. I am from the Russia sector in City of Vasha."

"Scott Everton, I am a Wind elementalist from South Carolina in America. I joined the Council in twenty-three-ten."

"Lí Scarlet, a Storm elementalist. I joined the Council the same year, only a couple of weeks after Scott. I am from Jingzhou, People's Republic of China."

"Dwayne Tebogo. I am from Botswana, and I control Life. I joined the Council a year after Scott and Scarlet."

"Eilene Vos from the Netherlands sector in City of Barren. I hail from a long line of elementalists, and I am the Water representative. I joined the Council a year after Dwayne."

"Series Pahona, I am part of the Hopi Nation in Arizona and New Mexico, United States," she said, "I joined the Council the same year as Eilene. I am a Fortune elementalist."

"Ethan Silverspoon—I feel a little guilty for admitting I am also American. We aren't terribly diverse, apparently. I've lived all over, so I can't say I really come from anywhere specifically. I joined the Council a year ago after it was discovered I am a Death elementalist."

Luana took control of the microphone again. "We are on the lookout for the return of the ninth element among our people. We want to be a Council of nine who can govern you with your faith in us. While we ourselves may not be terribly diverse, we do see the importance of our people coming from a global sphere. Our own country, the great Elementōrum Patriam, is full of the diverse cultures of the world and none are turned away. If we allow the humans to come against us, we will lose the unity we have with one another.

"The humans asked for war with us, and it is a war they will receive. We cannot back down when they want to take away everything we hold dear. As the call comes asking for you to serve our country, I hope you can accept. Our sense of nationalism, of globalism, is unparalleled by any other in the world. We understand what it is like to be oppressed, to be the one staring down the barrel of a gun waiting for others to see us as more than a mutation.

"We are stronger together." Luana stepped away from the microphone. The crowd below broke into raucous applause and cheering.

They would take questions from the waiting audience, but the most important part had come to an end—but really, they knew it would only be the beginning.

CHAPTER FIFTEEN
Denouement

Lakeland, Pointe Coupee Parish, Louisiana, United States of America

"Breaking News as we hear more about the declaration made by American Tyr Slattery who has garnered support from many countries around the world for his war against the elementalists. In rebuke of his speech, the Council made their first bold move in Elementōrum Patriam today. World leaders and citizens went online to watch their response and found themselves blown away by the unexpected. For the first time in history since the first separation of humans and elementalists, the leaders of Elementōrum Patriam, known collectively as the Council, revealed their faces.

"The Council is known to operate under firm secrecy to protect their friends and family, but it came crashing down today as they made their own declaration of war. We have a clip from the conference today," the newscaster announced through their television. Tyr perked up at the news, disinterested in everything else the media had to say. Mason and Ryan leaned against one of the counters in the kitchen, watching the TV as they ate lunch.

"We have lived in hiding for countless centuries. This will be no more. Our shrouded identities will no longer be such. We hope this will help you trust us and join our fight against those set to destroy us."

The Council removed the face plates from their masks and threw the material onto the ground in front of them. They pushed the hoods down, and the ceramic plates slipped from Mason's and Ryan's grasps. They shattered on impact, and their food splattered across the cupboards. Tyr sent them an annoyed glare over the mess but paused at their shocked faces. The eight people on the screen pulled the robes free from the rest of their body, and the red fabric joined the masks on the ground.

Mason watched his daughter run her fingers through her messy hair and smile. He saw the image of her five-year-old self with three missing teeth holding out a popsicle for them to share.

"I thought it would be more upsetting to reveal ourselves when we've lived hidden for so long, but there is something freeing in this action. It makes me feel closer to all of you. My name is Luana Ford, from Tennessee in America. I am the representative of Fire on the Council." She snapped her fingers and the robes burst into flames.

Mason's breath caught in his throat. Luana lived.

"Scott Everton, I am a Wind elementalist from South Carolina in America. I joined the Council in twenty-three-ten."

Ryan took several shaky steps forward, and the ceramic pieces burst into dust under his shoes. Messy footprints followed him across the floor.

They watched the introductions and speech in dead silence.

"We are stronger together." Luana stepped away from the microphone.

"I assume those are your supposedly dead children?" Tyr asked.

Mason nodded, unable to speak.

"When I asked for your loyalty, I didn't know you would be pitted against your children, but you understand I am still counting on both of you to lead this revolution with me. You cannot back out now." He clenched his jaw and looked between the two slack-jawed men.

"We understand," Ryan choked out. He thought he would never see either of his kids again, but Scott lived and led an entire country. He grew up to do great things, just as he expected. Ryan wouldn't be alone in the world without his family any longer—except he would be fighting against his son. He would tell him he didn't belong in the world, but he knew that was entirely untrue. Tears gathered in his eyes and spilled down his cheeks. His poor decisions would lead him right to potentially killing his son. Again.

"In light of this speech given by the newly revealed, Luana Ford, many countries are coming together to analyze their participation on either side of the mutually declared war. It is possible we will see our world changing soon in what many believe to be the bloodiest war we will see in our lifetime." The newscaster returned to the screen to finish out the segment, but Tyr turned the TV off before they could.

"Of course, this is the reaction I would hope for from our elementalist enemies. We can fight them one on one. We will not forgo the opportunity to stop other parents from having their families ripped apart." Tyr walked away from the room and left the two alone.

"I don't want to kill my son a second time," Ryan whispered.

"I understand." Mason placed a warm hand against his back.

December 10, 2317
The Bullet, Elementōrum Patriam

Eilene and Scott sat in a private car on the Bullet train. Luana sent them to the City of Sides to visit and work with the Industry District. They wanted to help them any way they could and improve their relationships with their people. Scott watched her mouth the words to the song as she stared out the window. They didn't expect any direct battles with the enemies yet, but they knew it would come in a matter of time. Several countries who initially walked away to back Tyr Slattery quickly tried to revert their decision while others expedited their decision to void the contracts. The changing relationships delayed many of their plans, unsure of how to react.

Scott nudged her foot with his. She courteously removed one of the earbuds from her ear.

"Song?"

"A three-hundred-year-old one," she laughed. He prompted her again with a raised eyebrow. "*'Castle on a Hill'* by Ed Sheeran."

She leaned forward and offered the available bud to Scott. He put it in his ear. After a few times on loop, she changed the song and moved to sit next to him on the seat. He stiffened but eased when she rested her head against his shoulder. The songs became familiar on the ride, and Scott mumbled the lyrics under his breath. They danced across Eilene's hair, and she fell into a nap with a soft smile on her face.

Industrial District, City of Sides, Elementōrum Patriam

"As you can see, we're ramping up our manufacturing of weapons, but there are a few assemblers which require a lot of maintenance. We have some of our best men on them, but just as one gets up and running, another one falls apart." The foreman escorted Scott and Eilene around the factory. Conveyer belts with Tēlōrum and Armōrum moved around them. "There aren't a lot of people who are willing to come and work out here because of its reputation, but in the last couple years we've been granted permission to give bonus checks for various things and raised the minimum wage we're able to pay the workers. It's all thanks to the Council as well."

"I'll see if we can't also help you get more workers." Eilene typed a quick note on her phone. "We may be able to pull workers from careers which need less help to aid in the war effort."

"We'll take any help we can get."

"What other things are the factories struggling with? What is your daily output?"

They continued their tour through the factories and spoke with several workers directly about their jobs. They didn't feel well-received by the people, nor did they look encouraged. Eilene wondered if their visit had the opposite effect and made them feel as if they had to work harder—not what they wanted.

December 11, 2317

Russia Sector, City of Vasha, Elementōrum Patriam

The days blurred together. The Council had their final list of countries who planned to continue the revolt. They had their first targets who were to mobilize their armies. Until the date of mobilization, they moved through the country and took care of various tasks. Hans made time between nationally important ones to take care of a couple of more personal tasks.

He greeted several children along the walk down familiar streets. Finally, he stood in front of his old home. The scent of his mother's cooking flooded his memory. He could see himself staring out the front windows with a book in his lap. He remembered Maxim's back as he stood on the porch, forced to leave their home as an Un. He saw his father throw Odessa out onto the street when she returned home after running from a Council summons to be killed. He felt the pain and relief as if brand new when the Council told him his father committed suicide.

Hans took the few short steps up the walk to the front door and knocked. The door swung open, and his mother threw her hands up to her mouth when she saw him on the porch.

"Mama," he greeted softly.

She stood barefoot, tears pooling at the corners of her eyes and spilling across her cheeks. She pulled him into a tight hug. "Hans, my baby."

"I am sorry for deceiving you," he whispered in Russian.

"I understand you didn't have a choice—I am so happy to see you alive when the Council announced the war." She pressed a soft kiss to his forehead. He bent low for her.

"I regret how otets died because of my promotion."

"It is hard without your father—without any of you." She brushed her thumb across his cheek. "You have come back to me. That is all I need."

"I hope to bring Maxim back to you, too, one day. You can't let anyone else on the Council know of this, however. It would put me in a lot of trouble. The Uns are still a hot debate for members."

"I will be satisfied either way—the both of you are safe and alive. I get to see you. I will earn my rest in the life after." She smiled, and it reminded Hans of her inevitable death growing even closer. Older now, she looked only a few steps out of the grave.

"I wish I could stay and visit, but I have Council duties I need to take care of."

"I understand."

"I will come back when I can to see you—a real visit next time."

"Be strong in the war. Stay safe."

"I promise." He gave her a final lingering hug before he parted ways once more.

City of the Uns, Elementōrum Patriam

Hans decided to walk between destinations, but the path led him along the trail directly next to the Uns encampment. People clamored near the fence to get a closer look at him. They didn't come within more than a foot of the electrified material.

"Are you really from the Council?" someone shouted.

"I am."

"Hans?" a familiar voice called from the crowd. He turned to face them properly and found Maxim fighting his way to the front. When he pushed through, it reminded him of the last time he saw him handling the uprising.

"Maxim, it's good to see you again."

"Again?"

"I was at the uprising. I made the earth stage."

"I'm an idiot. How did I not put that together? Of course, it was you," his brother laughed wryly. "I heard you will be going to war."

"It is true."

The crowd hardly dared to breathe, surprised by the ease with which one of their own spoke to the highly feared Council member.

"I want to wish you luck—if you need any extra support, please remember we exist. I know many forget about us behind our fences, but we're a part of this country too—though perhaps with a little less nationalism." Maxim swallowed.

"I will come back for you, brother." Hans placed his hand on the fence. Maxim followed the movement, but he didn't touch the material. The scars on his hand stood out in sharp relief. Hans said, "I will try to fix all the damage we caused."

"Tell Mama I love her." His brother turned away and walked through the crowd.

"Of course."

December 18, 2317

Miwok Sector, City of Wabaunsee, Elementōrum Patriam

The police found her.

Kristen groaned. Everything went so well for months. She escaped the return trip to Earth from Elementōrum Patriam with no one noticing vocally. Kristen liked the job she earned in the elementalist country, plus she had the comfort of knowing how the government took care of their people by providing housing and food. Even if she had a lower paycheck due to the heavy taxes it took to fund the large-scale operation, it meant the money she earned went toward the things she could enjoy—like video games or books. She loved it. A type of caring she never experienced previously.

However, the law caught up with her illegal ID number.

Kristen tore through the Forest of Light. Even running from the law, she noted the beautiful landscape. The officers behind her smashed through the forest, certainly destroying part of the ecosystem. Wind elementalists managed to keep up with her. She didn't want to use her powers to escape them in case it lit any red flags around the country itself. The last thing she needed was a nationwide manhunt when she could hopefully keep it contained to a few officers. *Maybe.*

She broke out of the line of trees and spotted the Bullet station. Before she could get there, a hand landed on her shoulder. Scared, she dodged under his arm and activated her ability. His eyes widened comically slow in shock when she vanished instantly in front of him.

Her feet pounded against the concrete. The police quickly caught up with her. Her eyes darted around the open space for an escape route and caught on an older teen, in the adult range, with red hair near a skinny alleyway between housing. She ducked around several more people with the ease of slowing down time, before she grabbed his hand and pulled him into the small space. Her hand slammed over his mouth before she pressed her lips hard against the back of her hand. His phone fell to the ground and shattered. He made several muffled sounds of surprise. She ignored him until he forcefully pushed her away.

Out of the corner of her eye, she saw the officers run past. One of them shouted into his communication device that they lost sight of her and needed backup to secure the area for a search. Kristen peered around the corner of the alley as the stranger inspected his broken phone. She pulled away and wiped her hand on her pants.

"I can fix that," she said.

He held the phone delicately between his fingers. "Does what you did count as assault?

Kristen looked into his warm, brown eyes. "Sorry, I had to get them off my tail."

"You appeared literally out of nowhere," he said.

"Yeah, it's my thing," she laughed nervously.

"You're an elementalist." He looked excited.

"I am."

"Why are the police chasing you?" He gestured back to the main square.

Kristen hesitated. It could be the moment between life and death for her. She could escape, and he would be none the wiser—he didn't know her. Although, he could get the information from the police still looking for her. She bit her lip, steeled her nerve, and fixed him with a hardened gaze.

"I'm not supposed to exist."

ELEMENTALISTS WEAPON GUIDE

Lūminis: Used to indicate a ranged (Tēlōrum) weapon.

Lūcis: Used to indicate a melee (Armōrum) weapon.

Arcus: A bow; recurve, compound, longbow, and barebow. Plural is Arcūs.

Manuballista: A crossbow; recurve, compound, reverse draw, rifle, pistol, bullet, and repeating. Plural is Manuballistae.

Sclopētum: A gun; handgun and long gun. Plural is Sclopēta.

Pyrobolus: A bomb; incendiaries, blast, time-delayed, command-initiated, postal, projected explosive, and commercial. Plural is **Pyroboli**.

Sagitta: Ammunition; all types. Plural is Sagittae.

Ēnsis: Single-edged sword; various styles in one-hand and two-hand wielding. Plural is Ēnsēs.

Rumpia: Double-edged sword; various styles in two-hand wielding. Plural is Rumpiae.

Jaculum: Spear; unlike a historical spear, the shaft of this spear can also be used as a slicing weapon. Plural is Jacula.

Fuscina: Trident; similar to the Jaculum, the shaft is a viable weapon as well as the base. Plural is Fuscinae.

Bipenne: Double-headed axe; offers one- and two-handed options. Plural is Bipennia.

Falx: Scythe; offers single-sided and double-sided head options. Plural is Falcēs.

Secūris: Handaxe. Plural is Secūrēs.

Scūta: Shield. Plural is Scūtum.

ACKNOWLEDGEMENTS

I always look at acknowledgment pages in the back of books, and think, "Man, that is a lot of people." I never really registered how much goes into publishing a book—not to mention when you're self-publishing. Although, from what I hear, it isn't much different in the traditionally published world except somebody else is footing the bill!

The idea for this book came from an unlikely source, and this story wouldn't exist without many nameless faces and faceless names I can't remember helping me along my journey.

Of course, I wouldn't be here writing without my parents instilling in me a love for learning and literature. My parents made dramatic efforts to make sure I loved reading. Both my parents are avid consumers of audiobooks, and I grew up listening to stories on cassette tape and CD. My mom wanted to write children's books when she was younger and has encouraged me immensely to chase my dreams. My dad always tells me how proud of me he is, and I know he's excited about this book almost as much as I am.

I became a first-generation college student, and now I'm creating worlds and stories itching at the back of my mind for years. This story took eleven years, maybe twelve, to get it to the point where I finally settled on self-publishing and sent my manuscript to an editor (the amazing editor Glysia Gretz who I'm happy to also call a friend). I learned a lot about writing from the original version of this story, which I still have, and I'm so pleased with where this story is. I think it's reached its full potential.

Of course, it wouldn't be here without all those amazing people behind me. Jeff Orren, a close friend, is one of my best support systems. I met Jeff while working a retail job after I graduated high school, and I'm glad that he's such a close friend. Obviously, I mentioned him in my dedication for a reason. I'm equally invested in the story he's crafting, and I hope he can publish it one day as well and share its amazingness with the world. Also, a big thank you to Jeff's wife, Aly, for allowing me to steal his time so often. His help is invaluable in crafting this story and many other elements.

In part of the process of getting this book ready for Glysia to take it on as my editor, I of course sent the manuscript to beta readers. Victoria MacDonald, Val Nelson, and Katy Magee gave me absolutely amazing help that changed the organization of the story, the structure of scenes, and many other small details which helped me create the vivid world of the elementalists. I'm so unbelievably grateful for their help. I'm writing the acknowledgement at a time when they still haven't seen a single part of the second book yet. I won't give a specific timeline, but they'll see book two in about a half a month, and by the time this is published, it will be at least a couple months since they've read it. I'm looking forward to hearing their thoughts on book two. I want every book to get steadily better.

This wouldn't be a proper acknowledgement without also addressing all the amazing people I met in my self-publishing journey. While I saw or met many of them on TikTok, I also attribute my relationships with them to our Discord communities where we video chatted while working or messaged each other frequently to discuss our craft. Believe me when I say that I will feel so guilty when I miss someone from this list, so if your name isn't here, please tell me, so I can issue you my profuse apologies. Without further ado, the amazing writing community includes: C.L. Carner, Trevor Billings, P.A. Powers, Julie Defisher, Elizabeth Krause, Mason Carlisle, K.D. Parker, R.L. Parker, M.K. Dockery, Zachary Jeffries, Joseph Harkreader, and R.M. Palumbo. Please make sure that you also check out the amazing things they are doing, including their writing. There's nothing like supporting a great Indie author community.

And an additional thank you to C.L. Carner who helped me with the final formatting changes for this novel. I appreciate the assistance.

I also just want to give a shout-out to some great people on TikTok who inspire me in my own writing. Jeff Spaur who is friendly, kind, and makes hilarious content. Jen Guberman who had a lot of great advice for authors seeking self-publishing (she is also incredibly friendly and bubbly). Chantel Burnham who is just generally amazing at everything (we also live in the same state, so bonus points; I swear I will meet her one day in person). And Michelle Sauer who is such a great person. I edited her debut novel, and I hope that I might be invited back again for the sequel. I highly recommend her fantastic urban fantasy with mermaids, demons, werewolves, and more.

It's a great murder mystery romance that deserves so much recognition. Yet again, I'm sure there's more amazing people who I missed.

Alright, I think I've reached the point where I finally sing the praises of Glysia Gretz despite mentioning her twice before. I'm so glad that I met her through the same groups listed above because my book would have way too many tautologies without her. That is apparently my writing kryptonite. My favorite moment, when getting general feedback from her, was when she told me she kept forgetting to edit my novel because she loved the story. These are the best words you can hear from an editor.

Publishing is truly a journey where you need a whole team behind you. I never imagined I would have a team quite as big as this because I didn't really know what the publishing world looked like. I'm so excited that Kristin Murray not only designed the cover for this book (and made it more stunning than I could ever imagine), but she is also designing the covers for the other books in this series as well. They're going to be lovely and match the spines as good covers should. I hope you love the covers as much as I do, because she captures the essence of my stories and vision.

Thank you to everyone who supported me over the years, including my past coworkers Tamara Harvey, Jared Scow, Rachelle Durrant, Aaryn Birchell, Michelle Bain, Camille Ward, Kristen Baumgarten, Liz Smith, Jana Bingham, LaDonna Christensen, and many others. I also wouldn't be here without the support of my friends James and Sacha Head and Devin Boyle. I am truly blessed to have such a long list of friends pushing me from behind to achieve.

You are my wings.

Thank you.

I love you all.

And now...

An excerpt from Indictment.
Book two in the Elementalists trilogy.

Novo Mesto, City Municipality of Novo Mesto, Slovenia

Once a haven of the elementalists, Novo Mesto became the humans' first successful stand against their oppressive power. Mason Ford crouched in the middle of the road leading into the heart of the city and watched the ash and snow drift to the ground around him. The pavement felt warm to his touch despite the darkening weather. He didn't want to be there, among the rubble, but he couldn't walk away—no—Tyr would notice. He kept Mason and Ryan close for his own reasons. Mason couldn't fathom those reasons anymore. Tyr went mad for his quest—and the world followed him.

"We're to head out in the morning." Ryan Everton stepped up behind him with nary a sound, and Mason jumped.

"That's his orders?" Mason's stomach dropped.

"Yes."

"And our task?"

Ryan took a shaky breath of frigid air; it rattled in his chest. "Testing center."

The faces of one of the families trapped in their house as Mason lifted the flamethrower under orders flashed through his mind. They didn't look scared but sad and resigned. He would stare at those faces forever and only add more to the number while trapped at Tyr's side. "What's he doing with the testing center?"

"Countries under his banner are investing in genetic testing."

Mason bit his tongue and tasted blood.

"Some have started ghettos," Ryan continued. "Tyr is sending us to work with the top brass on the testing center."

"Away from the fighting?" Mason lifted a hand to shade his eyes from the fading light on the horizon. He could see a mass of black dots growing bigger.

"For now." Ryan spotted the same shapes. "The elementalists are arriving."

"We should go." Mason turned his back on the smoldering ruins and followed the wet pavement.

Ryan fell into step next to him. "What's your rush?"

"If Luana is in that convoy, I don't want her to know I'm mixed up in all of this."

"Do you believe the same things as Tyr?"

"I don't know anymore."

January 30, 2318

Mason packed his last bag. They would ship out in a few hours. He had to be prepared to lift off from the airfield on time. The elementalists didn't bother to do much with their camp over the last sixteen hours; they focused on the town—or the piles of ashes. Mason and Ryan would help with the testing facility, but he also knew Tyr wouldn't keep them out of the line of fire permanently. No.

Tyr wanted them to meet their children on the field. He wanted the reality of the situation to drive a further wedge between the elementalists and the humans. Mason slung the strap of the bag over his right shoulder and stepped out of the nearly empty tent. The lower ranks would arrive later to pack away the beds and disassemble the tent.

He raised a hand to shield his vision from the bright sun overhead and saw the swarm of activity in the lower town. Green uniforms moved among the remains. Mason breathed a little easier. No orange uniforms meant Luana wasn't there. The same went for white; Ryan wouldn't have to face his son—yet.

"The Life branch." Ryan joined him with his bag over his left shoulder. "I doubt they're all Life elementalists, though. That'd be a stupid strategy."

"It'd leave the element without a military presence, and the others without medical aide."

"Exactly." Ryan scratched his eyebrow. "Either way, it's a smart idea to send the Life Council member. Have you seen what he can do?"

"Not personally. You?" Mason led them through the crowds of people to the airfield a little closer to the town.

"In video—and I heard from Tyr what he saw the day they took his daughter. It's intimidating to think someone has so much power to keep people from dying. How many of our people would kill for a blessing like that?"

Mason grinned. "I suppose that's why they're here." He stopped walking and watched a unit pull people out of one of the houses from a distance. They looked alive. Mason's brow furrowed. "Do you know where Tyr is planning to attack next?"

"You mean HISS?" Ryan asked.

Mason laughed. "I'm sorry, what?" He started to cough from laughing and couldn't focus on Ryan's identical grin.

"The Human Inquisition for Systematic Suppression. It's the new name they've fashioned for the movement—Tyr is at the head, but it makes the backers feel more involved."

"And they went with HISS?" Mason rubbed his hands across his face. "I'm glad I wasn't in that meeting."

"Same here." Ryan's eyes dropped to the city again. "I heard they want to go after all the safe cities first—HISS is planning on the Philippines."

"Want to make it more difficult for HISS?"

Ryan imitated a fish for a few moments. "How?"

Mason tilted his head toward the town. "There's a whole military down there looking for information. I think we ought to have a little conversation."

Join the Discord for Elementalists and get

engaged in conversation with others and directly

with the author.

Ä
Ö
Ü
β

A D F G V X Y B T
A D F G V X Y B
あ い う え お
ゴ サ し す
to te tsu
パ ボ ペ
ん を わ ろ

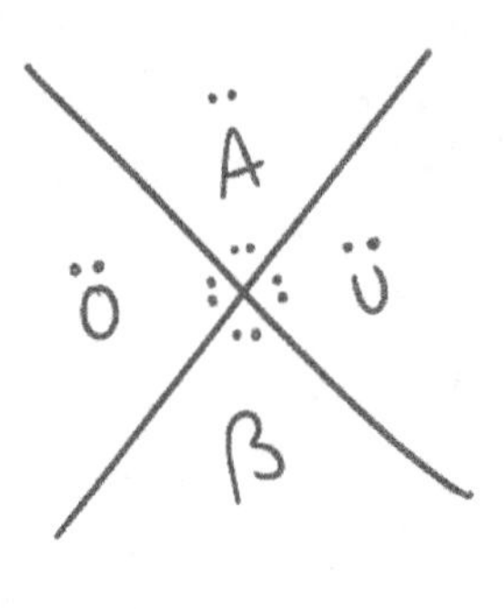

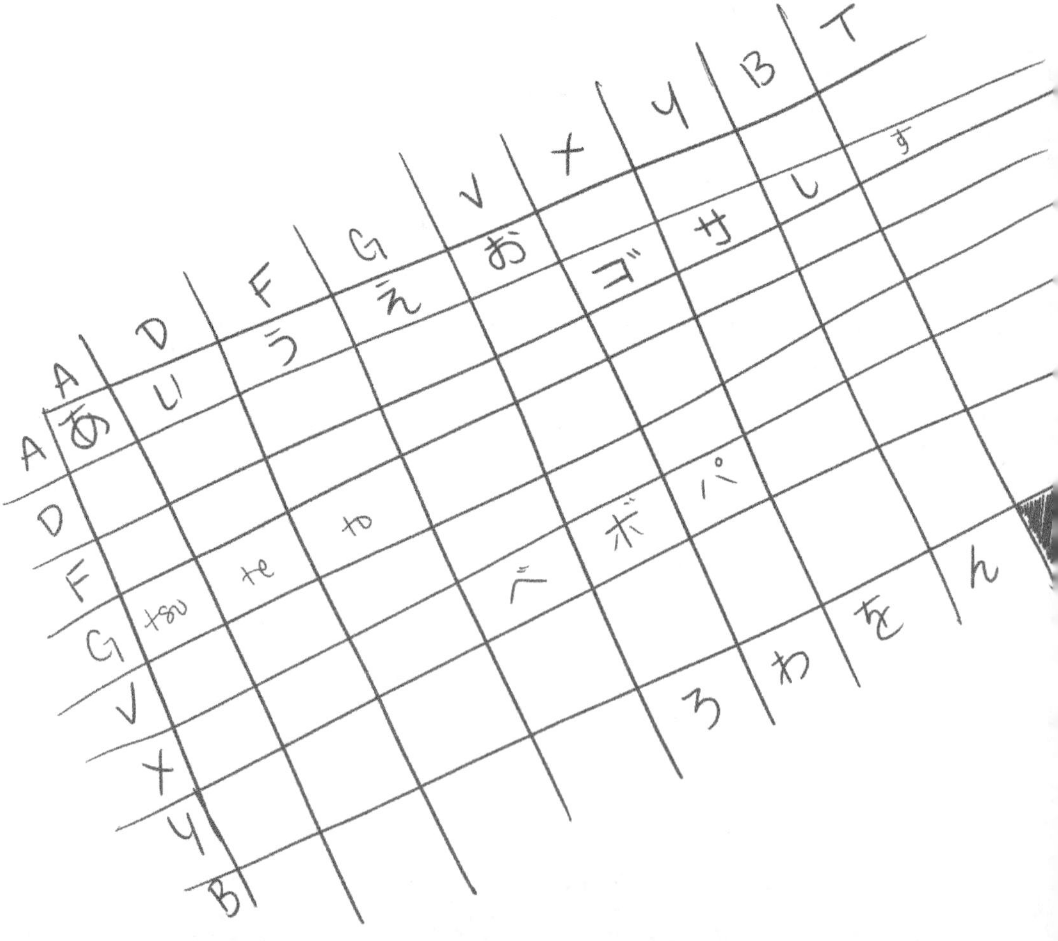

AUTHOR BIO

SI Foote loves English and well-written literature. Her favorite subject to study is linguistics. She is a supporter of the FanFiction community as it helps build great writing. She is a member of the LGBTQIA+ community as an Asexual (like several of her characters). She currently lives in Utah with her Teacup Yorkie, Cinnamon.

For More Behind the World of the Elementalists
Visit https://www.sifoote.com